# BEAUTY&
### THE BEAST&

## SOME GAVE ALL

# BEAUTY &
## THE BEAST

## SOME GAVE ALL

NANCY HOLDER

BASED ON THE SERIES CREATED BY RON KOSLOW
AND DEVELOPED BY SHERRI COOPER &
JENNIFER LEVIN

**TITAN** BOOKS

BEAUTY & THE BEAST: SOME GAVE ALL
Print edition ISBN: 9781783292202
E-book edition ISBN: 9781783292233

Published by Titan Books
A division of Titan Publishing Group Ltd
144 Southwark St, London SE1 0UP

First edition: May 2015
2 4 6 8 10 9 7 5 3 1

A CIP catalogue record for this title is available from the British Library.

Printed and bound in the United States.

TITANBOOKS.COM

# BEAUTY & THE BEAST

## THE BEAST

### SOME GAVE ALL

*From the moment we met,*
*we knew our lives would never be the same.*
*He saved my life,*
*and she saved mine.*
*We are destined,*
*but we know it won't be easy.*
*Even though we have every reason to stay apart,*
*we'll risk it all to be together.*

# CHAPTER ONE

Not quite dawn. New York City never slept, but New York detectives and doctors did.

In Greenwich Village, entwined in each other's arms, Catherine Chandler and Vincent Keller dreamed of mountains, and a cottage, and a dog—a small dog, since big ones weren't quite as fond of Vincent as Cat was.

Vincent's two brothers played tag football in the front yard, and Catherine's mother and father sat on the porch, paging through a photo album of Cat and Vincent's wedding. But in the gossamer way of dreams, time was an illusion, and the wedding was taking place beneath a glorious canopy of red roses and ivory sweet alyssum, and tiny nosegays of white baby's breath tied with lace.

Maids of honor Tess Vargas and Heather Chandler wore oyster-colored tea-dresses of antique lace, and like the groom, best man J.T. Forbes had on a tux. Luminous in a strapless white satin gown and a veil crowned with a freshwater pearl tiara, Cat carried a red rose bouquet. Around her slender neck, she wore a pearl choker centered with her mother's chimera pendant.

Golden wedding rings caught the sunlight; then Vincent

and Catherine were pronounced husband and wife. At last, heaven on earth.

*Lift me up…*

Vincent cupped Cat's face and she molded her hands over his. More velvety than rose petals, their lips touched. It was the second best day of their lives. The best: that morning back in the warehouse, when they'd first met.

*Come with me…*

In New York City, Cat nearly woke from sheer joy; then Vincent's arms wound round her as she settled her head on his chest, and his steady heartbeat lulled her back to sleep.

Vincent smelled Catherine's hair, her skin, and, reassured that she was really there, held her as he dozed. A smile softened the hard angles of his face. Bliss, utter bliss, so dearly won.

Their love had been sorely tested; now, precious and adored, Catherine and Vincent married in the mountains, with family, and their little dog, on a day shining with rainbows. Their union was their pot of gold, their triumph.

*Surrender to the afterglow…*

But which one of them had dreamed the dream?


Further out of the city, Tess Vargas rose from J.T. Forbes's bed, began to dress for the gym, and thought, *That cop is coming from L.A. soon. Tofu head. Cat is going to kill me.* J.T. stirred and Tess looked down at him with a pang. They had moved from the first thrill of romance to the calmer, more complicated long haul of a relationship. She just wasn't sure they had what it took. Wasn't sure *she* did. Maybe there was a reason for her less than stellar record with men. She thought of Joe Bishop, her old boss and former married boyfriend, and winced as she strapped on her watch and grabbed up her towel and water bottle. What a disaster, her affair with Joe. Had she gone crazy for a time back then?

She was nuts about J.T., but did their relationship make any more sense than that?

Courtesy of the door that anxiety had opened, the details of her day began to creep into her mind: trying to solve the string of horrible murders, possibly beast-related. Six so far. The mayor and the city were screaming for action. She was the newest precinct captain, so guess who was getting thrown under the bus because of the lack of results?

Well, hey, at least Cat would understand about Yoga Cop. Maybe.

*Yeah, after she kills me,* Tess thought.

She leaned down to kiss J.T.'s cheek, hesitated, straightened, and left.

After Tess closed the door behind herself, J.T. opened his eyes, giving up all pretense of slumber. Truth? He hadn't slept in hours. He'd watched Tess toss and turn.

Just now, he'd known she was getting dressed but he'd kept his eyes closed because he didn't know how to talk to her anymore. It wasn't going well between them, and he didn't know why. His experience with women was extremely limited. Face it, he was rusty. For over a decade, he had poured everything he'd had, mentally and emotionally, into keeping Vincent safe. Now his best friend had emerged from his cocoon, but J.T. hadn't fully emerged from his. Sara, the assistant chair of his department and briefly his girlfriend, had never forgiven him for bailing on meeting her parents. She'd seen right through his fake coughing fit. It wasn't his no-show that had made her so angry. It was that he had lied straight to her face. But how could he have told her it was a beast emergency?

The last time he and Tess had kind-of sort-of discussed their relationship, Tess had accused him of backing off. He thought *she* was the one who was being distant. They seemed to be caught in an outward spiral now, moving farther and farther away from each other.

*Was she just about to kiss me goodbye… and then didn't?*

Since his eyes had been closed, he didn't know.

He sat up and put his hand on her side of the bed. Her body heat was gone. He looked around forlornly. When Tess wasn't in his apartment, it felt so empty.

But sometimes it felt even emptier when she was there.

In the Bronx, an old man woke and checked the calendar. Today was the day. Maurice Riley began to cry. He had started nearly every day with a deep, pervasive grief since his daughter's death. But only recently had he met the morning in tears. It was the not knowing how, or why. Line of duty, they had said. But the letter he had recently received told a different story.

A horror story.

If answers brought justice, as the letter promised, then he wanted them. But if not… could he live with the truth?

*I won't have to worry about living with anything for too long.*

The doctors had given Mr. Riley six months to live.

Across from Aliyah Patel's bedroom, a monster prowled.

It had been shambling on the loading dock of the abandoned warehouse across the street for what seemed like her whole life. It was as tall as a gorilla and it growled like a tiger and its shadow flickered on her wall, merging with her drawings of houses with apple trees and threads of smoke rising from the chimneys, and a mommy and daddy in heaven, with wings and halos and happy faces. The silhouette pulsed like a heartbeat, vanishing and reappearing. Its arms made swimming motions and it had claws, not fingers, that sliced at the shadows over and over again, cutting the night apart.

The monster was looking for something.

Not, not some*thing*. Some*one*.

Looking for her, Aliyah Patel, eight years old, an orphan who lived with her Aunt Indira.

Hunched, huge. It was fast, busy. Seeking. Hunting. Because she was bad, and Aunt Indira had warned her many times that the boogeyman would get her if she didn't shape up.

Aliyah quaked in her bed, sheets pulled tightly up to her chin. Her large brown eyes welled as she held her breath and crossed all her fingers and then her thumbs to remind herself not to make a sound. That was what she did when Aunt Indira needed a break. It was really bad if Aunt Indira didn't get her breaks.

But not as bad as this.

It was still growling on the loading dock. It didn't sound like a tiger anymore. Aliyah didn't know what it did sound like. She had never heard a noise like this, not even in a scary movie. Not even in a nightmare.

She had more nightmares than people realized. She was sorry she was such a handful. That she made Aunt Indira's life a living hell. That she hadn't come as advertised—a sweet, good little girl. She understood why there was hitting.

It could see through her wall. Aliyah just knew it could. Just like Aunt Indira could see with eyes in the back of her head. She was always catching Aliyah doing bad things, like stealing cheese slices. It was just that she got so hungry.

She tried to breathe. She couldn't move. She was pretty sure her heart had stopped beating. She was getting dizzy; the room was spinning.

Her eyelids fluttered. *Lie still. Lie still.*

She watched the shadow. There! There it was!

No, it was gone again. Or else it was invisible.

It was still looking for her. She knew it. Could feel it.

She knew how to become invisible, too. It was her superpower and sometimes it kept her from getting in trouble. Not often, but when it did work, that was great. She took a breath and activated it. To remain invisible, you had to be quiet as a mouse. You had to look down. You had to not break things or say you were hungry. You also had to tell the people at the hospital that you fell.

Something scraped against the wall of Aliyah's building. She jerked hard, her gasp yanking her upward. She forced away a whimper as her bed springs creaked.

She had given herself away. Now it would know she was in here.

Her heart knocked hard against her chest. It beat so fast that it hurt. She was dizzier than ever, reeling, spinning. She couldn't make herself push out the old air filling her lungs. It was like being trapped underwater beneath a sheet of ice, suffocating on her own fear.

If she called out for Aunt Indira; if she just screamed—

Would she get in trouble?

It didn't matter anyway. She couldn't make a sound. Fingers all crossed, thumbs too, and now toes curled. She tried to shut her eyes but they wouldn't stay closed. First rule of invisibility: If you can't see them, they can't see you.

But her eyes wouldn't stay closed. She was too scared. Because if you can't see them, you don't know when they're coming after you.

Her lids fluttering, she burrowed into the corner of her bed, forgetting about the nightstand and the plastic water bottle and the ballerina lamp. The water bottle fell over and rolled onto the floor.

The silhouette of a head loomed on the wall. Now she'd done it. Now it would be sure that she was there.

The head moved left, right, then straight ahead. It was looking in.

Then it looked down.

Tears slid from the corners of her eyes and she bit her lower lip to keep herself from whimpering. It wouldn't be able to see her. Unless it could see in the dark. Maybe it was there because she was so bad. She broke things. She made noise. She was such a hassle.

The window rattled.

*I don't mean to be bad. I try to be a good girl.*

She bit down hard to keep herself from crying. Blood beaded on her lower lip.

*Rattle, rattle, rattle.*

*I'm sorry. I'm so sorry. I'll never steal cheese slices again.*

She should call out for her aunt.

*Call. I can call on my phone. They are always telling me press 911 for help if I need it.*

Her phone was on her nightstand. That would be better. She wouldn't bother Aunt Indira. Except that some things were *private* and if you told there was hell to pay. But this was different. Even she knew that, and she was so stupid she didn't even know how to count to one hundred by tens.

To get the phone, first she had to uncross her fingers and thumbs. Then she had to snake her hand up toward the nightstand.

She couldn't make herself do it. She lay still fighting for air.

Silence.

Then beside the window, the picture of her dead mommy slid to the floor and crashed as the glass shattered. She jerked, then squeezed her fingers together to make the crosses tighter. She couldn't manage one little whimper.

*Rattle.*

*Rattle.*

*Rattle.*

Silence.

She would do something. She would grab the phone or bolt out of bed or scream. But to do any of those things, she would have to stop being invisible and that might be her worst idea and Lord knew she didn't have a lick of common sense. So she would count to one hundred before she decided.

If she could remember all the tens' places. First was ten and then was twenty…

She got to thirty before the window exploded.

# CHAPTER TWO

## THE BRONX

Cat killed the engine and put her keys in her pocket. By then, Vincent was already out of the squad car, waiting for her in the snow. Stunning in his black suit and navy blue tie, his black wool calf-length coat hung open as it stretched across his broad shoulders. Like her, he wore a muffler around his neck and his short brown hair was covered with a black knitted cap. Her own cap was teal blue with a crocheted beaded flower; not really to her taste, but it had been the first thing she'd grabbed because they'd been bordering on late. Heather had persuaded her to buy it during a Saturday morning of sisterly bonding over coffees and vintage shopping. She planned to take it off before they met Maurice Riley. It was too frivolous for this solemn occasion.

They'd both awakened with smiles on their faces, then laughed at Heather's flurries of fabrics and feathers as Cat made the coffee and Vincent cooked breakfast. Heather was attending Silverado Academy of Design as a fashion design major. She was also working part-time as an events coordinator again. Each of her activities came with lots of stuff that she left out in the living room and/or her bedroom because she was "in process." Creating was interesting. Cleaning up afterwards? Not so much.

The chaos of Cat's apartment matched the chaos in their lives: A new kind of monster was terrorizing New York City. There had been six fatal maulings in as many weeks; savage, brutal, inhuman. Beast. It had to be. And yet Vincent had been at a loss to track it down, much less describe what new kind of atrocity had been created... and by whom. He had visited each crime scene and engaged his tracking senses, waiting for sensory details to emerge, meld together, and form a crystal-clear image of the event. In each of the six cases, that image had not come. Neither Cat nor Vincent knew what to make of that, and it was beyond troubling. The implications were too terrible to imagine: It was either a different kind of beast that he was unable to detect, or maybe Vincent's beast abilities were changing—leaving him defenseless against the new threat. True, they had grappled with faceless enemies before. But this was like Muirfield on steroids.

J.T.'s tests had come back negative for biological alterations in Vincent's own system. The biochemist assured them that Vincent was still Vincent. But what if J.T. simply couldn't measure a new mutation in Vincent's physical makeup?

Meanwhile, the island of Manhattan was up in arms, complaining about the lack of results from the NYPD. There were protests and demonstrations every day, people gathering in Central Park and in front of the 125th precinct with signs that read SAVE OUR CITY and TERRORISTS AMONG US? There was talk of vigilante justice and how *someone* had to do something because the cops were useless. It was scary talk.

A call came in from Tess.

"Good morning, boss," Cat said into the phone as she got out of the squad car. Her own boots crunched on dirty snow. New York in January was days of brown and gray slush alleviated by powdery snowfalls as white as sugar. She hoped it snowed again soon.

"We've got another one. Lucky number seven."

Cat looked at Vincent. His face went from somber to grim. She knew he could hear Tess as clearly as if the new captain of NYPD's 125th precinct were standing beside him. Courtesy of the "enhancements" Cat's biological father had equipped Vincent with, he could direct his blood to any of the five senses he wanted to boost. Right now it was his hearing. The process was second nature to him—he was a true apex predator. Or had been, until the six mysterious homicides caused him to question his status.

"Same as the others?" Cat asked.

"Worse. Much, much worse. That new ME's assistant threw up all over a key piece of evidence. I've got pictures on my phone that sent *me* to the ladies' room. We gotta catch this thing *fast*."

Cat frowned. "Do we have an ID for the vic?"

"Not yet, but this one's in our jurisdiction *finally*. I'm going over there now. Thought I'd check in and ask you if you think Mr. Riley can shed some light on this. Have you talked to him about his letter yet?"

"We just arrived. I'll touch base as soon as we interview him."

"Keep me posted." Tess hung up. She was a good captain, just what the traumatized 125th needed, but Cat knew her best friend was feeling the pressure of her promotion at the worst time in the recent history of New York crime prevention. Tess didn't need a serial-killer beast case on her plate right now.

Or ever.

Joining Vincent at the curb, Cat put her phone in her pocket and saw the anguish in his eyes. His gloved hands held a cherry-wood box with the desperation of a drowning man clasping the only piece of driftwood in a frozen sea.

"I don't know why I can't track whatever is doing this." Guilt and a misplaced sense of responsibility wafted in the air with the vapor from his breath.

She placed her hand over his. "It's okay, Vincent."

But it wasn't. She, he, J.T., and Tess all knew that the situation would only worsen if NYPD had to rely on traditional methods of solving crimes to stop this thing. How many years had the four of them suppressed evidence to keep the world from knowing about the existence of beasts? They were on a collision course with not only the 125th but every law enforcement agency in New York, the FBI included. And FBI meant her biological father, Bob Reynolds, a major player in Muirfield, the code name for the beast-creation program. He had justified his criminal activities—killing beasts and innocent humans alike—as a necessary part of his plan to wipe all beasts from the face of the earth. Although he had sworn he would never go public because he wanted to protect Cat, there was always a possibility that in his sick logic, he would decide she would be safer if he revealed everything he knew. Then Vincent could kiss any semblance of a normal life goodbye forever.

"J.T.'s barely slept in a week trying to figure out what's going on." Vincent sighed as if that were his fault.

Anything beast-related, Vincent took on as if he, and not the government, was responsible. He carried a massive amount of guilt for agreeing to become part of Muirfield by serving as a test subject.

"And I'm sure he'll break the case," she said, projecting a confidence she wasn't currently feeling. For a cop, each new crime in a connected chain of previous crimes felt like a defeat.

Together they faced a one-story house that, like them, had seen better days. Grubby white paint was peeling off the exterior walls and the porch had sunken in like a deflated soccer ball. A flag-shaped sign on the front door read THE RILEYS GOD BLESS AMERICA! in bleached red, white, and blue letters. The mailbox was flag-themed, too. Cat glanced at the box in Vincent's grip.

"Tess is going to the crime scene," she said. "She can monitor the situation. We've finally got one in our jurisdiction, so she's the captain in charge."

The New York Chief of Police had organized a task force comprised of special-crimes squads from the larger precincts, but most of the precinct captains seemed more interested in protecting their turf than in working together to solve the murders. Tess, as the newest captain, was fighting to hold her own. It frustrated her that she couldn't reveal everything she knew—that this was undoubtedly beast-related—a situation made all the more irritating because no one seemed to give credence to the few details she *was* able to share. She was new and she was a woman. Ergo, she must not know what she was doing.

He nodded. "That's good. With Tess we'll have direct access." His face masked emotions he wasn't sharing. She knew him so well, knew that he was keeping something back, and wished he would unburden himself. They had seen each other in their darkest hours... or so she had thought. But right then Vincent was in a bleak place he hadn't told her about, and she wanted to join him there. Not because she needed more tragedy and pain, but because she knew that if he let her in, she would bring him light. Maybe just one small candle flame's worth, but enough to remind him that he was loved. And that he was not alone.

"Look." He began walking down the gravel path through a rickety wooden arch. On either side, snow coated skeletal bushes and a sturdy oak tree, an outstretched limb sporting two long pieces of frayed rope and a splintered wooden board—a homemade tree swing. Neglected, forgotten, unused.

But that wasn't what Vincent was looking at. On the right side of the path, frosted with silvery white, a single red rose graced an otherwise barren rose bush. It was a lush velvety crimson, and as radiant as a jewel. Spring in the heart of winter.

*Even in the darkest place, there is hope,* the rose seemed to whisper. And as Cat admired it, she turned to Vincent, took off her glove, and cupped his icy cheek.

"I had a dream," she said.

He smiled very faintly. "I did too. I dream it every day."

"Mountains? And just a *small* dog." When he nodded slightly, her heart overflowed and she murmured in a rush, "Vincent, I love you."

He swallowed hard before replying, "I love you too."

"Whatever this thing is, we can deal with it together," she said. "We *are* dealing with it together."

His lips parted. Then he inclined his head and kissed her, wrapped her hand with his, and placed them both in his pocket.

"It's so cold today," he murmured. "Your hand's like ice."

"You know what they say: 'Cold hands, warm heart.'"

He gave her fingers a squeeze and she leaned against him for a moment. Then she put her glove back on. They were on police business, and it was a somber occasion. Still, it was so wonderful to wake up beside Vincent without double-checking for the whirr of helicopters that life was truly like a waking dream, even with all that was going on.

Together they walked up the path and Cat gingerly stepped onto the porch. A frayed American-flag welcome mat contributed to the pervasive patriotic theme. She held up her badge as she pressed the corroded doorbell. She heard no sound, and was about to knock on the door when it opened.

From yesterday's phone conversation, Cat knew that Maurice Riley was sick. Terminally ill, in fact. He had six months at most, he had told her. But she was still shocked by the cavernous hollows in his cheeks and the eggplant-purple circles under his eyes. He was wearing a white collared shirt, a pair of charcoal-gray trousers, and polished loafers. He had dressed for the occasion as well. In his left hand he held the letter he had told her about—the primary reason they were here. It had been Vincent's idea to make a special presentation to Maurice Riley in addition to the interview.

"Mr. Riley," she began. "I'm Detective Chandler. And this is—"

"I'd know you anywhere, Dr. Keller," Riley cut in. He tried to smile, but his lower lip quivered. "Roxie sent me pictures." He held out his hand, then glimpsed the object Vincent was holding. His eyes welled and he took a step back. "Please, come in."

"I should have come before," Vincent said as they entered his home.

Cat took in a worn sofa in a cabbage rose pattern, two chairs upholstered in frayed brown corduroy, and a fireplace containing ashes. Over the mantel, a large golden frame surrounded a studio portrait of a young woman in army dress uniform, with light brown skin and chestnut eyes shining with pride. It was Roxanne Lafferty, from Delta Company, one of Vincent's comrades in arms in Afghanistan.

And a fellow Muirfield victim.

A gold plaque mounted to the bottom section of the frame read ALL GAVE SOME BUT SOME GAVE ALL.

"How could you come any sooner, son? I saw you on TV. You talked about your... amnesia." Mr. Riley hesitated on the last word.

"I should have found a way," Vincent said, hinting that the amnesia story was a lie. He gestured with his head to the box he was holding. "For her, I should have done it."

"Well, you're here now." Mr. Riley's voice wobbled a little.

To Cat, he added, "You'll want to see the letter."

"First things first, Mr. Riley," she replied, although yes, she wanted to cut to the chase. She was itching to meet up with Tess at the crime scene. Instead she was standing there on idle and she was not a patient person. She wanted to fix things as soon as she knew they were broken. That was why she had become a cop—to solve her mother's murder, yes, but to fight for justice for other victims as well.

Catherine and Vincent took off their coats, caps, and gloves and laid them on the arm of Mr. Riley's sofa. Mr. Riley cleared his throat.

"We missed this part," he said to Vincent. "We missed all of it. But I guess you know that. That's why you're doing it."

"That's right, sir." Vincent helped Mr. Riley sit down on the sofa. Then former specialist Vincent Keller knelt on one knee and opened the box, lifting out a triangular-shaped wooden frame with a glass face. It encased a reverently folded American flag, stars up. He offered the flag to the dying man, in a traditional ritual that had been performed for over a hundred and fifty years at American military funerals.

"Sir," Vincent said, "on behalf of the President of the United States, the United States Army and a grateful nation, please accept this flag as a symbol of our appreciation for your loved one's honorable and faithful service.

"This flag flew over the firehouse where my brothers worked as firefighters before they died in the Twin Towers."

The man choked back tears as he received the archived flag, holding it against his chest as the tears came. At a military funeral with honors—such as Lafferty had been given—the flag in the box would have been the one that had draped the fallen warrior's casket, and would have been folded graveside by soldiers as "Taps" was played. Then it would have been presented on bended knee to Lafferty's next of kin. But Roxanne's mother had been too distraught to attend the service, and Mr. Riley had stayed home with her. When the time came for them to receive Lafferty's flag through the mail, it had never arrived. Mr. Riley had mentioned that fact to Cat on the phone, and Vincent had been so incensed that he had decided to give Mr. Riley one of his most treasured possessions. The flag had been given to Vincent's family at the funeral for his brothers, and Vincent had accepted it. J.T. Forbes had kept the flag safe after Vincent had enlisted in the army and left for the war.

Left for his destiny.

The man saluted, and Vincent stood and sharply saluted back. Vincent was no longer in the army, nor did he have any love for the military that had betrayed him, but Cat knew that he was returning the salute for Mr. Riley's sake.

And for Roxanne Lafferty's.

"Please," Mr. Riley said, and he handed each of them a shot glass filled to the brim with amber liquid from a ceramic red, white, and blue tray. Cat smelled whiskey. She was on duty, but like Vincent, she honored the moment, throwing back with the two men, then turning her glass upside down on the tray.

They shared one more silent moment, and then Mr. Riley said, "The letter."

Catherine reached into the pocket of her coat for a small pack of evidence gloves. She drew out a pair and slipped them on. The atmosphere in the room grew tense. Mr. Riley held out the letter, and Catherine delicately took it from him with both hands. He had read the words to her over the phone, but they still chilled her:

*Dear Mr. Riley,*

*We are a small group of concerned patriots who have banded together to fight a terrible conspiracy at the highest levels of government. One of us knew your daughter,*

Roxanne Lafferty, in Afghanistan. We know that you were told she died in the line of duty.

That is a lie.

The government pumped her full of poison and turned her into something unspeakable—a monster. She was last seen in the infirmary shackled to her bed, completely out of her mind with pain and fury. One of us, known as "Private X," attempted a rescue but failed.

We know that she never saw combat again, even though you were informed that she died in a firefight.

We would have contacted you as soon as this happened, but we had no access to her records to find her next of kin, and so there was no way of connecting "Maurice Riley" to "Roxanne Lafferty." We realized that she was your stepdaughter when the article about you ran in last Tuesday's New York Post, and it mentioned her by name.

We talked it over for a long time before we decided to contact you. There have been six murders in New York in the last six weeks where the injuries look similar to atrocities Private X witnessed in Afghanistan. We think someone got out of there—someone who has been mutilated like your daughter—and is out of control, like your daughter was. We think you may be in great danger—if not from this abomination, then from the government that created it. One of the six murdered people—Karl Tiptree—was one of the scientists who participated in the manufacture of the "serum" that destroyed your daughter's life. We have been investigating the histories of the other five in an attempt to link them to this travesty. We are confident that we will succeed.

The generals tied up loose ends in Afghanistan… with bullets. Private X barely got out alive and has stayed all these years under the radar. But he is ready to tell you everything he knows. We want justice for your daughter, and we want

*to stop this thing from butchering more people, even the
guilty. Please join us, Mr. Riley.*

*On behalf of the people of the United States, you have our
sympathy, and our respect. We're waiting to hear from you.*

*Sincerely,*
*FFNY—The Freedom Fighters of New York*

At the bottom of the letter was a phone number with a
212 area code.

Vincent had been reading over Cat's shoulder, and she
felt him trembling. She turned her head and looked up at
him. His face had gone chalk white, and when she raised
a brow, he averted his gaze and moved to the mantel. He
stared up at Roxanne Lafferty's portrait, perhaps unaware
that his shoulders were square and his spine was ramrod
straight. He was standing at attention. All that was missing
was another salute.

"I'm assuming you called the number," Cat said to Mr.
Riley.

He scratched his forehead with skeletal fingers. Cat
wondered if the rings under his eyes were from illness or
anxiety, maybe both.

"I've called it a hundred times. There's never been any
answer. No voicemail. I checked with the phone company and
they say it's not a valid number."

*We'll see about that,* Cat thought. The NYPD had
resources that were unavailable to private citizens.

"What *New York Post* article are they talking about?" she
asked Mr. Riley.

He sighed and picked up a newspaper off a coffee table
that was cluttered with prescription bottles. It was folded to a
small square of text that included a photograph of Mr. Riley
standing beside a thin little dark-skinned girl dressed in a

fuzzy pink sweater and lavender snow pants. She was holding a small, colorful piece of paper.

## FATHER OF ARMY WOMAN K.I.A. FULFILLS PROMISE TO DAUGHTER OF "LITTLE SISTER"

Last Tuesday, Mr. Maurice Riley, a resident of the Bronx, presented Aliyah Patel, 8, also of the Bronx, with a gift certificate to Palmieri's, her favorite ice cream parlor, good for fifty-two ice cream cones—one every week for a year. Riley's daughter, Private First Class Roxanne Lafferty, who was killed in Afghanistan in 2002, was the "Big Sister" of Aliyah's mother, Gheeta Patel, in the "Big Sister Little Sister" mentoring program. Lafferty promised Gheeta Patel that if she read fifty-two books before she graduated from high school, she would buy Gheeta an ice cream cone every week for one year. They wrote out a contract and both signed it. Sadly, Gheeta Patel passed away in 2010, leaving behind her daughter, Aliyah.

Riley recently discovered the contract while he was cleaning out his garage. With the help of social worker Angela Alcina, he was able to contact Aliyah's aunt, Indira Patel, who is her guardian, and present the gift certificate to Aliyah on behalf of her mother.

"Her favorite flavor is chocolate-chip cookie dough," Mr. Riley said.

"This was so kind, Mr. Riley." Cat was moved.

He made a face. "Not as sweet as it looks. That aunt of Aliyah's is a piece of work—the poor kid was covered in bruises. I called social services on her. And Miss Alcina, too. They all said they'd investigate but every time I call I go straight to voicemail. Last time I called—yesterday—Miss Alcina's message mailbox was full."

Cat took note. Theoretically, she would never have

enough time to follow up on that—it wasn't relevant to her investigation, and it was out of her jurisdiction—but she knew that before the end of the day, she'd be making a few calls.

"What about Karl Tiptree?" she asked. "Have you learned anything about him?"

"I read his obituary on my computer," he said. "It didn't say anything about a serum. It said he was a 'consultant.'"

"Yeah, I'll bet," Vincent muttered.

Mr. Riley's eyes traveled to Lafferty's portrait. Then he picked up one of the shot glasses and passed it from palm to frail palm. "Do you know what they're talking about? That *my* little girl was turned into a *monster*? What does *that* mean?" He swayed as he walked. He was so agitated that Cat worried about his blood pressure; she reminded herself that Vincent was a doctor, and he would intervene if he thought it was necessary.

"I haven't slept since I got this note. I don't know what to think. The world is full of crazies, you know? But if it's true... if someone *did* something to her..." He trailed off. "Do you think they're trying to tell me that she's still alive and *she's* doing these things?"

Cat slid a glance at Vincent. He was clearly conflicted, yet he kept his silence. She understood his reticence, but she had a thousand questions of her own. When they had first connected, he had told her that he was the only surviving genetically modified supersoldier of the army's Delta Company. But over time they had learned that there'd been others. Cat's biological father had a list of them, and he programmed Vincent to kill them one by one. Now this. "FFNY" was wise to fear for Mr. Riley. However, they were also putting him in danger by linking him to the tragic events in Afghanistan.

She reread the note and tried to remember if Vincent had actually told her that he had seen Lafferty die.

*What if she* has *evolved into this new beast that's tearing New York apart?*

Mr. Riley shuddered. "I can't go to my grave without knowing what happened to my girl. I've been her daddy since before she was born. I was on the older side, but I kept up with my little tomboy as best I could. Her real father was Hector Lafferty; a good man, a cop, shot in the line of duty. We had Roxie keep his last name to honor him, and I thought that was proper. But she was mine. My daughter." He heaved a sob. "When our girl died, my wife, Amanda, just faded away. She kept saying she was going to look for Roxie in heaven. That our angel still needed us..." Agony stretched his vocal cords like violin strings. He seemed to shrink before Cat's very eyes, fear and worry pressing down hard.

As Vincent turned around, a muscle jumped in his cheek, a vein pulsed in his forehead, and the merest hint of a yellow glow flickered in his eyes. The rising tension in the room was affecting him, too. But where Mr. Riley shrank before potential danger, Vincent responded with the first signs of beast aggression. Cat tried to subtly clear her throat as a warning for him to calm down. Mr. Riley was lobbing emotional grenades at a sorely misused veteran with a deep connection to him. Even a normal human would react to that.

"I'll find out the truth," Vincent said in a low, fierce voice.

"But did *you* see anything like that?" Mr. Riley blurted. "Her chained to a bed? In *pain?* This guy, this Private X, would you have known him? Or the other one, Karl Tiptree?"

The man's despair was hard to take. When he burst into tears and sank back onto the sofa, Cat sat down beside him and took his hand. Vincent turned away again.

"We'll find out," she assured him.

"Find out quick," Mr. Riley pleaded. "I don't have much time. I can't die like this. Wondering." He gestured toward the portrait. "They told me her death was quick. That she didn't feel a thing. There was no body to bury. But there's a headstone with her name on it in Arlington National Cemetery. Military honors. Killed in action. I've been there every single year on the day that I got the visit from the army with the notice. June twenty-first, two thousand and two. My roses… she always loved them so. I've let the house go, can't manage, but you should see my rose bushes in the spring. I put them on her grave. Her *empty* grave."

*Just like I put calla lilies on my mother's empty grave*, Cat thought. For over ten years, she hadn't known that her mother had been moved, her new plot marked with a headstone bearing only her first name out in a field behind an abandoned Muirfield safe house. Cat suspected that her biological father, former FBI agent Bob Reynolds, had done it, but she hadn't asked, and she was loath to have any contact with him whatsoever. His team had begun this nightmare, and he had made Vincent's life a living hell.

And Roxanne Lafferty's as well, if she was still alive.

"We'll help you, Mr. Riley," Cat promised. She glanced up at Vincent, who still kept his back carefully turned, so she couldn't see if the glow in his eyes was intensifying. She had to get him out of there.

"We need to go," she gently told the old man. "I have to take this letter for a while." Analysis for DNA and other forensic data would be strictly off the books, of course. And as soon as they left, she and Vincent would start looking for the FFNY, and digging into Tiptree's past.

"I made a copy of the letter," he said. "For me. I can't stop reading it. Staring at those words." Another tear rolled down his cheek and he gave his head a quick, angry shake. "Being sick has made me weak." He turned to Vincent one more time. "Son, you need to tell me what you saw. What happened there." His chest shook with the effort to inhale. "Why you had 'amnesia' for ten years."

Vincent finally turned around. The glow had vanished. He was entirely himself.

"Mr. Riley, I don't want to put you in any danger. The less you know, the safer you'll be."

The man smiled grimly. "I'm already dying. You're a doctor. Surely you can see that."

Vincent lowered his head, acknowledging the truth. "You must have other loved ones to protect."

"I'm alone. This is it." He swept an arc, taking in the room. "For the love of God, *tell* me."

Vincent glanced over at Cat, and she gave him a quick nod. This man deserved to know *something*. Maybe they couldn't tell him all of it, but Vincent would be careful with the truth. Cat trusted him to divulge as much as he deemed appropriate.

"There were drug trials in Afghanistan," Vincent said after a pause. "And Lafferty was among those who were experimented on. The drugs were supposed to make... the subjects... stronger, faster. To give... them... an edge in combat."

She noted that he was not including himself in the experimental group. That was wise.

"Things didn't go as planned. She had a reaction to the... medication, a seizure. A doctor gave her an injection, and then she was escorted away. I visited her in the infirmary later, and she seemed fine."

Cat listened hard. Was that the truth, or was he trying to comfort the old man?

"But did she return to combat duty?" the man persisted. "Did you see her die the way they said she did?"

Cat could practically observe Vincent's mind working as he considered his next words. "I visited her several times in the infirmary," he said, surprising her further. "I never saw her in the field again. But the infirmary was destroyed in the firefight you were told about."

Cat shielded her confusion from Mr. Riley by placing the letter in an evidence bag. Vincent had told her that when he and the other supersoldiers had gone on a rampage, the infirmary had been destroyed. Had Lafferty been inside? Did Vincent carry the guilt of that death as well as that of all the others that she knew about?

Cat's own mother had been at that camp, and put her life on the line to protect the "beasts" the government project known as Muirfield had created. She was the doctor who had given Lafferty the shot to stop her seizure, and J.T. had replicated that formula when Vincent had exhibited similar symptoms. Back in Afghanistan, Vanessa Chandler had requested time to work with the beast-soldiers, to reverse the medical damage that had been done to them. But all the government had wanted was to "shut them down."

To kill them. To do that, they were willing to kill her, too.

"So, if there was a mortar attack, an assault, she may have died in the infirmary when it was destroyed," the man said slowly, reluctantly. And suddenly Cat realized that he was hoping that his stepdaughter was alive. A monster, maybe, even a serial killer, but still here. The idea stunned her. Still, she herself had absorbed the shock that Vincent had killed people, and still loved him. Yet to hope that it was your child who was tearing innocent civilians limb from limb…

"That might have happened," Vincent said vaguely, "but I can confirm that she never returned to the field of engagement."

Cat's phone buzzed. It was a text from Tess. *NEED YOU PRECINCT ASAP*. She showed the message to Vincent and said to Mr. Riley, "We need to go, Mr. Riley. Before we leave, we're going to look around your property."

"Thank you. I have a garage out back. Here are the keys." As he fished in his pocket, he looked so relieved that she wanted to give him a hug. Instead she began to clear his house, walking slowly through the rooms, checking for signs of unusual activity, and for electronic surveillance equipment. Vincent was right behind her; away from the man's view, he beasted out slightly. She was depending on his tracking senses to augment her search.

When they were finished with the house, Vincent reported, "Nothing in here."

They left through the kitchen door into the backyard. About ten yards away, a detached garage sat in drifts piled up to the windows. If the old gentleman owned a car, he hadn't used it in a while.

She peered into the window and spotted a sedan, and beside it, a motorcycle. The forlorn motorcycle was coated with dust. Stepping back, she indicated that Vincent should look in, too. With a shake of his head to indicate that no one was hiding inside, he opened the garage door. Cat went in, and tried the car door. Locked. The car was so old that it didn't have an electronic lock. She found the correct key and opened up the car. It smelled old and abandoned, a thing of the past. A life shutting down.

They went back inside. Mr. Riley anxiously rose as if he'd been awaiting a verdict.

"How do you get to your medical appointments, Mr. Riley?" Cat asked.

"Usually? Subway." He raised his chin as if daring her to state the obvious: that a terminally ill man of a certain age shouldn't be taking the subway for any reason, much less for his cancer treatments.

Her phone buzzed again. Tess was impatient.

"I'd like you to get locks on your garage door," Cat said. She pulled out her card. "The city can help with that. And with transportation as well."

"I'm fine," he said reflexively. He kept his face neutral and respectful.

But when he turned his attention to Vincent, his face sagged, and it was obvious to everyone in the room that he was not fine.

"I'll be back as soon as I can. With answers," Vincent promised.

The man exhaled, as impatient for those answers as Cat was.

As she and Vincent left the house and retraced their steps on the path, Mr. Riley shuffled out after them. With a pair of gardening shears, he snipped off the single exquisite red rose and presented it to Cat.

"Be careful, Detective," he told her. "Live a long time. Longer even than me."

She took the rose with a faint sad smile. Her professional distance already sacrificed to her instinctive need to protect, she put her arms around the old man. He melted against her, utterly bereft.

"I'll be in touch soon," she promised him.

"Answers," he pleaded. "Justice."

Cat said, "I won't stop until we've laid this to rest."

Vincent remained silent and stared at the snow as it tumbled from the sky. Then he walked to the car, a towering figure all in black, moving with the stealth of an animal.

# CHAPTER THREE

## AFGHANISTAN, 2002

*T*he beast that was Specialist Vincent Keller bared his teeth at the flaming debris plummeting from the smoke-choked sky. He growled at the fiery rain, then threw back his head and shrieked as a burning ember sizzled against the fresh gouges in his cheek. He slapped his bloody hand against the wound as he waggled his head in rage, grabbed the nearest object, and flung it hard.

It was a soldier.

Others came and ran beside him as they reached the blazing building. Somewhere deep, beast-Vincent knew that this was a sacred place, the house of the sick. Infirmary. But the beasts' roars drowned out any rational thought and his heart, his muscles, his life's blood were screaming at him to rip, to shred, to destroy.

Against all logic, ammo had been stored in the same building as the wounded, and as the flames reached mortars and grenades, the building detonated like a bomb. The blowback knocked the beasts off their feet. Beast-Vincent landed hard on his back, bellowing, devoid of any sense of fear.

*Lacking any sense at all.*

*Then from the fragmenting structure, something ran. It was on fire, and chains dangled from its wrists. It was a pillar of smoke and bright orange flames; its screams shattered the eardrums of the human soldier it charged. The man blasted machine gun fire at the ground in front of it, a warning.*

*Impossibly, it kept coming.*

*The man shouted a name and dove to the ground.*

*The thing ran over him, crackling feet thudding hard on his back. His lungs compressed, the man groaned once, and then he collapsed into the embers and ash.*

"And that's what I remember," Vincent said to Catherine. They were headed back to the precinct. Catherine was driving and Vincent rode shotgun while she expertly wove in and out of the busy New York traffic. "About that day."

"Oh, my God," Catherine said. "That's horrible."

"Yes," he said. And there were other days, days that he hadn't discussed, and he knew that she could tell he was holding something back. *It's all right to tell someone your darkest secrets.* Catherine hadn't said that. Her little sister Heather had. But at that time, Heather had had no idea just how dark the world could be.

Sad to say, her eyes had been opened.

"And you think that the man the… burning creature… trampled might have been this 'Private X'?" Catherine put on her left-turn blinker and swerved around a street sweeper. She huffed and activated lights and siren. Tess had called again to share a few more details about the newest homicide. Even Vincent, a hardened soldier and an ER doctor, had been sickened by what they'd heard.

"I don't know," he said. "I do remember that there was something familiar about him. I think I'd seen him in the infirmary hovering around Lafferty, which jibes with that note. But with the soot, and the blood...

"After that, I ran into the barracks and saw your mother, and I was going to tell her about him. So she could help him. Then Colonel Johnson pulled out his gun to shoot her and I beasted out again. By the time I pulled myself back together, the soldier was gone."

He didn't add that he had risked capture and execution by retracing his steps to find the distressed man. And to look for Lafferty's burned body, if it had indeed been Lafferty's. No one could have survived being engulfed in flames like that.

He blinked.

Except... he *had* encountered a beast who could have survived. The psychotic arsonist Eddie Long had been made not only fire-resistant, but also somehow able to create fires and direct them at his enemies. Long had nearly killed Vincent, and Vincent's FDNY firefighter nephew Aaron as well.

"Something's bothering you. Something else," she prodded, but by then they had pulled into the precinct parking lot. Catherine rolled to a stop and Tess emerged from the precinct headquarters and strode toward them, filled with purpose. Vincent noted that she was dressing more formally these days. She'd lost weight, and not just from the job—she and J.T. were having a few issues and Tess wasn't handling it well. Since Tess and J.T. no longer had to work closely together to cover up Vincent's existence, they were a bit at a loss to figure out what they had in common, once they came up for air from their romantic encounters. He was pulling for J.T. on this one. Tess, too.

"So you said the little girl in the article that Mr. Riley showed you was named Aliyah Patel," Tess said by way of greeting, as he and Catherine got out of the car. "And her aunt is Indira?"

"Yes," Cat said. Vincent shut his door.

Tess grimaced. "Well, guess who's in interview room A. Completely catatonic."

Catherine took a beat. "Saying feels like choosing. I don't want it to be either one of them."

"Aliyah's in the room," Tess said. "We think Indira's our latest vic. *Beast* vic," she emphasized.

Catherine shared a look with Vincent. He was sure they were thinking the same thing: that it was way too coincidental that they had just been talking about the Patels with Maurice Riley. That a picture in the *Post* of Aliyah less than a week ago had presaged an attack on them... and now the girl was at the precinct.

"Crime scene is unbelievable," Tess said. "I've got a team from CSU there, blotting up the evidence. Tissue and bone samples have been sent for testing. Vic was unrecognizable, but we've ascertained that Indira was home when the attack occurred."

"Where was Aliyah?" Vincent asked.

Tess gave them both one of her patented you-aren't-going-to-believe-this eye rolls. "The attacker forced entry through Aliyah's bedroom window. Aliyah was in bed. Then it—I forgot, we're saying 'he'—tore her bedroom door—which was locked from the outside—off the hinges. *He* must have searched for Indira. He went into Indira's bedroom, then moved into the living room, where Indira had apparently fallen asleep watching TV. Hard to tell from what's left of the body. But there was an empty bottle of whiskey and plenty more crushed into the carpet."

"It definitely sounds like the beast was targeting the aunt," Catherine said. "He bypassed Aliyah and had to make an effort to get to Indira."

"Not much of an effort," Vincent observed. "When I'm transformed, ripping off an interior door is like tearing up a piece of cardboard."

"Right," Tess said. "Which is why I already have a call in to the social worker you told me about, Angela Alcina. Turns out she's left the job. But she wasn't the Patels' official social worker. She just helped Mr. Riley find Gheeta Patel's daughter and referred his complaints about alleged abuse to the proper channels. The name of their caseworker is Julia Hogan and guess what? She's missing."

"So… Mr. Riley alleges abuse by the aunt, caseworker does squat, now the aunt is dead and the caseworker is missing," Catherine mused.

"I already have a warrant to examine both of their financials," Tess said. "It wouldn't be a day without some computer time, eh, detective?"

Catherine made grumbling noises.

"I'll check out the crime scene for beast activity," Vincent said.

Tess smiled grimly. "Figured you would. Thanks." She pulled her phone out of her jacket pocket and pressed a couple buttons. "I've sent you the address. Just don't upset the CSUs. As has become standard operating procedure for us, we're going to have to monitor the samples that they bag and tag, and do everything we can to swap 'em out. So far there have been no reports containing the slightest hint of cross-species DNA in any of these seven cases."

"What about fingerprints?" Vincent asked.

"We've run them through AFIS and IAFIS and nothing's matched."

*Nothing to connect Lafferty to these crimes, then,* Vincent thought with a rush of relief. Catherine had tracked him down because of a partial print he had left on a *button.* As a member of the armed forces, Lafferty's prints would be on file, just like his.

"Be careful," Tess said.

"I'll be discreet," he promised her.

"Is Child Services with Aliyah now?" Catherine asked.

"Yes. Another social worker, this one named Miranda Kuhl. There was a child psychologist in earlier, too, a Ginger Gill, but she couldn't get anywhere and she had to go on another call." She glanced at Vincent. "Maybe you can take a look at Aliyah before you leave?"

"I'm not a pediatrician," he demurred.

"But you were an ER doc," Catherine pointed out. "You have experience with trauma."

Tess nodded at him. "I don't mean that you should interview her face to face. If you'd be willing to stand by, observe…"

"Of course," he said. There was very little he wouldn't do for Tess Vargas. She'd put it all on the line for Catherine and him more than once.

Their battle strategy worked out, they walked briskly into the building. He deferred to Tess and Catherine, walking slightly behind them—this was their place of business, their territory. The precinct was buzzing with activity but Vincent immediately detected the piston-like heartbeat of a young person, swathed in the scent of fear.

"Speaking of trauma, Catherine, I have something I need to tell—" Tess began, but just then a uni hustled up to her with a clipboard and asked her to sign off on a form. Next the desk sergeant informed her that two squad cars were overdue for maintenance and if anything happened while they were on the street, some ambulance-chaser of a lawyer could bust their balls for it.

"Cap," one of the other detectives called from the coffee station, "we got our warrant. Can we go?"

"Yeah. Just don't take car eight or eleven," she replied.

"Got it," he said. He saluted her with his coffee cup. "Thanks."

At a head bob from Tess, Vincent went into the

observation room to view the proceedings through a one-way mirror. There was another person in the room, a young guy Vincent didn't recognize. He was a few inches shorter than Vincent, with unnaturally blue eyes, white-blond hair, and a deep tan all the more startling given the fact that it was January. His charcoal-gray suit was impeccable, had to have cost thousands. Vincent had learned about things like that from his days squiring heiress (and beast) Tori Windsor around town. Not a hair was out of place. The guy looked like a fashion model. Or a Ken doll.

"Hey." The guy extended his hand. Were his fingernails *buffed*? "Sky Wilson. Just got here from Malibu."

*Sky? This man's name is Sky?*

"Here?" Vincent echoed, shaking hands with him.

"To the one-twenty-fifth. I'm NYPD now." He grinned. "Like in that Eddie Murphy movie, only backwards."

Vincent wasn't tracking. The guy—Sky—said, "*Beverly Hills Cop*. He goes from Detroit to Beverly Hills. I'm the opposite." He gestured through the glass. "There she is."

An African-American woman was seated beside the girl Vincent had seen in the *Post* article. Aliyah Patel. Catatonic was the correct word: She stared sightlessly down at the table, registering no response as Catherine and Tess walked into the room. A winsome stuffed teddy bear perched in front of her. The precinct had a collection of them to give to kids in upsetting situations. Usually the kids hugged the bears, squeezing tight for comfort. Aliyah appeared to be totally disinterested in hers.

"Has she said anything?" Vince asked Wilson.

"She…? *Oh*. The little girl. No. Nothing. I'm not sure she's even blinked."

Vincent arched a brow. Apparently Wilson's "she" was not Aliyah Patel.

"Hello, Aliyah. My name is Cat," Catherine said gently, as

Tess pulled out a chair and sat down. "We have some donuts. Would you like one? Mrs. Kuhl, how about you?"

"That would be nice," the woman said. "How about a frosted with sprinkles?"

"I'll bring the whole box."

Catherine left the room and Wilson whistled under his breath. "All that sugar and gluten. *She* sure hasn't been hitting the donuts, know what I mean?"

Vincent blinked. *Cat* was his "she." *What the hell?*

"What business do you have with Detective Chandler?" he asked.

The man grinned. "I'm her new partner."

Vincent's mouth dropped open. Cat hadn't said a word about that. Maybe she didn't know. But Tess would have had to assign him to her. Without checking? That was impossible. Tess wouldn't do such a thing to her best friend.

*To my* girlfriend, he thought heatedly.

"Are you a detective, too?" Sky—Vincent couldn't call him Sky—*Wilson* asked.

"No," Vincent bit off. He was done talking to Malibu Ken. He focused on the interview room.

Wilson's phone went off. He took the call. "Well, hello there," he said silkily. "It's Joan, right? Hi, Joan. How's your day going? Did you try out that breathing exercise I told you about? Yes, turmeric. Ginger works too. Yes, we're in the city and… wow, a broken pipe? Mom sure didn't see *that* on today's chart."

He slowly moved his neck in a slow circle, then made a circle with his thumb and forefinger and closed his eyes. "Well, we *did* perform that feng shui sweep and I *thought* the bathroom might be an issue. The *qi* flows naturally to water. We did a cleansing and my tantra partner suggested a white sage smudge but we're not pagans. All belief systems are valid, of course. The path is the journey."

*What the hell is he talking about?*

Vincent gave him a look, and Wilson held up a hand, begging his indulgence. He was wearing a bracelet of wooden prayer beads. "It's true that we were hoping for a good night's sleep in our beds. Our melatonin is off and yes, exactly. *Thank you.*" He smiled. "...salutes the Buddha in you. *Namaste.*"

He hung up, closed his eyes and slowly exhaled. Vincent cast a sidelong glance at him. "You live with your mother?" he asked mildly.

Wilson touched the wooden beads on his wrist. "That's just for the rent control. Mom's actually staying out in Malibu, she's renewing her aura-reading certification. We have a spiritual leader, Sri Shapur. She lives in the Malibu Colony."

*Colony of what?*

Catherine returned to the interview room with a pink box of donuts and a container of milk from the vending machine in the hall. She set them down in front of Aliyah. The girl did not move. The social worker reached over and selected a chocolate donut covered with chocolate sprinkles. She took a bite. Aliyah still didn't so much as blink.

"This tastes so good," the woman announced.

Wilson sighed. "Milk is poison. And all that processed junk. So much imbalance. That's what crime is, you know, karmic imbalance. We're all spokes on the wheel..." His voice became a whisper. "We must do everything we can to restore balance."

Tess leaned forward with her hands folded on the table. "Aliyah, my name is Tess. We know things have been very scary for you, but we were wondering if you might be able to tell us what happened this morning at your apartment."

"Does she know her aunt's been murdered?" Vincent asked Wilson.

"*We* don't know if her aunt's been murdered," Sky said with exaggerated patience, as if he was dealing with someone on the outside looking in—a naïve civilian. "We have a team at the alleged crime scene that's gathering up evidence."

"Alleged," Vincent echoed, but Wilson was staring through the interview window with his right hand slightly upraised as if he were blessing them.

"We know something scary happened," Tess continued, "but we're not sure what it was."

The girl said nothing. She was truly catatonic. The best thing for her would be to let out the terror that had locked her up inside. But if she told them that she had seen a beast and went on to describe it, it would make it that much harder to keep Vincent's own truth hidden.

The social worker would probably figure she was using the image of a metaphorical monster to process what she had seen. It bothered him that a vulnerable little girl would be disbelieved, as so often happened to children in horrific circumstances. That was one way that human monsters like murderers were created—through childhood abuse and neglect, with no one to turn to. Mr. Riley had already indicated that Aliyah's home life was bad... and that no one had come to her aid.

Mrs. Kuhl took a napkin from the pink box and set down her donut, then bent over to her right. When she sat back up, she was holding some paper and a box of crayons. She kept a piece of paper, then distributed a sheet each to Catherine and Tess, and one for Aliyah. Then she opened the crayons.

"What's your favorite color, Detective?" the woman asked, holding out the box.

"Red," Tess and Catherine said in unison.

"I also like blue," Catherine offered.

"Not me. Sticking with red," Tess declared, reaching into the box. Catherine took a blue crayon and Mrs. Kuhl pulled out brown.

Aliyah did not take a crayon. She didn't even look at the box.

"Let's draw a picture of our mornings," the woman suggested.

Catherine and Tess bent over their papers. The social worker mostly doodled, watching Aliyah, who remained inert. Vincent cocked his head, trying to make out what Cat was drawing. After about thirty seconds, she held up her picture so that Vincent could see it. A lovely blue rose.

Vincent smiled faintly.

"This morning I went to talk to Mr. Riley," Catherine said. "He's so nice."

Aliyah's heart skipped a beat. Vincent honed in on her.

"Yeah, hi, Mom," Wilson said into his phone. "Listen, there's a burst pipe in the apartment. See? That's what I thought, too. It's the *qi* issue. What do you think about a white sage smudge?"

Vincent glared at him and Wilson held up his "sorry sorry" hand again. This time Vincent didn't back down, and Wilson grinned at him and shrugged.

"Mom, I'll have to call you back. Police business." He put the phone in his pants pocket.

Tess held up a picture of a stick figure standing in front of a tall building and showed it to Aliyah. "I went to your apartment, because something happened there."

Although Aliyah sat frozen in position, her heartbeat picked up and she began to sweat. He braced himself for her to bust loose.

Her little heart pumped harder. *Bumpbump bumpbump bumpbump*.

Faster.

Sweat beaded on her forehead. Her fingers twitched. It looked as if she was trying to cross them. Her lower lip quivered.

Then her pulse rate skyrocketed off the charts. An adult with a heartbeat that fast might go into defib.

*Here it comes*, he thought.

All the color drained from Aliyah's face and her mouth dropped open. But instead of screaming, as Vincent had anticipated, she went limp. She would have fallen out of her chair except that Catherine grabbed her and supported her weight while Tess and the social worker lent an assist.

Vincent burst out of the observation room and rushed into the interview room. He bent over Aliyah and gently pulled back each lid. Her pupils were negative. Her pulse was racing, her skin clammy to the touch, and her breathing was shallow. The musky combination of animal and human pheromones filled his nostrils. Beast odor. He didn't think it was her scent, but that it had been left on her. His head swam and he concentrated his apex predator senses, using the clues at hand to piece together the beast's home invasion: window glass, carpet fibers, wood splinters.

The murder itself: blood, tissue, bone.

Rage. Such incredible fury. This was not a random beast attack. This was payback.

For what? And by whom?

"Vincent?" Catherine asked softly, and he locked gazes with her, gave her a little nod. Yes, he had something to tell her. He couldn't wait to get to the crime scene. It contained a story with a beginning, a middle, and a gruesome end; one that, this time, he might be able to read. He'd come up empty at the other crime scenes. But this time he might even glean enough to learn the beast's identity.

"She's in shock," Vincent declared. "We should get her to the hospital."

Tess nodded and whipped out her phone. Catherine and the social worker flanked Vincent as he scooped Aliyah up and carried her out of the room. Wilson met them at the door and trailed after them.

"Let me experience her energy," Wilson said.

"What are you doing here?" Tess blurted. "You're a week early!"

Wilson frowned. "Cap said I was all set."

Tess shook her head and spoke into her phone. "Emergency, the one-hundred-twenty-fifth NYPD precinct headquarters. That is precinct one-two-five. Minor needs immediate medical transport." She repeated the pertinent medical details, with Vincent nodding at her to let her know she was getting it right.

"She's blocking out what happened," Vincent said. He wondered if Catherine and Tess knew that there were flecks of blood on her arms, possibly her aunt's. His mind jumped to DNA. Beast DNA. Something was different this time. Would the lab results be different too?

*That would be a dangerous game changer,* he thought.

"The ambulance is arriving out front," Tess told them.

Unis, detectives, and staff swiveled their heads at Vincent and the others as they dashed through the busy precinct bullpen. A paramedic in navy uniform approached and Vincent reeled off the medical details of Aliyah's collapse. A stretcher appeared seconds later and Vincent gently placed Aliyah on it. Her fingers stretched as if she were reaching for something. She had cuts on her hands.

He turned and saw that Catherine had grabbed up the bear from the interview room table and was cradling it under her chin. She held it out and he knew to put it on Aliyah's chest. It bobbed there as the paramedics loaded the stretcher into the ambulance. Mrs. Kuhl climbed in and sat across from her. Her face was grim but otherwise, she was composed. Vincent figured a woman in her position had seen just about everything—except a beast.

"I'll keep you posted," she said to Catherine and Tess. Then one of the paramedics shut the ambulance door, and the vehicle screamed away.

Tess turned to Vincent. "Beast?" Tess asked quietly.

"Definitely," he said under his breath. "I could tell this time. There's not a doubt in my mind on this one."

"But not the other six," Catherine elaborated. "Well, we all know that human beings are capable of monstrous brutality. Sad to say."

"So it's possible that the first six murders are unrelated to this one. The crime scene's still crawling with CSU," Tess recapitulated. "But I agree that you need to get inside as soon as you can. It'll take the lab a while to process all of the evidence, even if it's designated highest priority, which it will be. But we don't have any insiders in the medical examiner's department the way we used to." She meant Evan Marks, who had gotten entangled with Muirfield, and died at their hands. "So whatever you can get for just us, that would be awesome."

Second strategy session completed. Vincent nodded.

"Okay, then I'll—"

"Shouldn't one of us have gone in the ambo with the witness?" Wilson queried, interposing himself between Vincent and Tess. "What if she snaps out of it and starts talking?"

*Wow, he sounds like a real police officer now*, Vincent thought dryly.

"Then we'll rely on Mrs. Kuhl's statement," Tess informed him.

"But the prosecution could argue that that's hearsay."

"Mrs. Kuhl is a mandated reporter," Tess riposted with a hint of irritation. "I don't want to harass our witness. That could taint her statement, too. She's got enough going on, don't you think?"

"You're absolutely right, of course," he said, smiling at her. His teeth were so white and even that they looked artificial. And his eyes were preternaturally blue—contacts, Vincent realized. Maybe his tan was the spray-on kind. "If we all send out our energy, maybe we can reopen her channels of inner peace."

"Yes, go do that," Tess said quickly. "Go do it now."

"I'm sorry, I don't think we've met," Catherine said to Wilson. She was smiling her little mush-mouth smile, the one that signified that she was feeling a little prickly. Vincent translated: She didn't much care for Detective Swami, either.

"Sky Wilson," he said expectantly, extending his hand. When it was clear that his name wasn't registering, he added, "Your new partner."

She blinked at him. Tess grimaced, then put on her boss face and said, "Wilson's transferring in. I thought assigning him to our most seasoned detective—"

"*What?*" Cat said shrilly.

"—on a temporary basis—" Tess added. She appraised Wilson. "Very temporary—"

"I promise not to get in your hair," Wilson said easily. "Smooth and shiny though it is—"

"Hey, watch it, no sexual harassment," Tess blurted, then she wiped her hand over her face, dropped her arm to her side, and said, "Wilson and I'll be in my office. I'll brief you and show you around," she told the new guy.

"Yeah, you'd *better* run," Catherine muttered in a voice so low Vincent knew only he would hear it.

"Captain Vargas?" A uni approached. "May I speak to you a moment?"

Tess huffed and walked away with the foot soldier. Wilson trailed after Catherine. "So can you fill me in, partner?" he asked Catherine sotto voce as she began to stomp toward her desk. "I get the vibe that you and Captain Vargas and *you…*" He paused a moment as he looked at Vincent. "I didn't catch your name, actually."

Over her shoulder, Catherine said, "That's Dr. Vincent Keller. He's my boyfriend." She picked up a stack of "while you were out" notes and paged through them.

"Darn the luck." Wilson clucked his big white teeth and gave his head a shake.

Catherine slammed the stack of messages back onto her desk blotter. "Excuse me. I have to go speak to the *captain* for a moment." She whipped out her phone and thumbed a text. To Tess, Vincent assumed.

Catherine blasted past Wilson and him and headed for the office that had housed the precinct captain, Joe Bishop; then Assistant District Attorney Gabriel Lowan, a beast and multiple murderer; then Captain Ward, who had been Lowan's stooge until near the end of his tenure at the one-twenty-fifth; and now Tess. A revolving door, indicative of the ripples that Catherine's discovery of Vincent's existence had caused on so many levels in so many lives.

"I'll catch you later," Vincent said to her stiff, angry back. She raised a hand to show that she'd heard.

"Great to meet you, Vince," Wilson said. "Let's do sushi soon."

"Sounds like a plan." Vincent ground his teeth and saw himself out.

# CHAPTER FOUR

Inside the apartment she shared with Cat and, occasionally, Vincent, Heather Chandler thrust her weight onto one hip, took a step, and pushed out her other hip. Then she sipped her Sauvignon Blanc.

On the floor, a dozen tiny pieces of green fabric fluttered like autumn leaves. There were scraps everywhere, and a half-finished moss-colored handkerchief skirt she had ultimately decided was way too Halloween Gypsy lay on the sofa. A bottle of red wine was open and breathing, but Heather had decreed that they could only drink white while working on her pieces. Also, they could only eat white Cheddar cheese and white crackers. The crackers were kind of crumbling everywhere but she'd get out the vacuum in a sec.

"See? Like that," she said to her audience as she took another sip. She was getting a little sloshed. "You're walking the fashion runway. Not guarding the Tomb of the Unknown Soldier."

"Sweet darlin', that is *exactly* how I am walkin'." Walker Chastain, who worked as a photographer at the Silverado Academy of Design, *also* holding a glass of wine and munching on nummy cheese and crumbly crackers, demonstrated his walk. Tall and lanky, he took one precise step forward, and then another. He was no fashion model, but he *was* fluid sex appeal. Plus he was a strawberry-blond edging into ginger, so very tasty. He even had nubs of red hair on his toes. Hazel eyes with gold flecks, a dusting of macho facial hair. And the most adorable freckles.

He was swathed with chartreuse raw silk, the bodice featuring an off-center, plunging neckline and slashed dolman sleeves inset with sand-colored muslin, then captured in a bamboo bustier. Heather had dyed the bamboo strips in green tea. The skirt—a second one, of chartreuse—she wasn't sure of yet. She had pinned it up to Walker's shins—her model, Bai Mei, was about an inch shorter than he was—but she hadn't yet discovered the *design* of her design, as Rudi, her silks teacher, would say.

Walker was the only person who had seen her creation thus far. She was entering it in the New Looks competition and it was going to be a winner. She already knew it because a bamboo corset? That was a whole new level of look. The prize was a photo spread and a "Designer to Watch!" write-up in *Couture Bleu* magazine. Cat and Tess had been working a case at the magazine when Cat had found Vincent. So it was very cool that Heather had a chance of being discovered there herself.

"My lack of walk is because I don't have any hips. Or chi-chis." He cupped his chest with his hands. He had great pecs. Beneath all the silk, his body was ripped. He had an actual six-pack, an attribute far less common in New York than back in Miami, where people walked around half-naked so you had to work at it. In Miami, a formal affair meant you wore something *over* your bathing suit. And flip-flops instead of going barefoot.

"Walker, fashion models don't have hips or chi-chis. And

no one says chi-chis. They are boobs. I mean, breasts." She poured him a little more wine in the hope of loosening him up. Maybe she was expecting too much. Walker was so talented it was hard not to imagine that he was good at everything. She had met him when he'd come to shoot her class's models in their silk pajama pieces. The pictures he'd taken of Bai Mei were fantastic.

After that, it had been a matter of trading business cards—she was still working part-time as an events coordinator and her boss had been looking for a good photographer—and about a week after the New Looks competition had been announced, he'd texted her to meet for coffee. He loved Il Cantuccio, the Chandler women's go-to for all things caffeine, which only added to the *yes* of him. They'd been going out for two weeks now, and she was truly touched by the interest he'd been taking in her project.

"Try the walk again," she urged him.

He pushed out his hip. He had the cutest butt. "We say chi-chis in the south," he said. "We have a more polite aesthetic."

Heather grinned and rolled her eyes. "'Polite aesthetic.' If this was a sitcom, you'd be my stereotypical gay best friend."

"But it's not a sitcom, darlin'. It's real life." He gave her a long, slow grin. "And you *know* that I'm not gay."

He seductively slid the corset around his chest to reach the linen fasteners she'd invented just for the piece. They intersected and formed square knots that would not pull apart unless you pinched them together. *Another* fashion first. She was born for this. He undid the first one and rolled his hips in a circle.

"Way not gay," he murmured, sipping his wine. He undid another fastener and rolled his hips the other way, as if he were circling a hula hoop. As comical as his striptease was, Heather couldn't help a little tremor of excitement. In addition to a body to die for, Walker totally knew his way around the bedroom. After having her heart broken back in Florida, Heather was up for someone who thoroughly enjoyed being with her and told her she was beautiful at exactly the right moment.

"Walker, please, we need to work. This is my entry," she said, and he smiled languidly.

"Maybe we need to work on mine." He waggled his brows and unfastened another loop.

She giggled. This was fun. She loved having fun.

"And you need more wine," he added as the corset began to slide to the ground.

"Oh, careful!" Heather cried. "I've spent a hundred hours on that!"

She swooped down to retrieve it, nearly spilling wine on it, and as she straightened, the chartreuse skirt splashed to the floor like a waterfall. Walker stood proudly in his underwear, all the more endearing because they were clean baggy boxers with a splash of red paint on them. He painted. He was a serious visual artist. He was amazing with oils, and she loved that he worked late at night in his boxers. She hadn't been to his place but he'd told her it was a cold-water flat, like a garret back in Paris. He was quirky and artistic.

"Careful with the hundred-hour dress," he intoned, and gently lifted her creation off the floor. He carefully folded it and held it out to her with a bow. She curtseyed and took it from him. Then he drained his wine glass, set it down, picked her up in his arms, and carried her toward her bedroom.

"*Entering* the hallway," he said. He turned. "*Entering* your bedroom. *Entering*…"

She kissed him. He returned the favor. Then he carried her to her bed and set her down. Blissed-out, Heather arranged her fashion items on her nightstand and held out her arms.

"You're the best," she said.

"Boom-ba-ba-boom." He thrust his hips from side to side.

The mattress dipped beneath his weight.

"We left kind of a mess in the front room," she said.

"Later, busy brain. Hip thrusters, we are go for launch!" He kissed her again.

And again and again and again.

*This cannot be more perfect,* Heather thought happily. *All my planets are in alignment. Nothing's going to mess this up.*


"Hey, buddy," Vincent said on the other end of the line. He was in the Bronx, waiting his turn to investigate the Patel crime scene. "Are there any cameras at east one-sixty-first? I've been looking and I don't see any."

J.T. sat at command central in the once-abandoned gentlemen's club that was his, and formerly Vincent's, home and hacked into the highly illegal-to-use surveillance system as he had done so many times before. Maybe now that Tess was the precinct captain, she could bail him out if he ever got arrested by the NSA.

The keyboard clacked like a concerto as he searched. "That's a big negative, big guy," he said glumly. "Guess no one is interested in what goes on in such a high crime area."

"I detect a hint of sarcasm."

"Sara's dating this guy who just got tenure. For research into bioluminescence. I mean *really.* Hasn't it all been done?"

"Except that you don't care about Sara," Vincent said, "because you're with Tess."

"Am I?" J.T. grabbed a gummy worm and bit off its head. Which maybe was its tail. "I never see her anymore. We don't talk."

"She's under a lot of pressure because of her promotion," Vincent reminded him. "And you know the one-twenty-fifth is under the microscope because of all the dirty laundry. Remember when your research wasn't going well? After Dolly the sheep got cloned and then it all went south? There was a long stretch there when we barely spoke."

"So you think I'm overreacting," J.T. said. A little flicker of hope warmed his sad heart. "That Tess is just preoccupied and I'm... not."

"Something like that. She's got so much going on, you know?"

"And I... don't." He grabbed another gummy worm. Bit hard down on its gummy midsection, savoring its gummy guts.

"It's like the old days," Vincent offered. "Before all the insanity."

*Back to square one. Me lonely and you... not back to square one.*

"Yeah, insanity," J.T. said. "Who needs it?" His phone signaled another call. "Hey, hold on, someone's on the other line," he said, and switched over. "Star Command."

That got a chuckle. "What if it hadn't been me?" Tess asked.

"Well, Vincent's on the other line and I don't get a whole lot of calls. So the odds were good."

"About that," she began, and then she cleared her throat. "I envy you. My entire day has been phone calls and meetings. If I'd had two seconds to think I would have given this to you hours ago."

"I'm listening." Something to do. Yay.

"Cat and Vincent got a phone number this morning that we think may have belonged to a Muirfield whistle-blower. Private X. Apparently he was in Afghanistan and he wants to talk. Our IT is coming up empty but I know you can go where no geek has ever gone before."

"Roger that, Jean-Luc," he said.

"Now you're getting obscure." She gave him the number.

"I'll run it," he promised her. "Jean-Luc was on *Star Trek*. He was *Next Gen*."

"Thanks. There's too many *Star Trek* shows. I mean,

aren't they all pretty much the same? What has Vincent got?"

*Pretty much the same?* A cold wind blew inside the gentlemen's club.

"He can't go in yet. The CSUs are still in there."

"Will the trail go cold for him?" Tess asked with a hint of worry in her voice.

"Not this fast. As I've said before, Vincent can track prey across the Sahara for, like, a year. And that's only a minor exaggeration."

"I still find that creepy. Okay. Call my cell but only if you get something, okay? Cat and I are going to have coffee."

"Nice gig," he said tightly. How long had it been since they had gone out for coffee? Or for anything?

"Not really. We're having it in my office. I have some groveling to do. It won't be pretty. Luckily I'm so busy that I have to keep it short."

He was intrigued. He wondered what was up. "So, will you have time for dinner tonight? I can go back through the history of *Star Trek* with you." He tried for a light, casual tone.

"It'll probably be Chinese at my desk. Right now there's a very large angry crowd in front of the precinct demanding to know why we aren't doing more to stop these homicides. I have to go out there and make a statement." She grunted. "I might have to skip coffee with Cat."

"That's… too bad?" he guessed.

"No. That would be good. It might give her time to cool off."

J.T. blinked. "What's going on? Are you two—"

"Gotta go." The call ended. J.T. grunted unhappily and switched back over to Vincent. "Tess just told me there's another demonstration in front of the precinct."

"That's bad," Vincent said. "All these murders. Remember Beth Bowman, Catherine's friend?"

"The reporter Gabe killed? By ripping out her heart?"

"We spun that one that he was committing vicious murders and trying to pin them on me. But he's dead and I've been exonerated."

"I follow where you're going," J.T. said. "There's no way to deflect these cases. Someone's going to figure this out. If you detected a beast presence when you were with Aliyah Patel, there's going to be evidence at the crime scene."

"Unless this beast is different and the lab equipment doesn't have the right markers."

There was a beat. Then at the exact same time, both of them said, "Or unless someone *else* switches the samples out."

"New beast, new beast-maker. New conspiracy," Vincent said. He sounded tired.

"We never seem to run out of them, do we." J.T. was not posing a question. "Maybe in this day and age we can't expect this just to stop. Digital files, info clouds... back when Rebecca Reynolds wrote out her journal in longhand, beasts could be kept a secret."

"Not really. Her beast, Alastair, was burned at the stake," Vincent reminded him.

"Tess called to put me on the phone number you got this morning," he said. "A 'Private X'? 'Private' as in 'for your eyes only' or 'private' as in 'army'?"

Vincent was silent for a moment. J.T. waited for yet another dire revelation.

"It's about Lafferty," he said with guilt and self-loathing in his voice. J.T. would recognize those qualities anywhere. Vincent had been quite the brooder before Cat had come into his life.

"*Lafferty*. What about Lafferty?" J.T. asked cautiously. When his best friend stayed mute, J.T. hunched forward, as if Vincent were sitting on the other side of the desk instead of spying on NYPD CSU. "Vincent, we've been over this. You had no way of knowing."

"J.T., you don't think… could this *be* Lafferty?"

"*What?*" J.T. was so shocked he rose from his chair. It fell over backwards with a crash.

"I mean, if they did something *else* to her. I thought she died. I thought I saw it. But maybe she survived… and went into hiding like I did but then something happened. Something *more*. Maybe, I don't know, she's here looking for me. Because of our past. Because of… what I did." He sighed. "I mean, what I *didn't* do."

"No, Vincent. We've been through this."

"But that was before the letter."

"No one has actually told me about the letter," J.T. said.

"I have a picture of it. I'll send it to you. Hold on."

J.T. held. Vincent's photo arrived and J.T. opened the letter up on one of his computer monitors. He read it.

"Karl Tiptree," he said. "I think I've come across his name in research somewhere."

"Cat and Tess are investigating, but if you can make any connections that'd be great," Vincent said. "I went to that crime scene back when he was murdered. I had no sense at all that he'd been killed by a beast, J.T. None. But today, when I carried Aliyah Patel to the ambulance, I knew she'd been in the proximity of a beast. Maybe that means there are *two* beasts besides me. One I can sense… and one that I can't."

"Oh boy." J.T. rested his hand on his forehead. "After this, can we all, like, go on a sabbatical or something? A cruise? With lots of drinking?"

"It does seem like we can't catch a break," Vincent agreed.

"We've been involved in more homicide investigations than there are people in the state of Wyoming. I know. I checked." He clicked his keyboard and zoomed in on a grid of NYC traffic. "I can't give you camera footage but I can say that the entire block where the attack occurred is completely blocked off. Which sounds redundant. Block and block."

"It's like a war zone," Vincent said. "I went up on a rooftop but the angle was wrong. I can't get into the abandoned warehouse across from the apartment building, either. Police presence."

J.T. heard the change in his voice. Vincent had repressed the guilt and remorse and was concentrating on solving the case. That was what Vincent lived for now—justice. And Catherine, of course. J.T. was glad his friend had found love, and a renewed sense of purpose, but he himself was beginning to question his own place in all of this. Tess had once urged him to be "less Robin, more Batman," but in the meantime, Vincent had fully embraced his inner Caped Crusader and J.T. wasn't even Robin anymore. He was the guy back at HQ doling out the information. Pretty much all the important superheroes had an IT guy: Professor X, Ron Stoppable on *Kim Possible*…

He ate another gummy worm and stared down at the phone number. Why give someone a bogus number? Two answers came to mind: one, the number hadn't been bogus when it had been given; two, someone was keeping track of the location of phones used to call the number.

"Or three, it's a code that they're expecting someone to crack," he said aloud. "The wrong phone number."

"Yeah," Vincent said slowly. "They had to figure Mr. Riley would go to someone. The army, or the police… But which side are they really on? Are they trying to get justice for Lafferty or dangling a baited hook to see who will bite? Putting Karl Tiptree's name in, too, and mentioning a *serum*?"

"So they're upping the ante? Doling out clues?" J.T. picked up another gummy worm, then went for an antacid instead. "Vincent, it sounds to me like they're trying to draw *you* out."

"But no one knows about me," Vincent began, and then he sighed. "Someone always knows."

"Maybe these guys are an old Muirfield cell, even." The antacid powdered his mouth. He grabbed another. "I'm getting fond of the 'trap' theory. There had to be reports about Lafferty in the infirmary. Cat's mom probably wrote them. They were observing you guys all the time. They'd know you went to visit Lafferty in the infirmary. They probably overheard her… asking…" He trailed off.

"Asking for my help. Begging me to get her out of there. And I didn't listen. I sentenced her to death myself."

"Hel-lo, Vincent, do not go there. You didn't know."

"She was Delta Company. One of mine."

"Exactly. She was a *soldier*." Suddenly J.T. realized something: Vincent had never left square one, when they had lived in hiding in the old warehouse and he had oozed guilt. They were both still half-in, half-out of their cocoons. Why didn't that make him feel better?

"I need to go," J.T. said, more gently. "I have to do my thing here."

"Yeah, me too. Thanks, J.T."

"Don't mention it." He hesitated. "Wait. Thanks for what, specifically?"

"Everything."

Vincent disconnected, leaving J.T. feeling warm and fuzzy, if a bit confused. He set up a protocol to dial various combinations of the phone number after accounting for known scam numbers. Once that was up and running, he started applying various decryption algorithms to attempt to break the encoded message, if such existed. He was tempted to start a Karl Tiptree investigation of his own, but he was up to his ass in variables as it was. So on that ass, he sat in his chair and listened to the phone calls his computer attempted. No service, no service, out of order…

"Logan's Pizzeria," a voice said.

"May I speak to Private X?" J.T. asked calmly.

"Say what? We're a pizzeria." The man sounded genuinely puzzled.

"Sorry, wrong number." J.T. ended the call.

The computer dialed another number. A phone rang.

"Fix-You-Fast Mufflers."

J.T. cleared his throat. "May I speak to Private X?"

"What?"

"Sorry. Wrong number."

It was going to be a long day.

"Look, Cat, I'm really sorry," Tess said, handing Cat a coffee laden with sugar and cream. "I was going to tell you about partnering with Wilson but he wasn't supposed to be here until next week."

"But why is he here *ever*?" Cat demanded. "I thought we had a hiring freeze. Why are we hiring Surfer Joe from California and *why* did you assign me to be his partner without even asking me?"

"Because I'm your captain now, okay?" Tess flared, but Cat didn't back down. They'd blown past the chain of command two years ago. Tess and Cat had both thought in black-and-white terms before Vincent had arrived on the scene, but that was then and this was now. The world was complex and gray and in the current case with Cat, bright red.

"Okay." Tess deflated. She picked up her coffee stirrer and tapped it randomly on her open palm. Cat gave her the moment she so obviously needed.

"Joe," she blurted out. She wrinkled her nose. "And it's corny and underhanded and I'm sorry, but he was... important to me. And I still care about him." She peered up through her lashes at Catherine, awaiting her reaction.

Cat didn't follow. Tess made a face and shut her eyes.

"You and I know the captain at the Malibu Police Department. Janice McAllister? She went to the police academy with us. She went out there and tore it up, zoomed right up the ladder with a ton of cleared cases. She heard about my promotion. We got to talking, trading emails, you know, work stuff. And then she said she'd heard Joe was interviewing around, trying to get back into police work. She said she would give him a job if we would take Sky in trade."

Cat's mouth dropped open. "*Tess.* Why didn't you talk to me about this?"

Tess shook her head. "The deal was sealed and then at the last minute he asked if you two could partner until he settled in. I was going to ask you, I swear. He got here early."

"Why do we have him?" Meaning *why don't they want him?*

"A female officer was about to file a big sexual harassment suit that bore no merit. Janice swore to me that it was going to be messy and expensive and would lead nowhere. The officer in question is the daughter of a film producer and her father has come in *every week* to see how his baby is doing."

"So no due process if he was charged and it moved forward," Cat said.

"You know I believe that sisterhood is powerful but this would not end in justice for anyone. And, Cat, it was for Joe."

Cat humphed. Tess tapped her stirrer against the plastic lid of her coffee cup. "Wilson said you were the best detective in the precinct. I told him it would only be temporary, maybe a month at most. And I *was* going—"

"You're my pimp," Cat cut in, furious. "My cop pimp. I don't even know you!"

"Temp-o-rary," Tess pleaded. "Hey, I put my job on the line a million times for you when you were covering for Vincent. You know I did."

"So now what? I owe you?" Cat asked indignantly. And then she calmed down a little. Because she did owe Tess.

"Argh, Tess. Now I've got him glued to my hip while we try to investigate a rash of beast killings?"

"Timing sucks," Tess agreed remorsefully.

"The timing on this would suck if the one-twenty-fifth never had another case, ever. Not even shoplifting."

"Don't hate me," Tess said.

"Does Joe know? Does this mean you're getting back together?" *J.T. will be heartbroken*, she thought.

"No, oh, god, no." Tess buried her face in her hands. "In fact, I made that a condition of the deal. That Joe would never know."

"How can you even make this happen?" Cat asked. "There's human resources and all kinds of hoops, right? I mean, I had to fill out three dozen forms to requisition a dictionary."

Tess shrugged. "It's different when you're a captain. And what do you want a dictionary for? Just go online."

"That's what every single person in every single department told me." Cat rolled her eyes. "There's nothing like a good, decent dictionary at your elbow..." She trailed off. "It became a thing. I was typing up a report and I went to the online dictionary and it stalled. And I got frustrated and decided to get a regular dictionary and when everyone started acting like I wanted the Crown Jewels I got stubborn... and this is not the point."

"Two weeks. Then Tofu Man is on his own. I swear it." Tess held up two fingers, Boy Scout style. "And not a word to J.T., okay? If he found out about Joe..." She caught her bottom lip between her teeth. "J.T.," she said softly.

"Things are still weird?" Cat asked, allowing her best friend to change the subject. She wanted it to work out between Tess and J.T., but more importantly, she wanted Tess to be happy.

"He's so distant. He's pulling away a little more every day. I don't know what it is. Maybe it's because I don't understand what he's talking about half the time. Three-quarters of the time. He's a brainy science guy."

"*We're* brainy. We're detectives," Cat reminded her. "And hey, look at all the amazingly complicated schemes we put together to protect Vincent *and* J.T." She tapped her temple. "Brainy."

"Yeah. But I can't even keep *Star Trek* straight." Suddenly Tess looked young and scared. Gone was the streetwise tough chick and in her place sat Cat's best friend in all the world, struggling under a very heavy load. Cat's protective instincts washed over her indignation like the Pacific Ocean on the sultry sands of Malibu Beach.

"It's not too late to sell hot dogs at Coney Island," Cat said, and Tess cracked a smile. That had been their backup plan when they'd been in the police academy, watching cadets drop like flies until only New York's Finest were left. "Or we could open a private detective agency. We're two-thirds of Charlie's Angels. We could recruit Heather."

"Your sister with a gun? She wouldn't pick her sparkly bullet casings up after herself. I'm going with the hot dogs."

There was a knock on the door. Tess exhaled slowly. "That will be my press conference with the mayor. Remember when it was some other poor schmuck who had to do this?"

"You'll do great," Cat said. "And J.T. loves you with all his heart."

"Yeah." Tess pushed away from her desk and stood. "Okay." She didn't sound convinced on either score. "Officially, you're working on the financial forensics for Indira Patel and Julia Hogan. Give Hogan to your very, very, very temporary partner so we can keep as close control as possible of beast-related activities ourselves." She broke her stirrer in half. "Talk about the *way* suckiness of timing."

"I'll be nice to Sky," Cat said, and then she mentally kicked herself. *Why* make a promise she didn't want to keep?

# CHAPTER FIVE

## The Bronx

At last the CSUs left the crime scene at the Patel apartment. Yards of yellow caution tape choked the perimeters of both their building and the abandoned warehouse across the alley. Inside the apartment building, more tape ran down the length of the common hall on their floor and looped a stairwell that glowed bright green with bloodstains beneath a black light after the Luminol had been applied. Vincent had eavesdropped on the evidence techs, who kept telling each other over and over that they'd never seen anything like this in their entire careers and hoped never to again.

It was seven-thirty in the evening. The sun had set, and the moon was a thin slice of bone. Large drifts on the ground would reveal his trespassing unless it snowed tonight or tomorrow's temperatures rose high enough to melt away the evidence. The surest solution would be to take the time to cover his tracks. Meantime, he would do his best not to leave trace evidence of his own, if indeed someone was looking for a beast that had escaped Muirfield's extermination plan. For that reason, he wore shoe covers over his boots.

He went into the warehouse first. The CSUs had stated their opinions that the perp had loitered there for some time, evidenced by a large quantity of fresh shoe prints—men's size eight. A bit on the small side, which indicated that the owner of the shoes would probably be on the shorter side—five-eight, perhaps. Each time he acquired a new piece of data, Vincent focused and tried to move into tracking mode. So far, he was drawing a blank.

A side door hung cockeyed like a drunk drooping from a lamppost. Since he could see in the dark, he had no need of a flashlight, and he slipped in with the studied silence of a Special Forces operative. He had been a good solider, strong and relentless, and now his body responded to his military bearing with seasoned reflexes. It felt easy and right, like stepping into a favorite old pair of shoes, or coming back home after a long time away.

Rats were blobs of red thermal flare in his enhanced vision. He smelled dead animals and, sadly, evidence that human beings had lived there since the warehouse closure. Homeless people, seeking shelter from the elements, though none recently, thank goodness.

He made his way toward the back of the warehouse, where the footprints had been individually flagged for photographs. Impressions had been taken, ostensibly of the best prints. He studied them and drew in deep breaths. An image clicked into sharp focus: shorter man, mid-forties, light brown hair with a military buzz cut. Steely gray eyes in a rectangular face. Wearing army fatigues and lace-up boots with soles that matched the impressions on the floor. A smoker who preferred cigars. He had been carrying an Uzi—an Israeli-style submachine gun.

The man smelled like gun oil, diesel fuel, Kevlar, fiberglass, styrene, and rubber, and Vincent got the distinct impression that he'd been on a covert mission.

*This guy is still military,* Vincent realized. *If this is Private X, he stayed in. And he's sure as hell not a private. Was he here with the beast creature? Deploying it against a female civilian?*

He heard his thoughts switching to military-speak. He hadn't even been in that long, but his indoctrination had been deep and thorough. One could even argue that the army was in his DNA.

After a minute or so with no additional input, he moved toward the stove-in back wall, where the docking bay was located. Ducking beneath a banner of caution tape, he proceeded onto the concrete apron of the dock. He saw the destroyed window in the building across the alley, a huge, ragged blast hole. Was it possible that the soldier had fired a rocket launcher at it? Surely that would have been apparent to Tess and her CSU team. She hadn't mentioned anything like that, however.

He took a few steps forward. And then a terror so intense, so all-encompassing hit him, and he gasped and contracted as if he'd been gut-punched. He was bolted to the concrete, shaking from head to toe. Hyperventilating. His mind beginning to shut down into catatonia, as Aliyah's had. His rational mind retreating, leaving his reptilian brain to deal with the crisis.

Correction: leaving his *beast* brain to deal with it.

"No," he whispered. This was bad, really bad. He had to get out of there. Now. Fast.

Too late. The change was coming. A tsunami of hormones flooded his nervous system, his blood, his muscles, every cell of his body. The world shimmered and shifted. Danger, everywhere. Sight, sound, touch, taste, smell: *imminent peril. Life-threatening.*

*Must kill.*

*Must destroy.*

A tiny part of him fought back: *I am Vincent Keller.* Reflexes and instincts braided together, tugging at him to attack the danger. What was the war zone mantra? *Kill anything that moves.*

But nothing was moving on the loading deck.

*The search field must be expanded then. Fan out.*

That was not his beast brain, but the programming he had undergone; first as a recruit, and later, as Agent Reynolds' private assassin. Soldier and monster were united; that was what the supersoldier program had been designed to create. Not mindless killing machines, but thinking men housed inside enhanced warrior bodies.

But he could not fan out. He was paralyzed. Then an ice-cold certainty yanked a roar from his throat.

*Enemy approaching.*

The interior of his brain was a blaring siren; it was exploding bombs; it was the imperative to *kill kill kill*.

But beast-Vincent still could not move. Something wafted around him, something in the air, which rendered him inert. The messages that were screaming in his brain to act were simply not being received.

*Kill kill kill*

No part of him acknowledged the order even though the threat was advancing. Blurring toward him. Almost on him.

Digging deep, fighting for survival, beast-Vincent's primal instincts sizzled and snapped, arcing in an effort to make connections, to get his body moving. To save his life.

*Kill kill kill*

His heart was rocketing toward a heart attack. Sweat washed down his face. He was shaking so hard he was beginning to seize.

The enemy was here.

*Kill kill kill*

But beast-Vincent did not kill.

Like Aliyah Patel in interview room A, he collapsed, limp and helpless, to the floor.

* * *

"Walker?"

Bleary eyed from sleep and wrapped in a sheet from her bed, Heather peered into the hall. She'd figured maybe Walker was taking a shower, but she didn't hear the water. She shuffled into the living room, taking pains to be modest because Vincent might be there. She was glad Cat had a sweetie and all, but it certainly did make life more… complicated.

Wow, had they left a mess. She grimaced and checked the digital clock on the microwave. It was past eight. No wonder she was starving. And where was Cat?

More to the point, where was Walker? Had he at least left her a note?

"Hey?"

Nothing.

She shuffled back into her room and put on an oversized T-shirt and a pair of flannel pajama bottoms. It was chilly in the apartment so she added socks and her bathrobe. A quick search of the rumpled bedclothes revealed no note. She did find one of Walker's business cards on the floor, though— WALKER CHASTAIN, VISUAL ARTS AND PHOTOGRAPHY—with the letter L written in ink on the back, and then a local phone number. Who was L? She felt a pang of jealousy as she set it on her dresser. She checked her phone for a message. Nothing.

She started to call him, decided that could become just too embarrassing, and concentrated on cleaning up the living room before Cat got home. Heather knew that Cat was keeping track of the messes and resenting them, which wasn't fair. Cat knew full well that surrounding yourself with the stuff you needed was part of the creative process. Look at how she had set up Mom's murder board and gotten out all those clippings when Vincent had appeared in her life.

*Yeah, and it was enough to make me move out,* Heather

thought. *All I've got is fabric. And wine bottles. And a few cracker crumbs. And some cheese under the couch.*

She was finished cleaning at a little before nine, and her sister still hadn't returned home. She was just about to call her when her own phone rang. For a second she couldn't locate it, but then she realized it was on the nightstand under her dress and corset. As she moved them, something registered about the garments—that something about them was different than when she'd set them down—but she didn't know what it was. Probably her imagination, and anyway, she'd just been, um, very active on her bed and of course they'd been a little disheveled.

"Hel—"

"Is Vincent there?" Cat whispered on the other end of the line.

"No." Massively disappointed that it wasn't Walker, Heather carried the phone as she scooted down the hall in her socks and opened Cat's bedroom door. "No," she repeated, more firmly. "Why are you whispering?"

"Has he called you?" Cat kept whispering.

*Why would he call me?* Heather thought, but Cat was freaking out so she said, "No. Is everything okay?"

"No," Cat said. "I mean, I'm fine, Heather. I just don't know where he is. He went to investigate a crime scene two hours ago and we haven't heard from him. I'm there now and I… " Her voice trailed off. "I just found his phone."

Heather swallowed. This was not good. "What can I do?"

Then she heard a man's voice on Cat's end saying, "The vibrations here are off the charts. This was an abnormal homicide."

"Funny thing," Cat said aloud. "In New York, we classify all homicides as abnormal."

"Cat? Are you okay? Who's with you?"

"My partner," Cat bit off. Heather's forehead wrinkled.

Cat didn't have a partner. "Hey, listen, could you check with J.T.? And call me back?"

"Um, sure. Yes," Heather said.

Cat ended the call.

Heather speed-dialed J.T. while she climbed onto the fire escape and went up on the roof, hoping that Vincent would magically be there. But she was all alone with a great view of the skyline when J.T. answered.

"Heather?"

"Um, yeah," she said. "Cat just found Vincent's phone at the crime scene and there's some guy with her. I guess she couldn't talk so she asked me to call you. Is Vincent with you?"

"No." She could hear the anxiety in his voice. "Hang on while I swallow an entire bottle of Tums."

"This isn't funny," Heather said, smoothing back her hair.

"Oh, believe me, I'm not laughing."

"Could he be with Tess?"

"Why would he be with Tess?"

"I don't know. Why is his phone at a crime scene?" She went back down the fire escape, and into Cat's room. She looked around for clues to Vincent's whereabouts.

Cat's top dresser drawer was open. Heather glanced inside. Nothing seemed out of place.

She closed it.

"Hold on," J.T. said. "Tess is on the other line."

Heather drummed her fingers on top of Cat's dresser. Then she left the room and went back to her room to look at her corset. *That's* what was different. The muslin loops had been refastened. *And half of the top one was missing.*

"Walker, what the hell?" she cried.

J.T. came back on. "That was Tess. She's at the houseboat. He's not there."

"Is there anywhere else he might go if he's in danger?" she asked.

"A thousand places. The sewers... *my office*," J.T. said. "That's one of our rendezvous points. I can't leave here. I have to watch the security cameras."

"I could check your office," Heather offered. She wasn't sure about offering to check the sewers.

"I've got the only key. Here, with me."

"Well, I could come over to your place and watch the security cameras while you go to your office." When he hesitated, she scowled as if he could see her. "J.T., I'm not some flighty kid anymore. I'm a grown-up woman and I'm more tech-savvy than Cat. And you wouldn't hesitate to ask *her*."

"Okay, yeah, I'm sorry. Yes. Come here and I'll go there."

"On my way," she said, then glanced down at herself. "After I change."

## PATEL CRIME SCENE

"I offended you," Wilson said. "Somehow. About...?" He smiled at Cat.

He didn't know that she'd palmed Vincent's phone on the dock, and that she was wild to get rid of her new partner so she could search for him in earnest. Wilson couldn't know that she was looking for anything specific, and he had spent half his time with his eyes closed, breathing rhythmically.

Panning the walls with her flashlight, she said, "No, it's just that I usually do this part alone. Immerse myself in the scene and try to imagine what happened." *Like an apex predator, only not one-tenth as useful.*

"The energy is very negative," he ventured. "Violent." He slumped and shook his head. "It's draining."

"Oh, wow, you must be jet-lagged," she said. "You should go home and rest."

"Well, 'home' is a hotel tonight," he said. "My apartment's got a plumbing issue. Unless I find some other place to stay…" He smiled at her.

*No way. I'm telling Tess.*

"I'm staying here," she said flatly. "By myself."

A text came in from Heather: *Vincent not home. J.T. going to university to look. I'll watch computers.*

Cat replied, *OK, stay in touch.*

Tess was right; even after the CSUs had carted away carloads of evidence, the crime scene remained a chamber of horrors. Although she couldn't track the way Vincent could, she could reconstruct some of the details of the crime. The violence, the savagery. The broken window had let in fresh snow and rooms were freezing; the blood that had been left behind was crystallizing. Destruction, everywhere. Aliyah Patel had witnessed at least some of this. It was getting to Sky, too.

"So I'll see you tomorrow," she prompted, giving him her patented fake smile. Then her eyes widened in surprise as he opened his arms and threw back his head.

"Divine Shiva, bless this place. Cleanse the evil from these walls and floors. Let the wheel turn!"

He began a singsong chant at the top of his lungs. Cat regained her composure, tapped him on the shoulder, and said, "All right. We're done here." She was the senior partner. He had to do as she said.

"This place is shimmering with a black aura," he argued. "It needs to be cleansed."

"Tomorrow," she said.

"You shouldn't stay here alone."

"I have my trusty aura-smasher." She pulled away her coat and showed him her gun.

"I'm serious. The vibes here are dangerous."

"We're in a dangerous business. I'm *telling* you to go."

He pressed his hands together and bowed. "Got it. I'll just grab a cab, then."

"Good."

He gave her one last look and then he departed the scene. She rubbed her arms for warmth and walked the rooms, searching for signs of Vincent. She explored the halls and the stairwells. The other residents had been told to find other places to stay tonight. Cat doubted any of them would be sleeping in hotels.

She went back outside into heavily falling snow and hurried back to the dock to look for footprints before they were obliterated. She was too late. The snow was rapidly piling up.

Then as she watched, she noticed that the snow wasn't accumulating in the eastern corner of the dock, and she hurried over. Pointing her flashlight downward, she saw that a sizable gash in the wood about four feet wide had been obscured from view by shadow and trash. It appeared to be new. A beast could have done it. So was a beast down there?

She angled the beam. *Bingo*. The gash had created an entryway into the city sewer system. She texted Tess to see if she could provide backup, but her former partner didn't reply. It was foolish to even pretend that Cat would wait for Tess to arrive. Still, she tried not to be too foolhardy as she sussed out how to descend without hurting herself. A coil of frayed rope lay atop a trio of paint cans. She gave it a few experimental tugs between her hands; when it held, she looped some around her waist, tied it to a pole, and then leaned back to put tension on it. Still good.

She unwrapped the rope and dropped it into the hole. Then she grabbed on and began to shimmy down. Her ear was cocked for any sort of noise. For all she knew, a beast that was not Vincent was down there.

One, or more.

\* \* \*

Heather arrived in record time with a giant purse that was apparently all the rage (what did *he* know?), and as soon as he showed her how to key in various search patterns on the cameras, J.T. drove to Northam University. The parking lot was almost empty and he walked quickly but cautiously from his car to the bio building. He kept compulsively checking his phone, praying that someone would let him know that Vincent had been found and was fine. Preferably that news would come from Vincent himself.

He was halfway to his office but nearly hung a U-turn when he caught sight of Sara and Mr. Tenure gazing at each other beneath the energy-saving fluorescents like they were about to launch into the big show-stopping love duet from *Phantom*. What were they doing here? There was a third person with them—a young, attractive woman in a black turtleneck sweater and a black wool miniskirt over black tights and boots that hugged her calves. She wore a spectacular pair of thick black-rimmed glasses that reminded him of Harry Potter, but in a cute-nerd-girl way. Not that he was checking her out at a time like this.

"Dr. Forbes," Sara said formally as he approached. Even beneath the bad lighting, he could see a flush spread across her cheeks. She was still pissed off at him. Why? She'd found true love. With a guy who had tenure. So it had all worked out for her, right?

"Oh, *this* is Dr. Forbes." The other woman's eyes widened as she pushed up her glasses—*cute*—and stuck out her hand. "I'm Heidi Schwann. I was just telling Dr. Holland that I was hoping to be your teaching assistant next semester and here you are."

None of this was computing, and J.T. didn't have time for it. But he took her hand and shook it.

"I'm Heidi's thesis advisor," Sara said. Then the flush

deepened and she added, "And of course you know David."

"Tenure. Bioluminescence," J.T. said with forced joviality. "Congratulations." J.T. wanted to punch the guy in the face.

"Thanks." David put a proprietary arm around Sara's shoulders. Smug bastard. "Life is good."

*Just die*, J.T. thought. "Great. Well, I have to get into my office. I'm running a protocol at my house but I forgot a key... piece of research that I only have in hard copy." He knew he didn't have to explain anything. But he was very nervous, and getting more nervous by the moment.

"Oh, may I walk with you?" Heidi Schwann chirruped. "I'd love to hear about your work."

"I have to make a couple of quick calls," he said apologetically. "Then I have to get back. I left my program running."

"Oh." Her head bobbled up and down like, well, a bobblehead... and then she continued to walk beside him. He was just about to make it clearer that he needed his space when he caught sight of the door to his office. It was ajar. It was always locked, always. Someone had broken into his office. Was it Vincent? Who else could it be?

Unfortunately, there was a long and mysterious list.

He reached for the knob and looked back at Heidi. "So, I'll catch you sometime tomorrow?" he hinted. Was she trying to look past him into his office? Yes. That was exactly what she was doing. Luckily the lights were off.

He waited. Finally she stirred. "Sorry, what? Oh, tomorrow. Sure. Of course." She jerked her hand forward in an almost inhuman way, like she was one of those octopus aliens in *Galaxy Quest*. Eager to be rid of her, he shook her hand briskly again and smiled at her to take out the sting of the quasi-rejection.

"Tomorrow," he repeated.

She pushed up her glasses again. "What time?"

It dawned on him that she might be even more socially

awkward than he was. He had no idea what time he would be in tomorrow. *If* he would be in tomorrow.

"Noon." A nice round time, easy to remember, easy to make excuses about if he needed to.

"Good." She almost hopped with happiness on the balls of her feet. She was actually quite charming. "Okay then." She gave him a little wave, *exactly* like the aliens in *Galaxy Quest,* and then she took a couple of steps backwards, as if she wasn't quite sure what to do next.

*Exit stage left,* J.T. mentally prompted her. Then, to his relief, she did just that. He watched her toodle down the hall until he was satisfied that he would be able to shut the door behind himself and get it locked if she made a U-turn and headed back to him again. Maybe he should start carrying a weapon. He wished he'd thought to bring the ol' tranquilizer gun. It had been nearly a year since he'd given it any thought— Vincent had made amazing progress controlling his beast side—but the time was definitely nigh to keep it handy. In fact, he wished he'd thought to give it to Heather before he'd left.

The door squealed on its hinges as he pushed it open. So much for the element of surprise. He thought twice about shutting it before he flicked on the light. The place was a shambles. File cabinet drawers hanging open, lecture notes strewn everywhere, his office canister of gummy worms lying on its side and a few colorful gelatinous delicacies scattered on the floor as if they'd crawled to freedom. Surveying the mess, eyes darting into the darkened corners of the room as he shut and locked the door—no way did he want Heidi or anyone else to stumble across his threshold, see this, and ask questions—he began to take inventory so he could figure out what was missing. All he kept in his office was university stuff. Papers to grade, hard copies of committee notes, cards and notes from graduates who kept in touch. Nothing seemed to be missing. All the good stuff was at his place.

*At his place.*

"Oh, God," he blurted, and dialed Heather. She picked up on the first ring.

"J.T.?" she whispered. "I think someone's outside sneaking around."

He went on red alert. "Are all the doors and windows locked?"

"Yes. I checked."

"Call nine-one-one."

"But what if they see all this equipment?" she whispered fiercely. "Won't you get in trouble? I should call Cat."

He blew out of his office, shut and tried to lock his door— the mechanism was broken—and dashed toward the front of the building. David, Sara, and Heidi were gone.

"If Cat's still at the crime scene, she's too far away. Power down and call the police *now*. If you don't, I will."

"Okay, okay. Oh, my God, I'm freaking out."

"Stay calm. I have a baseball bat under my desk. And the tranq gun's behind the bar. Get over there and grab it."

Heather squeaked. "I thought I heard a growl."

*Let it be Vincent. No, wait, not if he's growling.*

"Call the cops and get the tranquilizer gun, Heather," he ordered her. "Then get back on the line with me and stay on the line."

"All right. I'm putting you on hold but just to call the police."

"Good. That's go—"

He was talking to dead air. He took the opportunity to run flat out to the parking lot and leap into his car. Good thing he had login passwords on all the computers at the club. There'd be no actual motive for the police to interest themselves in his stuff, but to open anything up they'd have to have a warrant. Which they would not have.

As he turned on the engine and the headlights came on,

he registered the startled presence of Heidi Schwann in the empty parking space beside the one he'd used as he backed out. Had she been waiting for him? How did she know which car was his? And why wasn't she wearing her glasses?

He gunned the engine and went into reverse, scrutinizing her in the rearview mirror. The situation was fishy all around: a grad student he didn't remember hanging around campus at night, asking to be his TA, trying to follow him into his office, which had been ransacked. Maybe she was the beast-maker's spy. Or maybe she was the beast-maker herself. Any number of gorgeous women had turned out to be evil villainesses since Muirfield had come into their lives.

"Or they've been beasts," he said aloud, thinking of Tori Windsor as he wheeled the car around and shot toward the street.

*Could Heidi Schwann—*

He heard the car horn and the squeal of brakes before he felt the impact. Heard the crunch of metal on metal. Torso thrown forward, air bag deployed. It *hurt*. His glasses cut into his face. His head swam. He tried to move but nothing seemed to be working.

Footsteps.

Running toward him.

Someone shouting, "Oh, my God, are you hurt?"

Sounded innocent enough. Maybe this really was an accident. Maybe no evil government agent was running toward the car, attempting to kill him.

His door was flung open. Muzzily he lifted his head and was about to turn it to speak to his rescuer when a piece of damp, smelly cloth went over his face.

Then again, maybe it *was* someone trying to kill him.

From far away, he heard screaming. As he was dragged out of the car, he realized that it was coming from his phone, and that it was Heather.

# CHAPTER SIX

"Oh my God, oh my God!" Heather shrieked as she opened J.T.'s front door for the two uniformed police officers. "My friend was just in a car accident!"

The uniforms stared at her. One tall, one short, both of them were women.

"You called nine-one-one because your friend was in a car accident?" the tall one asked in an incredulous tone of voice.

"No," Heather assured her, sweeping backwards so they could come inside. "This is his house. I came over to, uh, turn off his curling iron and then I heard a noise so I called him. And he told me to call *you* and then I heard him in a crash!"

"We can check on that for you, miss. What is his full name, the location of his vehicle, and his license and registration?" the short officer asked. She whipped out a little notebook.

Heather got nervous. She wasn't sure if J.T. had found anything in his office. What if something was in his car? What if it was Vincent, beasted out and tranq'ed?

"Well, he's Dr. J.T. Forbes," she said.

"What do the initials stand for?" the officer asked.

Heather smoothed back her hair. "I don't actually know. But everyone calls him J.T."

"Do you know his location?"

"I'm not sure."

The officer gestured to her phone. "Is he in your 'Find My Friends' app?"

Wow, who knew the police could be so tech-savvy? She covered her face with her hand and held up her phone. "Wait. I can call him back!"

She hit redial and left it off speaker. The phone connected.

"J.T.!" she cried. "Are you all right?"

"This is Private X," a voice said. It had been electronically distorted. "Is this Heather Chandler?"

She jerked hard. "Who are *you*?" she demanded. "Private *who*?"

"We have Dr. Forbes. If there is someone with you, do not react to this call. Repeat: Do not react."

The hair on the back of Heather's neck stood straight up. She licked her lips and said, "Um." The uni looked at her strangely. "So hi, J.T. Are you all right?"

"He's safe. For the time being. If anyone tries to locate him... or us... that will change. Do you understand?"

"Ah, yes."

The cop cocked her head, and Heather really, really, really didn't know what to do. Help was standing right here. She could write them a note and they could send a SWAT team.

If they even believed her.

Then she heard J.T. rasp, "Heather. I heard you screaming." *Oh, my God!*

"I heard your accident." Then it dawned on her: kidnapped. This Private X had rammed J.T.'s car and abducted him.

"Oh, my God, J.T.!" she cried. The cop raised her brows. "What a close call!" Heather swallowed hard. "I'm so glad you're all right."

"Very good," said the electronic voice.

"Sure," she said cheerfully. She put her hand over the

phone. "It's my friend. He's okay, basically."

The uni reached out a hand. "Good. I need to confirm that you have his permission to be on these premises while my partner does a sweep. If I may?"

"Oh, of course." Heather cleared her throat. "So, J.T., right before your accident, you told me to call nine-one-one, remember? So they're here to check on that noise I heard and they want to make sure I have your permission to be here."

"What are you doing?" the electronic voice asked shrilly.

"So here's the officer now." She extended her hand to the woman. Surely she would see how hard Heather was shaking.

"Yes, sir," the officer said into the phone. "May I verify your name, sir? And that you are the legal occupant of this location?"

"Where did you hear the noise?" the other cop asked Heather. She was holding a massive flashlight.

Heather wanted with all her heart to pay attention to the phone call but now this officer was waiting for her response.

"Outside." She crossed her arms over her chest. "Like someone sneaking around."

"Could it have been a cat or a possum?"

"I don't know!" Heather cried, and then she tried to smile apologetically. "I'm sorry. I'm just… like I said, I was just supposed to stop by to make sure he had, ah, turned off his curling iron and then I heard about the accident and I'm kind of losing it."

The cop glanced at a framed news article on J.T.'s desk, complete with a photo of J.T. And his thinning, short—but curly—hair. The headline read: J.T. FORBES, PhD, RECEIVES BEST SCIENCE PROFESSOR AWARD.

"Curling iron," the cop said flatly.

"He got implants. Those plug things," Heather said. She was sweating like crazy. Her mind was racing. She was afraid she was going to start laughing hysterically because this was all way too insane and she was scared to death.

"Okay, sir, thank you," the tall cop said, pressing a button on Heather's phone.

"Don't hang up!" Heather shrieked. She caught herself. "I mean, I'm sorry, I'm just kind of on edge."

"That's all right, Ms. Chandler," said Ms. Tall. "That's why we're here." She flipped open a little book and wrote something down in it. "Are you by chance related to Detective Catherine Chandler?"

"Yes!" she cried. Then she caught her lower lip between her teeth and cleared her throat. "Yes," she said much more calmly. "She's my sister. She can vouch for me about the curling iron. I'll give you her number. She'll want to know about this right away."

"Very well," the tall cop said. She handed Heather back her phone. "Go ahead."

Heather nearly fainted with relief. Cat was smart. If she could make Cat understand what was going on, Cat would not only know what to do, but she'd take action. That was exactly what Cat was, an action hero. She dialed her sister.

Short Cop said, "I'm going to take a look around outside." She went out the front door.

The tall cop shifted her weight as Heather listened to incessant ringing. An image of Walker thrusting out his hips flitted through Heather's mind. He still hadn't called. That was the very, very least of her problems now.

Cat's phone rang some more. And kept ringing. The call went to voicemail and Heather said, "Cat? J.T.'s been in an *accident*. Like the one I was in a while ago? With David Scheckman?" Scheckman had kidnapped her to lure out Vincent.

Then Heather texted her *helphelphelpineedyou*

"Looks like she must still be on a case," she told the cop. "It figures. Tonight was the night *she* was supposed to make dinner."

The other woman smiled. "Isn't that always the way with sisters? I have three of them."

"Wow. That's a lot." Heather felt as though she was going to shatter from sheer nerves.

The other police officer re-entered from outside. She said, "There's a couple of homeless guys outside. They look harmless but I think we should escort Ms. Chandler to her car."

"Curling iron's off, right?" the tall cop said.

"It's funny how often people are just *certain* they forgot something," Heather agreed.

"They come with timers now," said the tall cop.

The short cop was scanning the room. Her gaze focused on something and her eyes narrowed. Heather traced her line of sight with her own. They were looking at J.T.'s chemistry equipment.

"So is Dr. Forbes conducting experiments here?" she asked.

That must have been some kind of code; the tall officer began drifting toward the glassware, Bunsen burner, and microscope as if they might jump out at them.

"Yes, he's just always working, trying to find a cure… for whatever he's doing. I don't really know." Oh no, they don't think he's making meth or anything like that, do they?

She returned to the computer console to pick up her bag. J.T. had been amazed by the size. He said it was big enough to carry around a bazooka.

That gave her an idea. She smiled at the two officers and said, "I'll just make sure I, um, flushed the toilet and grab my stuff."

They were still walking toward the lab setup. Heather zoomed toward the bar, ducked down, found the tranq gun, and stuffed it in her bag. Then she hurried into J.T.'s bathroom and looked for other weapons. There was a scattering of women's toiletries—had to be Tess's—and she glanced in the shower to grab a razor. So she had a tranq gun and a razor.

And some spray deodorant. She could use it like Mace, maybe?

The cops were peering into J.T.'s microscope. Suddenly she was extra-freaked. What if they weren't real cops? Maybe they'd killed the real cops on their way in and they were from the same group that had killed Vincent?

*I don't know that anyone killed Vincent. Vincent is not dead!*

She placed her hand in the bag, resting it on the tranq gun, and said, "Okay, I'm ready."

"I'll go out first, just in case," the tall cop said.

Heather whipped her head around to see what the short cop was doing. She was looking over her shoulder, then up toward the ceiling and around the room. Taking it all in. Her radio chattered and Heather jumped a mile. The officer replied in cop-speak that all was well and they walked outside together. Cat had used a squad car, so Heather had taken Cat's personal car and illegally parked in an alley, which the officers pretended not to notice as she unlocked it and slid behind the wheel. They waited until she started the engine and then gave her a wave.

She was numb as she slid into the traffic. She was hyperventilating. With trembling fingers, she opened "Find My Friends" and caught her breath when J.T. came up on it. It was an old result and it was about to refresh; she stared at the map hard, then took a screenshot and emailed it to herself, Cat, Tess, and Vincent. Then the map reported that there was no result for her friend; it had refreshed, and J.T. had disappeared.

She texted all of them: *J.T. kidnapped, was HERE. Call me asap.*

"Queens. Long drive," she muttered. As she merged into the traffic, she kept dialing Cat, Tess, and Vincent and there was never, ever any answer. Maybe they had all been kidnapped.

*I guess it's up to me, then.*

Every fear she had ever had rose inside her. She remembered when Cat had announced that she wanted to become a cop.

It was after she had watched their mother gunned down in front of her. All Heather had wanted to do was cry, and be comforted, and try to forget the awful nightmare. She had run away from the violence as hard as she could. But Cat had faced it, and not only faced it, but embraced it. Heather's big sister waded headlong into the deepest, darkest pits of human degradation every day and risked her life to bring innocent people justice.

As she drove, she looked at the hundreds of cars around her. Not one person inside any of them knew about beasts. Or kidnappings. If she asked for help, most, if not all, of the passengers would turn away. She was utterly alone in this. This is what it had been like to be Cat for two years. Unable to tell one person, not one, about Vincent, plus juggling trying to act normal around her own sister, Heather.

*And I was so angry with her all the time,* Heather thought. *I knew she was keeping secrets from me but rather than try to understand, I just got madder and madder.*

The only person in all the world who had known what Cat knew—besides Vincent himself—had been J.T. And *he* sure hadn't signed up for that life. He was sweet and smart, but he wasn't a fighter like Vincent and Cat. Or like Tess, for that matter. She wondered how that felt for him.

For her, it was extremely terrifying. But it didn't matter how it felt. It was what she had to do.

Then her phone map went completely kerplooey—the result of a bug in the new upgrade—and she tried to decide what to do. Just drive and hope the directions came back or what?

To her left loomed a stone pedestrian bridge completely covered in graffiti. Gang tags, she figured. The very worst place to stop. She drove on, scanning for a better spot, and realized she had just missed a merge.

"Damn it," she said, and swerved into a little industrial park that looked to contain nothing but auto body shops, and put the car in park. She squinted at her phone and tried to recalibrate, holding it close to the driver's side window to catch a few more bars. Nothing. She extended it toward her windshield, mentally willing the phone to behave. Time was racing by. For all she knew, J.T. was dead by now. Maybe she should call 911 again. No. Bad idea.

While she held the phone next to the window, she reached down into her bag and pulled out the tranquilizer gun. It was then and only then that she realized it wasn't loaded.

"Great," she muttered. "Fantastic."

There was a sharp rap on her window. She jumped a mile and looked up. It was a young, dark-skinned man in a hooded jacket smiling down at her. Beneath the glare of a streetlight she saw that he was tapping on her window with a gun.

She fumbled to put the car into drive and take off the emergency brake. But she was shaking too badly and nothing happened.

Then he pointed the gun straight at her. She gasped and then she pretended she was Cat and thought, *So what's he going to do when I just blow out of here? The odds of hitting me are much lower than most people realize.*

*But what if the odds are in his favor?*

She kept her eyes glued to his as she tried to find the gearshift. *Brake,* she reminded herself.

Then movement in her peripheral vision startled her into looking straight ahead for a second—

She jerked.

The car was surrounded by men. And nearly all of them had guns, and they were pointing them straight at her.

A dozen—a hundred—horrible scenarios rocketed through her mind—she liked the ones where she died instantly the best of all—and then the guy with the scars made a circular motion with his free hand. He wanted her to roll down her window.

*No way*, she thought, but it wasn't like she had bulletproof glass windows or anything. She remembered all her self-defense classes about fighting back and not appearing weak. She started to pick up the tranquilizer gun but realized that as soon as they saw it, they'd open fire. With a scream of "Aiya!" she laid on the horn, got into drive, got off that brake, shifted into drive, and rabbited forward. The men scattered and Heather slammed into a cinderblock wall. Her body jerked forward, then whipped backward, and probably the only reason the airbag didn't deploy was because she hadn't built up very much speed.

The guys broke into cheers and applause and Heather's hooded friend aimed his weapon at her again. All she had to do was figure out reverse. That was all—

—and then she heard a "chirp-chirp" and the guy opened her door himself. He squatted down on his haunches beside her. He was holding a remote control fob in his hand.

"Fire!" she screamed, which is what you learned in self-defense class, because no one would come to your aid if you screamed for help.

"Hey, calm down, girl," he said. "*Man.*"

She swallowed hard. "I'm a student. I work part-time. I don't have very much money and my sister is a cop."

He pulled in his chin. "No shit?"

"No shit. So don't try anything or she will put your ass in the electric chair!"

He and his thugs burst into laughter. She was aware that he was dangling his gun between his legs and she could push him over with a well-placed side kick and make a run for it. Except there was no place to run. This place was crawling with gangbangers.

"I just dialed nine-one-one," she informed them. "The police will be here any second."

"Nice try, but you ain't got no bars, baby." He held up his own phone… identical to hers.

"I *do*," she insisted. "I have a special police frequency."

This was hilarious to them. She told herself she would not burst into tears or plead for her life. And she *would* go down fighting.

*Attack him. It will scare the others.*

But it wouldn't. All he had to do was take one step backward and she'd be sailing into the dirt at his feet.

So she opened her mouth to plead for her life and instead of begging to be spared because she was her cop-sister's only family, she said, "Can I buy that gun off you?"

# CHAPTER SEVEN

Vincent came to with a sharp gasp. He was sprawled on his back with his right leg bent underneath his left; he hurt all over and there was blood on his hands. And his arms. He raised his head and looked down at himself. His jeans were soaked with blood.

*What happened? What did I do?*

By the overwhelming stench he knew he was in a sewer. It was pitch dark but his night vision was functioning perfectly. He performed a visual pan of his surroundings, his mind working hard to piece together how he had gotten here. He remembered going to the warehouse and reaching the loading dock. And then...

Vincent began to quake. Fear was like a net hoisting him up into the black night and carrying him away. It wrapped itself around him and tightened, cutting off his oxygen.

*There's nothing to be afraid of*, he told himself sternly. He pushed himself to his hands and knees, then rocked back onto his feet and stood. There were bruises on his bruises. With a doctor's practiced touch, he examined himself for broken bones. As he walked forward, he limped, but he was pretty sure he had only strained some muscles.

It was confirmed, then. This beast—or whatever kind of unholy creation it might be—could project fear onto prey or potential threats. It must have done the same thing to poor little Aliyah Patel. Even thinking about how he had felt—the abject terror—he wondered how a little girl like her could cope. Tess had told him they'd put her in a pediatric psych ward. As soon as he got out of here and checked in with everyone, he would look in on her. If only he could find words to comfort her without reassuring her that what she had seen was real.

He moved as silently as possible through the tunnels beneath the city, concentrating on tracking his adversary. He smelled the blood on his fingertips and tried to send his mind back to the stretch of time he had lost, but each instant that he began to form an image, a haze of fear blurred it. It was as though his mind simply would not allow him to face his attacker. How was it possible, and who had invented it? Karl Tiptree? This would be an amazing tool in combat: Terrify the other side into immobility, then pick them off one by one. Or as a means for conducting interrogations: Calibrate the fear-reaction and take notes as your subject babbles and begs not to be harmed.

*This stinks of Muirfield,* he thought. *Or of the people who funded Muirfield.* The world's rich and powerful, their tentacles deeply sunk into financial markets and advanced technology, ruling the world and serving up horrors for anyone who got in their way.

*I'd be happy to get in their way again,* he thought fiercely. *And bring them down.*

Had someone sent Mr. Riley that letter in order to flush out anyone who might be moved to strike against them? Or had the beast been directed to target Vincent through Mr. Riley, because he was the last loose end from the debacle in Afghanistan?

He feared for Mr. Riley. Unless, of course, the old man was in on it. Maybe he had invented the contract between Lafferty and Gheeta Patel and used it to gain entrance to the Patel home. Maybe the Patels had known something about what had happened to Lafferty. Hell, maybe Gheeta died because she knew Lafferty. All Vincent's letters home had been censored, but the army did make mistakes and allow sensitive, classified material through. Maybe Lafferty told Gheeta things no one should have known.

*But why would Mr. Riley help the very organization that had destroyed his stepdaughter?*

Maybe they had Lafferty and were using her as a bargaining chip. Or maybe he was just afraid of dying a more agonizing death than the one his cancer was offering him. Vincent had been waterboarded during his army training. It had nearly broken him, and by then, he'd been a hardened soldier. Do that once to a frightened old man...

Or simply appeal to his patriotism in some way, with some twisted story...

What about the string of murders here in New York? Was Indira the beast's first or its seventh? Had the beast eviscerated each one as payback for the terrible thing that had been done to it? To him? To her? Or was it under the control of the army?

*And how am I going to fight this thing if I panic like this?*

Just thinking about it made him tremble. It engendered fear at a deep, base level. It would take more than a force of will to stay in command of himself.

He reached for his cell phone. Gone. Lost? Or taken? He thought of the names and messages on it, the damning connections to people he never wanted to put in danger. He had to get topside and find out what had happened while he was out. He hoped to God Catherine was safe. And J.T. and Tess. That they had information he could use to destroy this thing and shut down the operation that created it.

Sloshing through runoff, he employed the left-hand rule—keeping track of his route by following every twist and turn on his left—as he examined the roof of the tunnel. His hope was to see either city lights or daylight. He had no idea how long he'd been out, but he wasn't hungry or thirsty, so that told him it was probably still night.

Finally he saw a break in the unrelieved uniformity of the curved ceiling, and to his left he spotted a ladder leading up toward it. Manhole. He climbed the ladder and pushed on the cover. It didn't budge. Vincent closed his eyes and pictured Lafferty in her misery. What had been done to her in the name of advancing the cause of warfare.

Anger surged through him. His body responded, his beast DNA soaking up the chemical changes caused by his emotions and feeding on them. Charged, nourished, the DNA presented and he beasted out just enough to push the cover off the manhole as if it weighed no more than a sheet of paper. By the time he poked out his head, he was back to human.

He had emerged in a busy street, which was both good and bad. Bad for getting out of there as safely and discreetly as possible; good because there would likely be transportation—buses, subways. He'd have to clean up first.

Traffic stopped—had to be a red light—and he slid out beneath a rumbling semi. He lay flat as the air brakes chuffed and the truck moved forward, then quickly rolled to the side of the street and crawled into the shadows. A sign on a chain-link fence read KELLY'S TRUCKING YARD. According to the address, he was in Queens.

About twenty feet away stood a small building, practically a shed. He darted over to it and tried the side door. It opened, and he found himself inside an office. An olive-green jumpsuit and baseball cap hung on a hook beside an interior door. A quick glance inside revealed a bathroom. Vincent stripped, cleaned up quickly, and put on the jumpsuit and cap. He found a roll of plastic trash bags among some cleaning supplies inside the sink console and put his bloody clothes in one.

Fortune continued to smile on him as he found a landline on the desk. He called Catherine.

"Chandler."

"Catherine, it's me."

"Oh, my God, Vincent. Where are you? Are you all right?"

"Yes." He knew Catherine better than anyone else on the planet, and he knew something was very wrong. "Tell me."

"J.T.'s been kidnapped and Heather's gone after him—"

"*What?*"

"You weren't at the houseboat so J.T. was going to check his office. I was down in the sewers and I missed Heather's calls. I've been calling her back and I can't get through. Where are you?"

He fished through some papers on the desk and found a couple of invoices with Kelly's' full address. He read it off to her.

"On my way," she said.

"No one knows I'm here. I helped myself to some clothes. And I don't have my phone."

"I have it. I'll get there as fast as I can. If I can."

He understood. If she heard from anyone, she'd take immediate action that might preclude picking him up.

"I'll check in with you in half an hour," he told her, figuring he could manage that long and maybe longer if he stayed quiet and didn't trip any alarms. So far so good on that score.

"Okay." They hung up. He wished he'd told her that he loved her. The way their lives were going, he should tell her that as often as possible, in case it was the last time he spoke to her.

\* \* \*

Heather and her companion had been driving forever. Queens was filled with one-way streets and construction zones not marked on her phone's map, and Heather, for one, was getting tired of all the detours.

"Heather," Cat said on the other end of the line, "wherever you are, stop and pull over. Do not do this. Leave it to me."

J-Bag—that was the name of the guy who had sold Heather the gun—held the phone up to Heather's ear because she hadn't wanted to put the conversation on speaker. She had given him 70 dollars for the gun, although she was sure she had more in her purse earlier—hadn't she withdrawn that cash she owed Cat on the way home with Walker? Still, it made J-Bag do a touchdown victory dance, because he had gotten the gun for free.

She was grateful down to her soul that he had offered to go with her. They were in a derelict section of the borough, passing blocks so squalid she doubted that even rats went inside them. A burned-out car had run up over a curb and she had never seen more litter in her life. J-Bag had told her not to be afraid and promised to look out for her.

"I'm only one block away," Heather argued with Catherine. "And you're going to go pick up Vincent first!"

"As it happens picking up Vincent is practically a straight line from there to where J.T. is being held. Listen to me. I am a cop and Vincent is… Vincent. There's no reason for you to do this."

J-Bag pulled a joint out of his baggy pocket with his free hand.

"Oh, my God!" Heather shrieked. "Don't do that in my sister's car!"

"Do what? Who's with you?" Cat demanded.

Heather hesitated. She didn't know what to say. "My backup. A friend. You don't know him."

"Let me guess. Walker?"

"No." And Heather died a little inside because Walker hadn't ever called back. "The thing is, Cat, J-Bag is very street-smart."

"*J-Bag?*"

"I heard that," J-Bag said indignantly.

"Okay. Listen," Heather said. "We won't go in. We'll drive past and I'll take some pictures and send them to you. So that way you can plan your attack."

"Attack, damn." He sucked in the smoke from his joint, held it, rolled down his window, and blew it out into the night. He smiled pleasantly at Heather as if to say, *See? I'm civilized.* When she batted his shoulder, he muttered, "Okay, okay, jeez, you're worse than my mama." He spit on his fingers, then clamped them over the business end of the joint. Then he stuffed it back in his pocket.

"Not even pictures," Cat insisted, but Heather could tell that her sister was liking the idea of pictures. She just didn't want to tell Heather to go into enemy territory to snap them.

"Who they attacking? Cuz guess what." He reached into his jacket and pulled out a gun at least twice as big as the one he had sold her.

"Oh, my God!" Heather cried.

"What? What's happening?" Cat shouted.

"Girl, listen, I'm good with this," he insisted.

"Heather, pull over immediately," Cat barked. Before Heather could protest, she added, "If I recall correctly, the people who kidnapped J.T. rammed his car. You're one block away from their last known location. In the car of Vincent Keller's girlfriend. If they knew enough to ram J.T.'s car, they know enough to ram yours."

"Oh." Heather's voice was small. "Right."

"*Turn around now.*"

"Okay."

"I have another call," Cat said.

"Okay, bye."

J-Bag stared at her. "Just like that? You're the person closest to a friend who is in trouble and you bail?" He shook his head. "You are not the woman I thought you were."

"So?" she flung back at him, but she was stung. He was right. "But she's a cop."

"Yeah, and what? If you don't do what she say, she gonna to throw your ass in the electric chair?"

She opened her mouth. "You're right. What the heck, J-Bag? Right?"

"Damn straight. Park and we'll check it out. You can take pictures and send them to her anyway. Probably get her ass—I mean, herself—here a lot faster, she know you stuck around."

"Deal."

He grinned at her. "I knew you had it in you. I knew you were a real woman, not some baby girl."

"You must not have any brothers or sisters."

"I got so many of 'em I don't even know all of 'em," he assured her. "And tell me one more time what the hell this thing is?" He held up the tranquilizer gun.

"I used to volunteer at the zoo," she said, grabbing it from him and putting it on the back seat. "That's for wild animals. *Real* ones."

"You're the strangest person."

"I'm really not," she said earnestly. "Trust me on that."

The problem with parking was that there were too many places to park. Except for the burned-out car, there were no other vehicles, no bushes or trees; only shadows could make them inconspicuous. Heather rolled into the deepest, darkest shadows she could find and handed J-Bag her phone.

"Could you take some pictures, please?" she asked him. "I can't really see past you."

"Sure, baby. Here, hold this." He held out his gun. She

took it with one hand and would have dropped it, but she gripped her other hand around it and lowered it to the seat.

"It weighs a ton," she said. "How do you even hold it?"

"Feel my arm muscles." He grinned and flexed.

"I'll take your word for it."

"You're missing out."

She sighed. On the way here, he had told her about himself. She'd been hoping J-Bag might turn out to be an undercover cop or a journalist doing a piece on gang life, but this was no fairy tale. He was a high-school dropout, his sister was a heroin addict, and he had killed two people. They had deserved it, he assured her.

*We are each the heroes of our own stories,* she thought wistfully. What was the story of the people who had kidnapped J.T.? They had wanted someone to know what had happened to him, which was a good sign. But they hadn't made any demands, which was a bad sign. And no one had heard back from Tess since she left the houseboat. Which was a very, very bad sign.

"I think you should smoke some weed," J-Bag said. "You are so tense."

"If you don't stop with that, I'll kick you out of my car." She looked past him to the post-apocalyptic city block across the street. She tapped her fingers on the steering wheel. "It's going to take them forever to get here. What if they're torturing him?"

He whistled. "Okay, so *not* the little kitten. You got spunk, woman. You could be my old lady if you want."

"That's so sweet, J-Bag, but trust me, you don't want me. I'm way too neurotic. And messy. I leave stuff out everywhere."

"But I'll bet my kitten is a tiger in the sack."

"*Please.*" She thought about batting him, but he was taking the pictures for her with her cell phone. Her mind filled with the images of Miami Beach palm trees and a moonlit beach, contrasting them with her current situation. She'd thought things would be just peachy in New York now that she knew Vincent was not Vincent Zelansky, also known as Ass. But she still had to fight to get one moment of Cat's attention, and three was a crowd no matter how nice and un-ass-like Vincent Keller was. Maybe if she signed on as Cat's sidekick she'd get some quality time.

*Or die,* she thought fearfully.

"Got 'em," he said, "and get ready to roll, because a car is coming down the street."

She reached for the keys in the ignition, but he stayed her with a gentle squeeze on her wrist.

"No, wait. It's a low-rider, and there's a chance they won't see us. You go screaming out of here, they're going to follow you."

"Great. Just great." She locked all the doors and rolled up all the windows. "We should probably hide."

She slumped down behind the wheel. He hunkered down too. She held her breath and made a promise to herself to take a gun class. Cat shot guns all the time. And not just at paper targets.

J-Bag's hand rested on her thigh. "Move it," she said between clenched teeth.

He made a little whimpering noise. "The ladies fight over me, Heather. And here you got me all to yourself."

"First of all, I don't fight over guys. Secondly, we are on a life-or-death stakeout."

"All the more reason we should seize the moment."

"Get your hand off me or I'll shoot you."

He chuckled… and did as she asked.

"Don't ever tell anyone I behaved myself," he said. "I could never live it down."

"Don't worry. No one will ever know you were in this car."

"It's not too late for me to call my brothers and tell them to show. They'd do it for me."

"That's so thoughtful," she said, "but let's wait for my sister." *So she completely loses her mind when she sees me.*

"I could go across the street, do a recon."

"Just stay put, J-Bag, okay?"

Before she realized what he was doing, he clicked his door, opened it, and crawled out. Using the door as a shield, he duckwalked toward the back of the car. She sat up and stared into the rearview mirror but didn't see him. Seconds ticked by. Her stomach filled with fluttering things. What if all this niceness had been an act? And he was going to sneak around the other side of the car—her side—kill her, and take the car?

*What was I thinking?*

But no, she trusted him. Still trusted him. Of course, she had trusted Walker, too. And look where that had gotten her.

*We don't know about that yet,* she reminded herself. *Walker is To Be Continued.*

Her chest hurt; she had been holding her breath. She exhaled, and just as she ran out of air, her phone pinged. "Find My Friends" showed a new location for J.T.

She messaged the information to Cat, and then she phoned her. Cat answered on the car's speaker. "I see it. I'm getting close to Vincent. I am seeing you on *my* app, Heather. Get out of there *now*. And who are you with? Does he… *know?*"

"No."

"Then take him home and wait to hear from me."

"Cat, J.T. is my friend too."

"Do it."

The door behind her opened and J-Bag popped into the car. Heather said, "Okay, Cat, you're the cop," and glanced into the rearview mirror to see what effect those words had on J-Bag. It was too dark to see him.

"Someone's on my other line. It's probably Vincent," Cat said. "Go home."

Heather started up the engine; keeping her headlights off, she slowly hung a U. She said to J-Bag, "My friend's on the move and my sister's closer to him. So I'm retreating."

"Yeah, now that I'm in love with you I'm all for that. I can't have my woman getting messed up."

"You're freaking me out. You're not going all stalkery, are you?"

He cocked his head. "You have not had good experiences with men."

"You can say that again," she blurted. And then she shook her head. "We are not having this conversation now. Lives are on the line."

"Cuz the heart's already been broken."

"Where do you want me to drop you off?" she asked doggedly.

"At your place, sweet thing," he said. "Of course. But I don't want you to go back to where we met. That's a bad place. Probably best you take me to a subway station."

"Is it even running?" she asked. Actually, weirdly, it wasn't all that late.

"Doesn't matter." He patted her shoulder. "This has been an interesting evening."

"Can I sell you back the gun?" she asked him. "I can't bring an unregistered weapon home. Cat would kill me."

"You should be packing like *Grand Theft Auto*, your sister's a cop," he said. "They even got tanks now, I hear. But yeah, I'll buy it back. For ten dollars."

"*What?* I gave you seven times that!"

"Yeah, and now it's used. And plus, I didn't make any money tonight, driving around with you. I have to account for myself with my brothers. All I'm coming home with so far is sixty bucks. You're lucky I'm buying it back."

She sputtered. "This is robbery."

He grinned at her. "If you think this is robbery, you've

never been properly robbed. C'mon, look at it from my point of view. I'll get my ass kicked, I come home with nothing."

"All right. Give me directions."

"Give me your phone. I'll key them in."

"Suddenly I'm feeling a little more protective of my stuff," she informed him.

"You do okay."

That was some sort of a compliment, so she said, "Thanks."


Vincent melted out of the shadows as Catherine glided to the curb. He got in and Cat moved off quickly. She told him about the new location and he asked the same questions she had asked herself: Who had sent the address? Was it real? Or were they being sent on a fool's errand?

"Any word from Tess?" Vincent asked, and Cat shook her head. "Did Heather remember anything else? Anything they might have said that would give us more information?"

"No. She had someone with her. I think it was a guy and I have no idea why she didn't drop him off before she started looking for J.T. She knows that we have to keep the existence of beasts a secret. I'm going to have to have a talk with her."

"Give her the benefit of the doubt," Vincent said. "Heather's grown up. She had to have a good reason."

"You're right. It's hard for me to see her as anything but a flighty teenager. It was very brave of her to light out after him like that."

They drove in silence, both tense and worried. Before Vincent had rejoined society, J.T. had worried for their safety, but he'd never actually been harmed.

"All I can think is that they're trying to lure you," Cat said. "Otherwise there would be demands by now."

"Unless something went wrong," Vincent murmured. He

didn't finish the thought: unless they had killed J.T., either by accident or design.

"We'll get them, Vincent," she promised. "And we'll kick their butts."

*Unless we're too afraid to*, he thought.

# CHAPTER EIGHT

J.T.'s head was pounding. Whoever had chloroformed him had clocked him with a blunt instrument as well. Probably a gun, because these guys had a lot of them. He wasn't up on his advanced weaponry but he knew submachine guns when he saw them. Also black matte handguns that were so enormous they looked fake. There were maybe six men, and they were dressed in olive fatigues and combat boots. They wore black hoods and bandanas covered the lower half of their faces, which gave him hope of survival. If they planned to kill him, they wouldn't care if he knew what they looked like.

They told him that they were the FFNY. The FFNY was a paramilitary operation "assisting" someone with a "mission," and he wasn't sure it was precisely the mission they had written Maurice Riley about. He didn't think they seemed very concerned about Mr. Riley's safety. They didn't seem concerned about anyone's safety. They wanted J.T.'s help capturing the beast, not destroying it. They wanted to use it for their own ends. What ends those were, he didn't know. They hadn't yet shared their manifesto or whatever with him. But weren't all manifestos pretty much the same?

Your side is wrong, our side is right. Join us or die.

His hands were cuffed behind his back and ropes around his chest and ankles kept him tied to a chair in the middle of a large warehouse half-filled with long wooden shipping crates. There were three men standing on the crates, legs spread wide for balance, Uzis around their necks. Parked in a row were two panel vans, one white, one black, and a quartet of nondescript sedans. J.T. tried to memorize license plates but his vision was blurry and the bare light bulb hanging directly over his head made it difficult to see much.

They offered him water, which he accepted. Those action movies where the brave heroes display their machismo by refusing all food and drink from the enemy? Very bad training films. You had to do anything you could—within your moral compass, of course—to last long enough to thwart the enemy. You couldn't do that if you were dehydrated and starving. Vincent had taught him that.

"One more time," said the man who identified himself as Private X—the ringleader of the FFNY. "What have Vincent Keller and the NYPD discovered about the creature?"

J.T. noted his use of the word "creature." Everyone connected with the experiment—including Cat's father, Agent Bob Reynolds—referred to Muirfield's creations as "beasts." These guys didn't. Did that mean that they were on the outside looking in—not members of the original conspiracy? On the other hand, if they knew about Lafferty— and potentially Vincent—*and* they knew that Karl Tiptree had invented a "serum," then they had some knowledge. Again, the point was not to die a hero—it was live to see another day—and J.T. tried to calculate how much he had to divulge while keeping them as ignorant as possible.

"This new murder seemed different," he said. "The police suspect the first six murders were committed by a human. That would mean that last night's murder would be the creature's first murder in New York City. That they know of, anyway."

The masked men looked at each other. This was news to them. Whether welcome news or not, J.T. had no idea.

"Why do they think that?" Private X asked as he strode up to J.T. The light from the bulb gleamed on his Uzi. He was wearing black leather half-gloves. He seriously creeped J.T. out.

"I'm not sure. I haven't had a chance to talk to Vincent about it and—"

Lightning fast, Private X punched J.T. in the jaw. J.T.'s head whipped back and his glasses went flying. Now he would *never* be able to memorize those license plate numbers.

"Don't lie to me. Even if you haven't talked to Keller, you've talked to the cops. We have your phone."

J.T. hesitated. Private X threw back his arm and J.T. flinched. His interrogator snickered.

"Civilians," he said derisively. "Always weak and in the way."

"I thought you cared about people," J.T. said. There was something dribbling down his chin. It was either blood or drool... or pulverized bicuspids. "That you were doing all this to stop the bloodshed."

Now a couple of the other men snickered. J.T. didn't like all the snickering. It put him in mind of schoolyard bullies, which he'd had plenty of experience in dealing with while growing up. Bullies took real pleasure in inflicting pain. Yes, maybe they did it to compensate for deep-seated feelings of inferiority or *whatever*; the point was that pain was their thing.

"Weak, in the way, and *gullible*," one of the crate-standers said.

*Go ahead and laugh*, J.T. thought. *Because... I can do nothing to stop you.*

"Tell me why they think the first six murders weren't committed by the creature," Private X said.

J.T. tried to think of a plausible lie. Then he decided that a variant of the truth might actually work.

"There was no creature DNA at the first six murders." That was the truth. Then he remembered that their side was worrying about a possible mole in the department or the lab. Private X might have put them there. Now he wasn't sure how to move forward. "But at the Patel crime scene, there was a strange reading when one of the CSU techs applied Luminol for the detection of blood. Another substance presented under the black light." It was a total lie, but it was the best he could come up with while the cartilage in his nose ran down his face.

Private X was listening hard. J.T. didn't know if the man was waiting to see how much he would lie, or if he was buying what J.T. was selling.

"What did it look like under the black light?" Private X asked.

"I don't know. I wasn't there and I haven't gotten to see it. It could have been a false reading."

Private X turned to one of the other men—way buffed out—and said, "We'll have to check into that." Mr. Universe nodded as if making a mental note.

"Now I want you to tell me something else, and I don't want you to lie to me. I have done some terrible things in the service of my country, and I will not hesitate to do terrible things in the service of the FFNY."

J.T. thought about asking him what the real name of their group was. They definitely weren't doing all this in the name of freedom. But the time for banter was over. No more fun and games. Things were about to get real serious. Possibly fatal.

"Okay," J.T. said. "Got it."

"Did the army do to Vincent Keller what they did to Lafferty?"

Shock warred with elation and J.T. fought to conceal them both. *They don't know. Vincent's secret is safe.*

"I don't know," he said, which was true. Cat's mother had given Lafferty a serum to combat her violent fugue states and hustled her away. Vincent had visited her in the infirmary a few times, when she had begged him to help her "escape."

Which, to Vincent's loyal mind, meant "desert."

"Don't lie to me," Private X said, giving his Uzi a pat.

"I really don't know. I don't know what they did to Lafferty."

Private X smiled thinly. "But you do know what they did to Vincent Keller."

*Damn it*, J.T. thought. Had this been Private X's plan all along? To find out if Vincent was a beast?

"I know they gave him some steroid injections. The effects appear to be permanent. He's got mood swings, and there was the amnesia…" He trailed off. He was too afraid to say anything else.

Private X just stared at him. Then he looked across the room at someone behind J.T. and gave a sharp nod. J.T. was afraid he was going to wet his pants. He took a deep breath and mentally said goodbye to everyone he cared about— he even included Sara (but not David)—and saved his last goodbye for the best—

"Tess, no!" he shouted.

Because Tess was there. Bound and gagged, her hands tied or cuffed behind her back, she appeared at his side, then was pushed face down to the ground by a soldier who had a tattoo of a skull on the back of his right hand.

"Are you all right?" J.T. shouted.

Tess rocked herself until she rolled onto her side. She looked hard at him as if she were trying to tell him something. He pursed his lips and gave his head a quick shake; he didn't understand.

Private X stood over Tess and aimed his Uzi at her head. J.T. fought against his restraints but it was no good.

"Tell me the truth about Vincent Keller."

Tess blinked at J.T. and gave her head a nearly imperceptible shake. *It's not a choice between them*, he reminded himself. If he told these men the truth about Vincent, the world would change.

But if Tess died, *his* world would change.

*I can't do this. I can't.* He felt himself beginning to check out and shut down. He could not do that to Tess.

Private X stared at him with flat blue eyes. They seemed to have no spark of life in them, as if the man were dead. Or soulless.

"He-he's strong," J.T. said. "And his reflexes are off the charts. But if you're asking me if he's the creature that killed that woman last night, the answer is no."

"You *know* that's not what I'm asking you!" The soldier planted his boot on Tess's head. On her *head*. "Damn shame," he said. "I told you not to lie. We have eyes and ears everywhere, Dr. Forbes."

He aimed his weapon straight at Tess's face. Time slowed horribly for J.T. He saw her eyes above the gag, enormous; he saw the gun move into position. The men in the room strained to watch—

J.T. contracted his body with every fiber of strength at his command, attempting to throw his mass between the imminent fusillade of bullets and Tess's body.

All he succeeded in doing was throwing himself off balance; the chair smacked the concrete floor hard, and his head slammed against it. He was dazed, and he figured he must be hallucinating, or dying, because his blurry field of vision burst with the image of Private X dropping to one knee beside Tess and aiming high, sweeping the positions of the three men on the crates with a torrent of ammo. They dropped one-two-three. The other nine or so FFNYs had time to react, fanning behind crates and returning fire.

Private X dragged Tess by the feet behind the nearest crate. Then he returned for J.T. Bullets were zinging and pinging all around them; J.T. had no idea why they hadn't yet been hit. He shouted with fear as somehow, Private X dragged him and his chair behind the same crate as Tess. He didn't question it; he just kept his head down and prayed to God he wasn't about to become dead weight in the literal sense.

*This guy is outnumbered,* J.T. thought. *There's no way any of us are getting out of here alive.*

As if on cue, Private X gave a shout. One minute he was standing over J.T. and the next, blood was spurting out of his arm and he was collapsing behind him. Then J.T. felt a sharp, nearly electric pain and he grunted because he was too scared to yell.

"Damn it, do the rest," Private X said in his ear.

*The rest? What rest?*

And then J.T.'s bound wrists magically came apart. It took him a few seconds to realize that Private X had cut through his handcuffs. Then the most wicked-looking knife he had ever seen in his life was slapped into his hand. His circulation had been cut off and hundreds of fire ants were crawling over his skin, but he bent forward and sawed through the rope around his chest. Private X was working on his ankle restraints. The guy had taken a bullet and he was still going.

*Oh, my God, could he be the beast?*

J.T. had no more time to wonder because now that he was free, he crawled over to Tess. Private X shouted, "Fire in the hole!" and J.T. instinctively threw himself over her. He had watched enough war movies to know that that meant something bad was either incoming or outgoing. He prayed it was out.

The world shattered as sound waves shut down his eardrums. He couldn't hear anything, could barely think. Knife, he had a knife. Tess was underneath him. Enormous chunks of debris were crashing down all around him. Something struck him on the back and he held on more tightly to Tess, protecting her.

Dust, dirt, and smoke clogged his nose and eyes. He pushed himself up, elated to see that he still had the knife, and sawed at her restraints. She yanked a hand free and pulled down her gag.

"I wasn't choosing Vincent over you," he said. Or hoped he said. He couldn't hear anything.

Her mouth moved but without his eardrums or glasses he couldn't make out what she was saying. Then she pushed him off herself and scrambled toward Private X, who was lying in a pool of his own blood. His eyes were half-open. For a moment, J.T. thought he was dead, but when Tess patted— not slapped—his cheek, he stirred and blinked his eyes. She bent down and put her ear to his mouth. Then she shook her head and tapped J.T. on the hand, pointing to his ears. He gave her a thumbs-down.

Machine gun fire strafed the area where they were sitting; now it was Tess who threw herself around J.T. She took one of Private X's arms. J.T. took the other. As they began to drag him, bullets ripped down his torso. Tess let go of him immediately and grabbed J.T.'s hand. In a low crouch, she rushed forward, and he understood that they had to leave Private X's body behind.

The warehouse was burning. Bullets chased them. J.T. still couldn't hear anything. Tess and he were running side by side and then something blurred past him. He prayed to God it was Vincent and then he prayed that it wasn't because these guys had massive weaponry and Vincent wasn't Superman; he *could* be hurt.

Or killed.

Then the smoke thinned and they were outside, falling to their knees in the gravel. Wearing a bulletproof vest, Cat appeared from behind a Dumpster and gestured toward them. Then someone was helping him back up and guiding him toward the Dumpster.

*Heather?*

Cat's sister threw her arms around him and kissed his cheek. He tried to extricate himself so he could get back to Tess, but a guy in a do-rag was run-walking with Tess toward them. Once Tess reached them she kissed J.T., hard, and then she joined Cat. Cat pointed to her left leg and Tess squatted down, yanking up Cat's jeans leg and pulling a pistol out of a holster. *Wow.*

Tess and Cat started moving in unison toward the burning warehouse. J.T. bounded after them. Tess whipped her head around and gave him a stern look. He frowned at her—he was going back in, too, damn it—and then she pointed at him and made a cutting motion across her neck.

A big strong hand clasped his shoulder and dragged him backwards. It was the do-rag kid. J.T. was in no shape to take him on and reason began to seep in along with his circulation: He was unarmed, he was injured, and he was exhausted. He didn't know battle tactics, either. Loath though he was to admit it, he would serve Tess better by remaining out here with the other non-combatants.

One beast, half a dozen well-armed soldiers of fortune.

It wasn't a fair fight.

And when it was over, still partially beasted out, Vincent carried the steely-eyed, cigar-smoking man out of the blazing inferno, his memories rocketing back to that horrible day in Afghanistan. And he thought, *Yes. This is the soldier I went back to save, and didn't.*

He had come full circle.

Except… against all odds, the man had survived that day.

He would not make it through this night. His luck had run out. The only reason he had lived this long was the Kevlar armor he was wearing under his fatigues.

Catherine approached and said, "Vincent, he saved Tess and J.T. I don't know if he's undercover, or what, but he was a plant."

As if speaking for him, defending him, Vincent inclined his head to indicate his understanding. Then he waved her off with a twist of his chin. As relieved as he was to see her, he needed to be alone with this man in his dying moments. Cat got it, and gave him room.

Vincent dropped to his knees, cradling the broken body in his arms, cushioning the man who had given his life to save J.T., protecting him from the broken glass and gravel on the ground. Private X was coughing up blood. He didn't have long.

"Was that you in the warehouse?" Vincent asked him. "Last night?"

"Tried to stop it," he said. "Too much fear... oxygen. *Tell me,*" the man pleaded. "Did they do it to you?" He coughed again and blood ballooned from his mouth down his chin. "Not wearing a wire. No one's listening."

But Vincent couldn't know that. If someone crouched nearby with a parabola antenna and a good set of earphones, his secret would be out.

He wanted to give this mysterious man the peace of a definite answer, but that exceeded the parameters of the mission. Instead he said, "Who is it? How do we stop it?"

"I loved her," the man murmured. He was fading. "I would do anything..."

Vincent jostled him. "Stay with me, soldier. *Is it Lafferty?*"

The man clenched his jaw. He was in agony. "Tiptree," he ground out.

"The beast is Tiptree?" Vincent asked. "Tell me."

"Muir..."

"Muirfield?" Vincent filled in. "Are you part of Muirfield?"

"Pocket." His eyes widened as if in surprise, then focused on something behind Vincent. As if the Grim Reaper were standing right there with a scythe. Vincent turned and focused too, confirming that there was nothing there. Whatever the man was seeing, it was a sight reserved for the dying.

"Pocket. Take it," he ground out urgently.

After extricating the ruined body armor from the man's chest and abdomen, Vincent began gently going through his pockets. From a Velcro pocket in Private X's parachute pants, he pulled out a military ID and stuffed it in the pocket of the jumpsuit he had stolen. He found an ammo clip and a knife with a serrated edge.

"These?" he asked Private X.

The man's eyes shifted from the ghost behind Vincent to Vincent himself. Steely blue and fearless. His heartbeat was slowing.

"Bone... do..."

His mouth worked, but no sound came out. He continued to look at Vincent as if willing him to understand. Vincent touched the man's breast pocket. It was empty.

"I'll get it done," Vincent said. "Stand down."

For just one flicker of an instant, the corner of the man's mouth struggled upward—maybe it was a smile—and then his body failed him. Vincent locked gazes with him in case the brain hadn't yet finished working and there was still something there; he felt a kinship he hadn't experienced since everything had gone south in Afghanistan. When he'd enlisted, it had meant something to him. The betrayal had shaded his wish to defend his country with terrible undertones of conspiracy and corruption. But seated here in the dirt with a man he didn't know, whose agenda he was uncertain of, he still felt a small restoration of his faith in good soldiers.

He closed the man's eyes.

He had just finished a recheck of the pockets when Catherine darted up to him. She held up her phone. "We have to go. Fire and police are on the way."

"I want to take his body," Vincent said. "He was at the crime scene. For all we know, *he's* the beast."

"Do you sense that?" she asked him.

"I'm sure he was there. But the beast? I can't tell, but there's so much about this Beast two-point-oh that we don't know…"

She frowned. "It's too risky." She leaned in and took several pictures of the dead man's face with her phone. Next she reached down and pressed his limp fingers on the phone's glass face, and then his thumb. She took the knife from Vincent's hand and without hesitation, cut off the tip of the man's right index finger. Vincent opened his pocket and she placed it inside.

"Best we can do," she said.

"We can't leave him for the vultures to find. He was undercover and… I don't want them to find him anyway."

She squeezed Vincent's hand. "I understand. And I agree." She looked over at the fire. "What do you think?"

Vincent rose to his feet and trotted toward the warehouse, the man still in his arms. He reminded himself that in the days of the ancient Vikings and Greeks, a funeral pyre sent the souls of brave men to paradise. He didn't know this man's story, but he wanted to respect his final chapter.

Amid the flames and charring bodies, Vincent found a large pile of burning wood. He climbed onto a nearby crate and laid the man carefully down. Overhead, the burning roof was bowing inward and would fall soon.

"Day is done," he murmured.

And then he left.

# CHAPTER NINE

In Cat's apartment, Vincent was already in the shower, and Cat, filthy, shaken, and angry, couldn't wait to join him. Heather was angry, too, which Cat could understand, except that Cat was angry with *her*.

"I told you to go home," Cat yelled at her. "And not only did you *not* listen to me, you brought a *felon* with you!"

"He's *not* a felon," Heather shot back. Then she flushed. "Well, okay, except for murdering two people. And he only *said* that he did it. He was probably just trying to impress me."

Cat stopped pacing and stared at Heather.

Heather exhaled. "That came out wrong."

"I certainly hope so."

"Oh, Cat, don't be so huffy," Heather snapped. "I helped you tonight. All of you. You can spin it however you want—that I'm your stupid little sister, your comic relief—but *I* saved J.T. and Tess tonight. *Me*. And you can go *on* about how I didn't listen to you but it's a damn good thing I didn't listen to you. So let's all cheer, 'Go, Heather, for following your own instincts. Because you saved the day!'"

Heather made a show of patting herself on the back. Then she stomped into her room and slammed the door. Cat cooled down a little. Heather had a point. She *had* saved the day.

"Hey, Heath," she called after her. "Listen, I'm so—"

She didn't get to finish her apology because Vincent, dripping water and wearing nothing but a sodden towel, grabbed her up firefighter style and carried her into the bathroom. She was draped over his shoulder, laughing; then she helped him peel off her filthy, bloody clothing and let him lift her over the lip of the bathtub. The shower was still running and she lifted her face to the moist, divine warmth. The heady floral scent of her shampoo billowed around her, and then Vincent was washing her hair. It was only one of the many sexy, loveable things he routinely did that underscored how very thoughtful and special he was.

He moved from her head to her neck and shoulders, then on down her back. She leaned against him and tipped up her head, the view of his chin just splendid.

"So," she began. "Let's recap. You were in the warehouse. The one by the Patel apartment. And you felt—"

"I felt nothing that I hope to feel in about twenty minutes," he said. "As we leave the world behind for the rest of the night. We deserve this, Catherine, and I'm not going to deny either of us."

She, too, flared with passion. There were a hundred leads they should follow; as many theories to investigate. But her mind, her body, and her soul needed a moment, *this* moment. Needed him. Or else she would be no good to anyone. Being with Vincent tonight was as necessary as breathing.

"Make it ten minutes," she said.

Languidly, he picked up a bar of scented soap and a loofah and gently washed her arms and legs. She did the same to him, with her bare hands, her fingers trailing over the contours of his body. Reacting, his stomach muscles jerked and then his arms were around her.

"Make it two minutes," he said, bending to kiss her.

"Make it now," she whispered.

*I want to make you feel wanted...*

Drowsing, it took Cat a moment to realize that Vincent was idly braiding, then unbraiding, a tendril of her wet hair. She rolled over and nuzzled his beard with her cheek. Luxuriating in his presence in her bed, and in her life, she consciously blocked all the questions and tangents vying for her attention.

"Every time I wake up, you're here," she said with delight. She laced her fingers through his and kissed his knuckles. The joy in his eyes made her tingle all over and she reached for him.

"I'm not going anywhere." He smiled lovingly at her. "Is there something that you'd like?"

"You. Again," she whispered.

"My pleasure." He gathered her up in his embrace. Again, all care and worry slid away and they were in a world of two. Last year, that world had been threatened every second of every day. But now, it was their safe place, and Vincent's heart was her sanctuary.

"We should go on a vacation," he said later, playing with her hair again. "A real one. For a year."

"I agree." She closed her eyes and began to drift. She was sated, and she could barely stay awake. "For now I'll take eight hours of uninterrupted sleep. I'll call in. Sky can be a trained professional law enforcement police detective without me."

"I don't trust him," Vincent muttered.

"I don't, either; we'll talk about it in the morning."

"That's my line." Vincent kissed the crown of her head. Cat snuggled against him, happily returning to her drowsy bliss.

Then Heather shrieked and yelled, *"Why is there a severed human finger in our refrigerator?"*

"Leftovers," Vincent yelled back, and Cat beaned him with her pillow.

Tess flopped beside J.T. with a happy groan, then rolled over on her back. She moaned with pleasure.

She said, "Thanks. I needed that."

He grinned and the relief of the warming afterglow gave her a pang. There had been so much distance between them that she hadn't been sure he'd want to make love tonight. Sexual nirvana aside, they still had issues. She would have thought that after staring death in the face tonight, they each would have confessed their undying love and sworn that there was nothing in the world that was more important than their relationship. They had *survived*. If that didn't change your priorities, what would?

Except… it didn't feel like that inside her heart. It still felt a little too cold and a lot too lonely for someone who had a steady guy.

Maybe J.T. sensed the shift in atmosphere. He rolled onto his side and propped his head up with his elbow. She braced herself for The Talk, or some version of it, but remained silent. She wanted to let him have his say.

"It wasn't a matter of choosing Vincent over you," he said. "When Private X had a gun to your head."

Another wave of relief swept over her. This was not The *Talk* talk, then.

"I know. I'm good. I would have made the same call." She was teasing him a little, but it was true. Revealing Vincent's secret wouldn't have saved her life, and it might have ended Vincent's.

"Oh. Well, good," he said, way too fast.

"I would be dead either way," she went on. "So cheer up." She smoothed the frown lines on his brow. "J.T., I'm teasing you. Chill."

"It's just difficult to hear the words 'I' and 'would be dead' coming out of your mouth. I just... seeing that gun aimed at you. It really hit home that there are guns aimed at you *a lot*."

She too felt a little chilled. Was it inevitable that guys tried to bench you once they started to really care about you? Joe had completely sidelined her. If she had *wanted* desk duty, she would have asked for it.

J.T.'s frown lines deepened. Maybe he realized he was overstepping. She watched him make a willful effort to change the subject and the warmth came flooding back. He really was a good guy.

"Hey, so there's a lot of stuff to research," he said with relish. "Heidi Schwann, that warehouse, facial recognition searches for Private Dead Guy, hacking into the lab to see if there are any pertinent test results from the Patel crime scene. And also, finding out if my insurance will cover the damage to my car."

It had been discovered parked in a lot not far from campus with a major dent in the side and a crumpled hood. Reparable, in Tess's estimation. Growing up with five brothers, she had absorbed a lot of information about car repair.

He was trying to process his ordeal. When cops made it through dangerous situations, they slaked off the adrenaline at the shooting range or a karate dojo. This was the nerd version of that. She understood that, but it underscored to her the difference between them. She was brawn, he was brain. Sooner or later, wouldn't he get bored with her? And how could he stand to sit around all the time? She thought of other men, physical men who went on runs with her, sparred with her in the kickboxing ring, even roller-bladed, for God's sake. His baggy clothes did nothing for his physique—he was in pretty good shape but she could tell by the way he carried himself that he harbored memories of being a chubby kid.

"Tess?" he queried.

She'd zoned out. What was *wrong* with her? Okay, maybe he didn't aspire to becoming the next Rambo, but *he acted like a detective. They were working on cases together.* Wasn't this the dream? A guy who understood the life of a cop? And not only understood it, but participated in it? And who wasn't a cop himself?

She put her arms around him and kissed him. His lips were velvety soft and warm, and as their tongues touched, a million sparks lighted down her spine and spread throughout her body. J.T. was the most physical man she had ever known, and when she was with him, she was aware of her own body in so many new and delicious ways.

She said, "Let's do all that stuff in the morning. And do some more of this stuff now."

"Great minds think alike," he said happily.

She almost laughed, but knew that might spoil the moment.


Just a few hours later, the sun was trying to shine through curtains of snowflakes and Tess and J.T. resumed their discussion of everything that had gone down the night before. J.T. was ready to put on his Superhackerman cape and Tess was all for solving the many mysteries that had popped up last night—and also figuring out who had come up behind her on Vincent's boat, knocked her unconscious, and taken her to the warehouse. She figured whoever it was had died in the gun battle, but it would be nice to be sure.

"I started investigating Karl Tiptree. Why don't we proceed with him?" she suggested.

"As you wish," he said, beaming at her.

That was a pop culture reference he'd made before. She took her time to come up with the answer. "That's what

Riker says to Picard on *Star Trek: The New Generation*."

He chuckled. "The correct title is *Next Generation*, but no. It's what Westley says to Princess Buttercup. In *The Princess Bride*."

"Wait, but isn't Wesley in *New… Next Generation*?"

"That's a different Wesley. Wesley Crusher."

She had it now. "Wesley Crusher is the robot. Because he *crushes* people." She made two fists and smacked them together. "Crush!"

"That's Data. And speaking of data…" He kissed her again and put on his glasses. "Let's crush some."

They put on robes and he flipped on the Double-Oh-Seven console of his wall of machines. She leaned over his shoulder. The universe of J.T. Forbes popped into being.

"Warp it, baby," she said into his ear.

"Mmm." He moaned with pleasure. "Shields are down."

She needed coffee so she padded into the kitchen. He drank a lot of diet soda. He had a vast array of junk food snacks and microwavable meals. But actual *food* food was in short supply.

While the coffee dripped, she went through the messages on her phone. There was one from Cat with a number of photos attached, including one of a human fingertip labeled PRIVATE X. Good move. It appeared that Cat had also taken the guy's prints on the surface of her phone and then dusted them. She had sent Tess pictures of those as well. A treasure trove of data.

*I still don't get who the robot is…*

When she returned to the computer station with two cups of coffee, her man was nibbling on a gummy worm and scrolling through addresses. Then he double-clicked on a link and cried, "Yes! I have a match. I found the warehouse. Last night's, I mean. Thank you," he said, holding out his hand for the coffee without looking at her. "Look at this. The warehouse was leased to something called the Thornton Foundation."

"I've never heard of them." Interest piqued, she pulled up a chair and sat down beside him. "Can you find something on them?"

"Is this an official case?" he asked her.

"Parts of it are official." She grabbed a gummy worm. It was actually not bad with the coffee. "The parts that we can share. You know, business as usual for Team Beast."

"How much of this business do you think we have left?" he asked her. "Where we have to selectively edit what we reveal, and make up cover stories about what's really going on? Every time I think living like this is all over, something else happens. It's like we're on a Hellmouth."

She knew "Hellmouth" was another pop culture reference but for the life of her, she couldn't remember what it was from. What the heck.

"Like in *Ghostbusters*," she said.

"Yeah." He sounded a little vague. Maybe... disappointed? She winced. She needed a book on this or something. Maybe there was an app.

His phone rang. He took it. "Yeah, hi, big guy." To Tess, he mouthed, "Vincent." He said into the phone, "Sure, no problem, of course, bring it over. Oh, good, okay, that too."

He disconnected and kissed the back of Tess's hand. "He wants me to take tissue samples off Private X's finger. Also, the guy had a military ID card on him but it was a fake. He's bringing that, too. He said Cat sent you photographs and fingerprints. Off her phone."

"Yeah, I opened them when I was in the kitchen."

"That's so cool."

Tess glanced at the clock on his computer. Nearly nine! How had the time flown? She had to go to work. Suddenly, with all her heart, she wanted to stay. She wanted to sit beside J.T. in her bathrobe and perform computer searches and float theories about the murderer's means and motive. She did not want to face another angry mob demanding that she make their streets safe. That was why cops got the big bucks. *Not.* Yeah, putting their lives on the line day after day, against criminals who carried semiautomatic weapons and grenades and wore body armor. Go up against that for a public that mistrusted them. Stand up to creatures who could rip your sternum from your chest with a nonchalant tug.

She still believed in what she was doing, and she was proud to be a cop, but she understood that the department had to earn back the public's trust. Ending these homicides would be a giant step in that direction.

She put her phone to her ear and called her secretary. "Hi, Senya. How's it looking?"

"It's bad, Captain," Senya said. "Oh. Detective Chandler just poked her head in. Yes, it's the captain," Senya said away from the phone.

Cat was on the other end in record time. "You have to get rid of him," she bit off. "He told me that my chakras need tuning, for God's sake."

Tess grimaced. "Has he done anything wrong? I mean, besides diss your chakras? Because I can't start a file on him for being a New Age weirdo."

"Tess." J.T. leaned toward the monitor and pointed. "We have a match."

Tess leaned forward too. "Cat, J.T. just got a facial match on Private X. Here's his name: Theodore Coffey." She spelled it out for Cat. "Date of birth... he was forty. From Los Angeles."

"Malibu is in Los Angeles County," Cat pointed out. "Sky the vegan king's old stomping grounds."

"Do not tell me that he's a vegan," Tess said, groaning.

"He *is*. Except he got permission from his guru to wear regulation leather shoes, even though it really bothers him.

And it really bothers me that he and Coffey are both from the same part of the United States."

"Cat, ten million people live in Los Angeles County. And that's not what's interesting. What's interesting is that Coffey is already supposed to be dead. Killed in action in guess where. Afghanistan."

"Beast," Tess, J.T., and Cat said in unison.

"Give me the finger," J.T. said, and grinned.

"I heard that," Cat said. "Vincent's on his way over with it. I wish I was too. You have got to unpartner me. He brought gluten-free donuts this morning."

Tess couldn't help a grin. "Tofu-filled? Because those are the best."

"*Tess.*"

"No, listen. It's not weird that he's from Los Angeles and so is dead Theodore Coffey. But it *is* weird that he's here a week early. Janice said that he said he was going to take some time off before he started here. But he practically came to the precinct straight from the airport. When I asked him about it, he said he wanted to 'jump right in.'"

"But into what?" Cat asked rhetorically.

Tess pressed her lips into a thin line. "Exactly. But he would *know* that that would look suspicious to us. If he's involved, wouldn't he have lain low so he wouldn't attract our attention?"

J.T. held up his hand. "Like in *The Princess Bride,* when Westley is trying to figure out which goblet is poisoned. The reason he survives is because he knows that they'd know and that he'd know that they know."

Tess stared at him. "You have a TV reference for every single thing in the world."

He huffed very slightly. Maybe a police detective wouldn't have noticed it, but she *was* a police detective. She was trying his patience. Because she lived in the real world.

"*The Princess Bride* is not a TV show. It's a movie," he said. "And the Hellmouth is from *Buffy the Vampire Slayer*."

*This relationship is doomed.*

Vincent arrived about an hour later. He, Tess, and J.T. stared at the computer monitor, hoping for results. They had uploaded the fingerprints of Private X, also known as Theodore Coffey. Vincent took in the complex pattern of whorls and swirls on both sides of the screen. A definite match.

"Run it again," he told J.T.

"I've run it three times," J.T. retorted. "And it's come up the same each time. Those fingerprints do not belong to Theodore Coffey. They belong to Richard Howison. And Richard Howison is currently listed as deployed in Okinawa."

Vincent exhaled. "How likely is it that the system is giving us a false reading?"

"Pretty darn *un*likely," J.T. said. "I can give you the statistical degrees of uncertainty if you want. Of course, one can concede that it can make errors."

"Even Data made errors," Tess said, sounding strangely proud of her statement.

"Then, if the result is correct," Vincent began, "Coffey is an alias or Howison is, but the point is, this guy was undercover."

"Maybe this guy had plastic surgery to pass as Theodore Coffey," Tess speculated. "Hey, why didn't you two ever do that with you, Vincent?"

"Where would we have gotten major plastic surgery done?" J.T. asked, making a quarter-turn in his office chair to face her square on. "At the Spies R Us Plastic Surgeons Lair? We *are* just regular people, you know. Except for Vincent." He swung back to his keyboard. "I'm bringing up the photographs Cat sent us on Tess's phone."

He did so. The dead man's face filled J.T.'s largest monitor. Before Vincent could make the request, J.T. zoomed way out and guided the mouse to roll over the image very slowly as the three inspected it.

"There," Vincent said. He pointed to a shot that Cat had taken as the man's head had lolled toward Vincent's chest, exposing the skin behind his right ear. A shiny purple scar proved Tess's theory.

"We could assume that Richard Howison is a ranger, if he's undercover army. Elite fighting forces." Vincent held up a plastic bag containing the military ID card he'd taken from the corpse's pocket. "This identifies him as Major Alan De Graizo."

"This guy has more names than a character in a Russian novel," J.T. muttered. "Let's see how far down we can drill with *this* alias."

J.T. squinted at the name and typed it in. The screen filled with red letters that proclaimed TOP SECRET CLEARANCE PASSWORD REQUIRED ALL OTHER ACCESS DENIED.

"You've got your firewall up, right, buddy?" Vince asked tersely. Muirfield had been able to tie Vincent to Catherine because she had uploaded an old photo of him with two of his friends from Delta Company. They had wiped her computer clean and initiated a manhunt for him. Their lives had never been the same.

"My firewall's up but with security tech it's like playing an infinite game of Submarine, you know? We're hidden for now, but if they lob something new at us and they get the right square…" He made an explosion sound.

"Then get out of there," Tess said. "It's not like we're going to be able to come up with the password while we're standing here."

"Try 'Chimera,'" Vincent said.

J.T. complied.

WELCOME, MAJOR HOWISON, the screen said. Now in blue letters.

J.T. opened a drawer and pulled out three surgical masks and a container of computer monitor wipes. He handed out the masks; everyone put one on. Then he turned off every single computer except for that one, and draped the top of the screen with several wipes, arranging more wipes at the bottom of the monitor.

J.T. grabbed a pen and wrote on a yellow sticky note, *For all we know, some tech is staring at us right now*.

By mutual unspoken agreement, they walked out of potential viewing range. J.T. wrote on another sticky, *Bugs? Cameras?*

*We just did an electronic sweep yesterday,* Vincent reminded him. *Place was clean.* And suddenly it was three years ago when they spent a good part of each day making sure they were still safe, still off the radar. Some people kept track of trash day, they'd kept track of sweep for bugs day. Vincent felt the walls closing in again and anxiety nibbled at his nerve endings. He could actually sense his hormone levels rising.

*I'm supposed to be free now. All this is supposed to be over,* he thought.

In an act of defiance, he tore off his mask and walked outside into the busy New York sunshine. A driver in a car studied him and Vincent lowered his head, just like in the old days. A homeless man shuffled down the street and Vincent narrowed his eyes. Was he undercover?

A helicopter flew overhead. He flinched. Then he moved in a slow circle, taking in a hundred pairs of eyes, a dozen people talking on cell phones, and his heartbeat pounded harder and harder.

*I'm surrounded.*

A hand touched his shoulder and he whirled around so fast he staggered. It was Tess. Her big brown eyes were filled with concern. She put both hands on his shoulders, steadying him.

"What's wrong?" she asked him.

"I don't know," he replied. "My blood pressure's ramping up and I've got the cold sweats."

"You're afraid?"

He raked his fingers through his hair. "Yes," he said after a beat. "I want to run. Everything in me is shouting at me to flee."

"Like when the other beast attacked you?" She put her hand on his shoulder. "Vincent, this must be some kind of residual effect of the thing that set you off. Maybe there was some chemical in the warehouse last night, or on Howison's ID. Something is affecting you but it's not real. You're here, with us."

He took a deep breath and exhaled. Another. He stared into her eyes and saw reassurance there. "He wanted me to go in his pockets. He wanted me to take something. All I found was the knife, an ammo clip, and the ID. And I took them all."

"Maybe there's something on them. Like a chemical that elicits fear."

"But you're not reacting."

"Maybe you have to be predisposed. Like cross-species DNA must be present for it to take effect. We'll check it all out."

"I don't think he wanted me to be afraid. I don't know. Maybe I missed something. I was hurrying." He thought back. "You know, he mentioned Tiptree by name and it was in connection with a serum of some sort. I remember when Lafferty lost it. I always assumed she was moving into rage because that's what I've felt every time I beast out. But what if she felt fear? And they figured that out and they used her response to create a serum that causes terror?"

"That makes perfect sense," she said. "There have always been efforts to demoralize the other side into not fighting. Displays of power, propaganda that questions the morality of the confrontation—or persuades the fighters that they are going to lose, so they might as well give up. This would take warfare to a new level."

"Your tax dollars at work," he said sourly. "The people who funded Muirfield still have access to huge amounts of money. After we shut Muirfield down, it would start burning a hole in their pockets. They'd find a new project, or finesse the results of the old one."

"Well, it's working. You're scared. And all of New York is scared, and you know that New Yorkers scare easily."

"I hate being scared. It makes me feel helpless." He quirked a grim smile. "Which is exactly what they want. But knowing that doesn't help me. I can tell myself that I *know* I shouldn't be afraid, but it doesn't stop me."

"You're trembling."

"I can't seem to stop. I think I'm just going to have to ride it out."

"Then come inside." She looked around at the busy New York street. "It's sensory overload out here. It's even scaring *me*."

That brought a little smile to his lips. Together they walked back into the club. J.T. looked up. He still had on his mask. The sight unnerved Vincent but he fought it back. *It's just a mask. It's still J.T.*

"You okay, Vincent?" J.T. asked cautiously.

"Yeah," Vincent said, at the same time that Tess cut in, "He's having some kind of reaction. Can you examine the ID he brought you, see if there's any kind of drug adhering to the surface?"

"Reaction?" J.T. half-rose from his chair. "Of the very violent fugue variety?"

"No, J.T.," Vincent said. "Just… more fear." He wiped his face with his free hand. "I was telling Tess that Howison—or whatever his name really was—wanted me to find something in his pockets. He told me to take it. Those were his exact words. I'm wondering if he had something else on him—maybe an antidote for whatever this is. I think whatever is affecting me is a distillate of some kind of pheromone that triggers terror."

"Well, if it's in his pockets, that would be too bad since you performed a home-grown cremation," J.T. said.

"Maybe it was left behind," Tess offered. "I mean, the military makes structures that can withstand nuclear bomb blasts. Why not a small bottle or a vial that can survive a fire?"

Vincent reached for his jacket and gloves. "I'm going back to the warehouse to look around."

"Wait until I check these objects," J.T. said. "You might not need to go."

"No. Arson investigation will be combing through the ashes. I need to go *now*."

"If arson's there, they won't let you get anywhere near the scene," Tess argued.

He shrugged. "Then I'll try to blur in, examine where his body was burned, and blur out."

Tess looked at J.T., who moved his shoulders with an air of resignation. She cocked her head at Vincent and smiled faintly. "Why do I get the impression that this isn't really a discussion? You're going to go no matter what we say."

"Yes." He turned to J.T. "See what else you can get on Tiptree. Howison mentioned him with his last dying breath. We need to find out what we can. And, Tess, can't you get Wilson a new partner? We need Cat on this and she's hamstrung because he's looking over her shoulder."

Tess made a growling sound. "My first and only new hire as Captain."

"Yeah, what's he got on you?" J.T. teased her.

"Nothing," she said quickly. "It was just like a foreign-exchange program, only with police officers. I did it for the goodwill."

J.T. clacked his keyboard. "No good deed goes unpunished, Tess."

"While you're working on that, I'm going to look into the Thornton Foundation," Tess said. "Off the books. It's just like having two jobs rolled into one." She flashed them an artificially happy smile.

"I think it's time to pay another visit to Mr. Riley," Vincent said. "I'll go to his place after the warehouse."

"Poor old guy." J.T. clucked his teeth. "He's probably a wreck."

Tess said, "We should also go by the psych hospital and talk to Aliyah. Still no word on the social worker, Julia Hogan. I'm betting she's dead."

"This is a nasty business," J.T. declared. He slipped on a pair of gloves and picked up the military ID. "And as for *this*. It reminds me of when the government used to give the Native Americans blankets permeated with smallpox. They had no immunity and it wiped out entire tribes. So if there's a scare-factor pathogen on here, it was engineered to hurt anyone they thought was a threat."

"If you can find a way to give me immunity, I'd appreciate it." Vincent pulled some tissues out of a box on J.T.'s desk and dabbed his forehead.

"Still feeling it?" Tess asked.

"Oh, yeah," Vincent replied. "But you know what they say: 'Feel the fear and do it anyway.'"

*I just hope I can.*

# CHAPTER TEN

## Silverado Academy of Design

Heather was proud of herself as she straightened the pie-crust collar of an emerald-green silk blouse she had made herself and pushed through the revolving door with a smile on her face, not revealing that her heart was thudding in her chest as she scanned everywhere for Walker. Cat and Vincent had been stuck in a sewer, and J.T. and Tess had been kidnapped. Those were the reasons they hadn't called her. Good reasons. What was Walker's excuse?

Behind the receptionist's glass desk, Elaine Tugong was wearing a scarlet baby-doll kimono top and flared black crepe pants. She had on very shiny eyeliner and wet-look scarlet lipstick that matched her top perfectly, but truthfully and not in a catty way? She looked dated. Being one of the receptionists at Silverado was a plum student work-study job because they got to meet all the visiting designers, who were always on the prowl for new talent. That was why the magazines held contests like New Looks. But if Elaine was going to catch their eye in a good way, she needed to put an accent on *new*.

Elaine was texting; she gave Heather a little wave without

pausing. Heather was just a student, hence, inconsequential. Today on Heather's schedule was History of Design followed by Silks. As she headed for the lecture hall she caught sight of Mr. Summers, who owned Silverado. Now *there* was someone who knew how to put a look together: perfectly cut black wool trousers, Italian loafers and no socks, and a white shirt that had to be custom-made, accented with simple onyx cufflinks. His hair was white, trimmed short, and he had black eyebrows.

"Good morning, Mr. Summers," she sang out, giving him a wave.

"Heather, isn't it?" he said, and smiled at her. "Green is your friend."

Buoyed by the encounter, she walked into the lecture hall for HoD and Georja and Tyna, two of the girls in her class, bounded up to her. Everyone was changing the way they spelled their names to set themselves apart. Georja had told Heather she should change her name to something new, too, because "Heather" was boring.

"Did you hear?" Tyna trilled. "Walker had an argument with Mr. Summers and walked out! He's not working here anymore."

Heather jerked, her cheeks as hot as if Georja had slapped her. Mr. Summers was totally in with everyone in New York fashion, and she couldn't imagine *anyone* with an ounce of ambition having an argument with him. That had to be why Walker hadn't gotten in touch. But it still didn't explain why he'd left the apartment without a single word *before* that argument.

"What did they argue about?" she managed to ask.

"The door was closed. All I heard was 'record,'" Georja said.

*As in criminal record?* Heather thought, astounded. No, that couldn't be right. And anyway, they did background checks before they hired people, right? She'd had a background check for all three of her events coordinator jobs.

"Wow, so, okay," Heather said. "Gosh. Has anyone talked to Walker? Is he okay?"

"No clue," Georja replied, and Tyna lifted a brow.

"I kind of thought you two had gotten together," Tyna said. "Didn't work out, huh?"

Humiliated, Heather tried to put on an enigmatic smile. She had a feeling she looked like she had indigestion. But Tyna had a point. They *had* gotten together.

Before she could respond, the two turned and headed for the lecture hall. They caught sight of a guy they all knew— Jimm—and hurried up to him. Heather heard Walker's name and whipped out her phone.

*We did get together,* she told herself. *That gives me certain privileges.*

She texted him: *Walker? At SAD. U quit????*

The message was delivered. She waited to see if he read it. Everyone was walking into the lecture hall for the class but she loitered, getting a drink of water from the fountain, checking her lipstick in the hope that Walker would respond before class started. Canada Browne, her HoD teacher, had a zero-tolerance rule for texting. Get caught even once and she'd throw you out of class. History of Design was a required course to receive the coveted design certificate.

The message remained unread.

Then Heather's irritation plummeted into the deep-freeze of worry. What if something had happened to him?

*You're thinking like a cop's sister,* she told herself. *It's not like every single person you know gets murdered or something.* But it *was* true that her sister's boyfriend was a beast who had killed one of Heather's own boyfriends to keep him from killing Heather. And that her mother had been murdered, and probably her father too.

*I'm allowed to think the worst,* she thought petulantly.

Then she went into her History of Design class and didn't hear a single word about the evolution of the bathing suit.

Meanwhile, back at the precinct... or the seventh circle of hell, as Cat now liked to call it:

"The keyboard goddess has smiled on me," Sky informed her. He took a hefty gulp of wheatgrass juice like it was champagne. "I found no unusual activity for Julia Hogan *until* four days ago, when a transaction she began at an ATM in Brooklyn was never completed."

Cat's heart skipped a beat. The chase was on. "Tell me you've found out the location and subpoenaed the footage." She crossed her fingers that the footage did not contain a beast attack. She would have to intercept it. The jury was still out regarding whether Sky's arrival in the 125th was just an escape from a sexual harassment suit.

"I have ordered the footage." He pressed his hands together and inclined his head. "I shall seek enlightenment."

He was making fun of himself a little. Cat warmed a bit. Maybe he wasn't so bad.

"And may I say that if you would stop eating sugar, you wouldn't wrinkle. It's called White Death for a reason."

"Wrinkle?" she repeated.

"Oh, it's very faint," he assured her. "Only someone who would really scrutinize you would notice."

*Like you? Like Vincent?* Cat rarely took the time to be insecure about her looks. She had more important things to worry about. But this answered the basic question: Sky *was* bad.

"And you should try a colonic. Lemon and ginger. A great detox."

Cat wasn't sure what a colonic was. But it had the word

"colon" in it so she figured that she had a good idea what it entailed. No pun intended.

She cleared her throat. "Okay, let me know when the footage gets sent over. I'm going to run down some leads. We can meet up later. How about we debrief over lunch?"

He hesitated. "You don't mean in the precinct dining room. What they serve in there is *not* food."

"When have you had time to eat there?" she asked skeptically.

"I had breakfast there this morning." He made a face. "Or what they're calling breakfast. I can feel my bowels shutting down."

"Well, we could eat someplace else. You worship Shiva, right? So, Indian food?"

"I don't *worship* Shiva," he began. "How about I pick out a restaurant and introduce you to food that will extend your life, not send you to an early grave."

"Sounds yummy," she quipped. But he didn't realize she was joking. "Just text me the name and I'll meet you there."

She took her leave and dialed Tess's cell phone number. She was going to go back over the six original crime scenes to see if she could find anything that might connect them to the fresh leads J.T. had sent over. Tess didn't pick up. Cat looked over at her closed office door. Senya Fitzwilliams, Tess's secretary, was seated at her desk outside. She caught Cat's eye and said, "Captain Vargas got waylaid on her way here. There's another demonstration."

*Poor Tess,* Cat thought. She went out the back and then circled around to the front of the building. Since as a detective Cat dressed in street clothes, there was no way for any of the protestors to identify her as a cop unless they spotted her badge. She made no move to conceal as she joined a large mob—there might have been as many as five hundred people completely blocking the street. Police officers on horseback watched carefully; squad cars with blue marbles pinballing in their grates had closed the street completely, and traffic cops were diverting angry motorists. In New York, you had to file for a permit to hold a demonstration. But this looked spontaneous. Men and women were jeering and booing at Tess, who was standing on the steps leading into the precinct flanked by the mayor and the NYPD Chief of Police. Signs read STOP JACK THE RIPPER and VARGAS STEP DOWN. There were camera crews. People were recording on their smartphones. What a mess.

"We have every faith in Captain Vargas," the chief was saying into a microphone as Tess gazed calmly at the surging mob. Rarely had Cat been more proud of her. And she was grateful that it was Tess up there and not her. She had no ambitions toward becoming a captain.

She waved at Tess, but she didn't think Tess saw her. Then she phoned J.T. and said, "There was footage of Julia Hogan at an ATM machine in Brooklyn. From four days ago. Her transaction was never completed. Sky's going to get the footage."

"I'm guessing that we're both thinking beast attack," J.T. said.

"We are. Tess is stuck here. There's another demonstration. I'll go to Karl Tiptree's apartment myself."

"With or without Sky?"

"Without," she said firmly. "I'm not bringing him into this at all." She grimaced. "Which leaves him on his own if the footage shows up in his inbox while I'm gone. And if there's evidence of a beast attack…"

"On the bright side, if he is the beast-maker or the operative of same, he already knows what he's going to see on the footage. He'll have to lie to you about what's on it. Since I'll make sure I get it blind copied to my email address, we'll catch him lying to you."

"There is that," she deadpanned.

"Is Tess okay?"

Cat considered her words. "Tess has always been able to take on whatever's been thrown at her. I don't think she's loving this, but it won't break her, if that's what you're asking."

"It is," he said softly.

*He really loves her. I hope this works out for them.*

"I'm sure she's glad you're here," she added.

"It's just… you guys *like* this kind of stuff. All this danger."

"No, J.T. We like solving cases." Actually, he had a point. Chasing after perps, preparing for action, even the firefight last night, tragic as it had proven to be, had given her a rush. A detective's job was both physical and mental. The perfect combination, as far as she was concerned.

They disconnected and she took a squad car to Tiptree's last known address. Vincent had visited the crime scene after CSU had cleared it and come away with no beast evidence. The 125th had received the workup from the citywide homicide squad. To Cat's exacting eyes, it had been light on facts. No one had dug deeply into Tiptree's activities. Maybe someone had told them not to.

Maybe that someone was the beast-maker who had bought serum from Tiptree.

The apartment was empty now and Mrs. Steinmetz, the landlady, accompanied her, unlocking the door herself. Mrs. Steinmetz told her that the police had given her the name of a company that cleaned crime scenes. They had ripped up the carpet and scrubbed the walls with bleach. It had taken four coats of dark green paint to hide the bloodstains, and the floor had been completely ripped out and replaced. But word must have gotten out that someone had been murdered in the apartment, because she was having no luck getting it rented out. In fact, three tenants—the ones directly across the hall and on either side of Mrs. Steinmetz—had given notice. The savagery of the attack had started a panic.

"Please feel free to do all the looking you want," the woman said, leaving Catherine to it. "I would prefer to stay out here." She swallowed hard. "I'm sure you understand."

That was good; Cat could conduct a more aggressive search without a landlady hovering over her. Mrs. Steinmetz shut the front door, effectively sealing Cat in, and Cat went to work. First she did a sweep of each bare room. It was so much easier to clear a crime scene devoid of furnishings and possessions. But that also meant that all the good stuff had been taken. Even the curtains were gone. No doubt bagged and tagged and on their way to testing.

She was nothing if not thorough. Wearing gloves, she pulled out the plug-in stovetop burners and looked underneath them. She unscrewed the air vents and felt around in the space. She examined the toilet tank. She walked across the living room. A board creaked. She stopped and walked back over it. More creaking. Dropping to her knees, she pressed on the board. It was loose but it hadn't been pried up.

As she began to rise, she happened to turn her head to the left. A faint outline on the wall flush with the baseboard suggested that it had been patched.

Meaning that the wall had been damaged—not too surprising given the level of violence described in the police report. She got up and walked over, then used a martial arts back kick, employing the force of the sole of her foot, to break the plaster exterior. Jagged pieces fell to the floor, revealing a small hole. She crouched down.

And in that hole was a metal canister—about the length of her index finger, and the circumference the approximate size of her index, middle, and ring fingers compressed into a bundle. A vial.

"Huh," she murmured. It was a miracle that it hadn't been spotted by whoever had done the repairs. She'd check into that, make sure they hadn't meant to leave it there until the heat died down and someone came to retrieve it.

It was crimp-capped shut, meaning that she couldn't simply unscrew the lid. Not that that was a good idea anyway. For all she knew, what was in here was some kind of nerve gas that created irreversible brain damage.

She took a picture of it and emailed it to J.T. Then she felt along each wall, knocking at intervals to see if there were any more hollowed-out hidey-holes. She took her time, since this might be the only opportunity she would have to get in here. A swift glance at her watch told her that she needed to call Sky to cancel lunch.

She dialed Sky's phone and he answered right away.

"The bank's cooperating," he said by way of greeting. "They're looking for the correct date and time to get the footage to us. They said most likely scenario would be that they'd just email it."

"Good work," she told him, crossing her fingers that J.T. would hack in faster and take a look without leaving a footprint that he'd done it. The longer she knew J.T., the greater her admiration for him. He might save an extra dose of snark for her now and then, but the combination of his loyalty toward Vincent and his brilliance and dedication to solving cases and keeping Vincent safe made him a keeper.

The front door opened and Mrs. Steinmetz said in a small voice, "Did you find anything?"

Cat had already debated informing her of the hole, and decided not to. For all Cat knew, Mrs. Steinmetz was an accomplice, or the beast-maker. Not disclosing damage during a police search might not gain the department any new fans, but she had to control the investigation as best she could. If she told Mrs. Steinmetz about the hole, it was possible that the bad guys would know she'd found the serum. But it might be quite a while until Mrs. Steinmetz discovered the damage—hopefully after the case had been solved. Since the landlady claimed that she never actually came into the apartment, Cat pinned her hopes on that scenario.

As with all police work, Cat had to assess how much of her resources—in this case, time—to allot to each aspect of a case. She could spend a week going over each square inch of this apartment, or she could assume that she had already found the pearl in the oyster and move on.

"I'm finished," she said, deciding on the latter. "I was actually here just to verify some of the measurements in the report."

"Oh, I have a floor plan I can give you," the woman said. "Come with me."

Cat followed her into an overheated apartment that smelled of boiled cabbage—to Cat, a stereotypical New York City smell—and she occupied herself with looking at the many framed photographs on the walls as Mrs. Steinmetz fetched a stack of folded flyers from a dresser.

"I had these made up for potential renters," she said, handing one to Cat. "I haven't gotten rid of a single one."

Cat unfolded it to see a floor plan, a breakdown of utilities and deposits, and a little bit of history about the building. As she put it in her purse, she said, "This will be very helpful. Thank you." She gestured to the photograph. "I couldn't help but notice this picture. The young woman looks so much like you."

The woman smiled proudly, her anxious demeanor transforming on a dime. "That's what Dr. Tiptree said. He said she had my eyes. That's my grand-niece, Heidi. She's a graduate student at Northam now."

Something tugged at the back of Cat's mind. She took a quick picture of it with her phone as Mrs. Steinmetz returned the flyers to the dresser. "What's her field?"

"Biology of some sort."

Another beat as Cat worked to keep her poker face. She *had* to be J.T.'s lead, Heidi Schwann.

"I'm afraid it's a little too advanced for me. She and Dr. Tiptree used to talk about it together. I'd let him know when she was coming for a visit. We'd have some tea and cookies and play cards." She paled, as if the fact of his death was creeping back into the forefront of her mind. "I think he might have been a little sweet on her but of course he was way too old for her. He was always respectful. I don't think she ever knew."

Maybe, but maybe not. Cat tried out a scenario where Tiptree recruited Heidi to assist him in beast-making, or possibly, creating the fear serum. Maybe he simply examined her research. A third option was that she had spied on J.T. for him. It was possible that she'd ransacked his office and given the signal to have him kidnapped.

"Does Heidi live here with you?" Cat asked.

"Oh, no. She has a place closer to the university. I'm glad of that, especially with everything that's happened." Mrs. Steinmetz cocked her head. "I did tell the other police officer about this. I believe he even went to speak to Heidi about Dr. Tiptree."

Cat went on high alert. She had seen the file for the Tiptree homicide and there'd been no mention of a Heidi Schwann. Either the documents she'd seen had been redacted— censored—or someone had impersonated an officer and come to dig for information. Possibly they'd been searching for the vial, too.

"Huh," Cat said casually, "I must have missed that report. Do you happen to remember the name of that officer?"

Mrs. Steinmetz managed a wan smile, nothing as genuine as the real pleasure she had taken in talking about her grand-niece. "Yes. It was Officer Coffey. I thought that was such a funny name."

*Whoa,* Cat thought, and a kaleidoscope of possible scenarios spun through her mind. She allowed them as much of her attention as possible, since each one could demand a different set of answers. That meant that she would have to ask Mrs. Steinmetz different sets of follow-up questions. But she was starting to feel the pressure of time, so she attempted to keep her next question as broad as possible, to cover as much ground as she could.

"Did Dr. Tiptree have any visitors on a regular basis?" She smiled. "I know that might be in the report, but since I'm here, I may as well ask."

"Would you like some tea?" Mrs. Steinmetz said hopefully. The interview was shaking her up. For that, Cat was sorry. But although she would like to be gentle, her focus had to be solving the case. Preparing tea would make the elderly lady feel helpful and create a bond with her. Cat would make a bit of time for that.

"Yes, that would be so nice. Do you have a restroom I might use?"

"Down the hall. First left."

Cat thanked her and went into the bathroom. She whipped out her phone, hoping for bars, and murmured "Yes" when she found she had excellent cell coverage. She immediately called J.T.

"I got the picture of the cylinder," he said as soon as the connection was made. "Did you open it?"

"Couldn't," she said, "and I didn't think I should, anyway." She moved on quickly. "I'm in the apartment of Tiptree's landlady. I'm sure she's Heidi Schwann's great-aunt. I'm sending you shot of a photograph on her wall to confirm." She texted it.

"Hold on." He came back on the line. "Oh, my God. It *is* Heidi."

"Well, she and Tiptree were friends. Or friendly. He would

come to Mrs. Steinmetz's apartment when Heidi was over and she'd talk about her work."

"Which was…?"

"Mrs. Steinmetz has no clue. She just made the tea."

"I'm supposed to have lunch with Heidi in about an hour," J.T. said. "To talk about her becoming my TA next semester. She emailed my university account about twenty minutes ago to confirm."

"Are you kidding? So she doesn't have a clue that you were abducted right in front of her?"

"Or… that's the way she's playing it."

"I have more. Mrs. Steinmetz just told me that the *other* police officer who interviewed Heidi about Tiptree's death was named Officer Coffey."

J.T. was silent for a moment. "It's time to reconsider the plan to disappear into the Yukon," he said dolefully. "Luckily, Vincent and I look good in flannel."

"But remember, 'Coffey' didn't know if Vincent had been transformed into a beast by Muirfield. I think that's significant, given what he *did* know. And if Heidi's keeping your lunch date, she may really be unaware of what happened to you last night."

J.T. exhaled slowly. "Or she may be incredibly ballsy. So now what?"

"I'll bring you the cylinder. Then I'll follow you to your lunch with Heidi. I'll protect you, J.T. She won't see me and I'll be armed. And you'll wear a wire."

He moaned. "And the fun just keeps on coming."

"I. Will. Protect. You," Cat enunciated clearly.

"Yeah, that's what they said to President Kennedy," he quipped. "Where are my Tums?"

"I'll be over soon."

"I'll be here. So, hey, have you heard from Vincent? I've called him three times and no answer. And you know what that meant last night." He made a "grr" sound.

"He must still be at the ruins of the warehouse," Cat said, prickling with anxiety.

"Don't you want to go check on that? Instead of spying on my lunch with Mata Hari? So I can cancel?"

"We don't know that she's complicit."

"And the moon is made of green cheese."

"Don't worry, J.T.," Cat said. "I'll be there soon."

She ended the call and walked back into the living room. Mrs. Steinmetz was busily arranging china plates laden with slabs of coffee cake and silver forks on a small table. Her pleasant bustling contrasted sharply with Mr. Riley's poignant efforts to deal with Lafferty's death. Cat renewed her pledge to him to get to the bottom of all this. Maybe right this minute, Vincent was finding answers.

"I can't stay long," she said gently, taking a seat and picking up her fork. "I hate to be so personal, but do you happen to know if Heidi is seeing anyone special?" Detectives were always looking for connections, preferably with threads that could be followed and investigated.

"I believe she is," the woman said sweetly. "She's very excited for him. He just got tenure at the university. He does research into... let's see... things that glow."

Cat stifled her surprise. "Bioluminescence?"

The woman cocked her head thoughtfully. "I believe so. His name is David. He's been over here with her."

*That has to be Sara's new boyfriend. I'm hitting the mother lode.* She picked up her fork but didn't eat, pointedly waiting for Mrs. Steinmetz, as hostess, to take the first bite. She wanted the elderly lady to sit down and really spill.

"Wasn't Dr. Tiptree in some kind of biology field?" Cat asked disingenuously. "A consultant for the government?"

The teakettle screamed. Mrs. Steinmetz zoomed into the kitchen. "Yes. Oh, what was it. There's a word," she called out to Cat. "Something scientific. All three of them used it all the time. It starts with *ph*."

"Phosphorescence?" Cat called back.

"That's close. It has to do with smelling. Like when animals want to attract mates."

*Pheromones.* Cat's fork hovered over the cake as she mentally willed Mrs. Steinmetz to say the word. She didn't want to put words in the landlady's mouth. She wanted to make sure she got as straight an answer as was possible.

"Oh, golly, my memory's not what it used to be. The four of us used to play Scrabble and they came up with such outlandish words that I finally bought a Scrabble dictionary so I could look them up."

She reappeared with a teapot covered by an embroidered cozy and two pretty china cups. She set everything down. "Let's see. Where did I put that dictionary?" She bustled down the hall.

About half a minute ticked by. Cat checked the time on her phone. If she and J.T. were going to keep his lunch date, she'd have to leave in five minutes.

"Here we go." The woman reappeared with a paperback book in hand. She was holding a pair of glasses. "'Pheromones.'"

"Oh," Cat said. "Is that what Heidi's studying?"

"Well, I guess they had a project they were working on together. She and David. They were consulting Dr. Tiptree about it."

Cat considered. Could be coincidence. But she sure didn't think so.

"Have some tea, dear."

Mrs. Steinmetz poured and, needing to hurry, Cat bolted back the steaming hot liquid. Her throat blazed. Stifling a gasp, she put down her cup and said, "Thank you. I wish I could stay longer, but I have an appointment."

"A lady police officer. We've come a long way." Mrs. Steinmetz looked very impressed.

"Yes." Cat scooted back her chair. "Thank you. May I call you if I have any more questions?"

"Of course. And if you know anyone who wants to rent a nice apartment…"

"I'll let you know. Thank you again. The cake was delicious."

"You barely touched it. No wonder you're so thin." She sucked in her breath. "Do you have allergies? Poor Heidi has all kinds of them. She has a terrible immune system."

"I'm fine," Cat assured her, keeping careful track of every scrap of information Mrs. Steinmetz was giving her.

She made her goodbyes and left the apartment.

## CHAPTER ELEVEN

At the warehouse, Vincent remained in the shadows until the arson investigation team left. The chief investigator had put forth a theory that the warehouse had been burned down because of a gang war. From one perspective, that was true.

He found it impossible to believe that no other players were hiding in the shadows, as he was, waiting for the officials to clear out. Had all the FFNYs died in the shootout? With them and Major Howison dead, who was minding the beast? Or had the FFNY ever even seen it?

The combined odors of the warehouse reminded him of the flight deck of an aircraft carrier—metal, rubber—and he chalked that up to whatever had been originally stored in there. His boots kicked up ashes and the smell of humanity wafted around him like ghosts. Next he focused on visuals, then sounds, confirming that he was alone. Although the pyre had burned, Vincent easily distinguished that pile of embers from the others by the scent of Private X distilled into the charcoal-like sticks. The bones of the victims had been reverently collected and transported, with more dignity than he would have accorded all but one of them. Now he squatted before the remains of the pyre with a pair of thick protective gloves. Methodically sifting through the debris, he concentrated on the last moments of Major Howison's life.

*I loved her.*

*Take it.*

*Bone do…*

He sifted through the fine gray powder, and his memory cast back to a day in the desert when he had sifted the hot, arid sand through his fingers in just this way, trying to quell his anger.

AFGHANISTAN, 2002

*Lafferty was in the infirmary, goldbricking. Faking illness to avoid combat. At least that was what the medic who was attending her claimed. She just lay there staring at the ceiling in a T-shirt and shorts and telling Vincent that she didn't feel right in her skin.*

*Then once the medic was out of hearing range, she clasped Vincent's hand. Her face was flushed and tears welled and spilled.*

*"You're going to get me out of here," she whispered. "I figured out how. He does rounds at twenty-two hundred hours, checking on all of us. Making sure we're still alive," she added bitterly. "And then he leaves. He goes and plays video games or watches some stupid movie and I'm lying here on fire. I am in agony, Keller, and they're making it worse."*

*"What about Dr. Chandler?" he asked her. "Doesn't she check on you?"*

*"Swear to God, if I had a gun, I'd shoot that bitch. She did this to me," Lafferty grunted. She wrapped both her hands around his wrist. "This whole thing is wrong. We shouldn't even be in Afghanistan. We're not helping the*

*locals. We're only getting them killed."*

Vincent stiffened. *"Lafferty, we're soldiers. We don't see the big picture. We follow orders."*

She glared at him fiercely. *"Our orders are wrong, Vincent. All of this is wrong. You should refuse to fight. Or better yet, take over the camp."*

He was shocked into speechlessness. He understood her anger and confusion—they were in a war zone, and it did often seem that they were doing more harm than good, same as the army was doing to them. But Dr. Chandler had backed off on the injections, and now she was monitoring symptoms as they arose. He had faith in her.

*"Yes, I'm talking mutiny,"* she said. *"And desertion. I say you stockpile some weapons, start talking to people. There's an officer, he agrees with me. I'll put you together with him."*

Vincent shook his head. *"No. No way."*

Suddenly she caught her breath and clamped her jaw shut. She began to writhe back and forth. Contracting into a fetal position, she wrapped her arms around her abdomen and made guttural, growling noises that made his hair stand on end.

*"Jeez, Lafferty."* That was Adams, the medic. He was carrying a hypo. *"Can it, will you?"*

*"Don't drug me!"* she screamed. *"Don't!"* Her eyes were huge, wild, as they fastened on Vincent. *"Do something!"*


*By the time I did something it was too late for Lafferty,* Vincent thought, pulling himself out of the memory and back into the present in the warehouse. He wondered if Howison was the officer she had wanted him to connect with back then. If Howison had gotten her out… if he then helped her heal from the burns she had sustained in the infirmary explosion and kept her off the grid for all these years. It wasn't so far-fetched.

*If this is Lafferty doing all this, her crimes can be traced back to me. She was one of mine. I should have believed her. I'd known her to be a brave soldier. Why did I walk away?*

He knew the answer: That was when he had begun to seriously question what was going on. Lafferty had been giving voice to his own doubts and he'd moved away from her as if her fears were contagious.

Fear. That word again. Just remembering how afraid he had been yesterday made him shaky.

Resolutely he continued to sift through the ash. His fingertips made contact with something solid. He dug down and wrapped them around an object about an inch in diameter and two inches long. Coated with powdery gray, it resembled a large ammunition shell casing. He cleaned it off with the tail of his shirt and cradled it in his palm.

It was a metal vial. He must have missed it while going through Howison's pockets, either because it was so small or he had missed the pocket itself during his rapid search. He pulled out his phone and turned it on. He hadn't wanted to risk detection; even the vibrations of a silenced phone could be picked up by sensitive surveillance equipment... or the ears of a beast. But surely he had been noticed by now—if anyone was even watching.

Pretending to aim the phone camera at the pile at his feet, he took a video that included a zoom of the vial. Then he sent it to Catherine and J.T., surreptitiously slipped the vial into his boot, and continued to dig in the ash in case he was being watched. Observers might assume that whatever had caught his attention, he had rejected. He kept himself on alert for the *snick* of a weapon, whether it be an AK-47 or a tranquilizer gun. If no one was watching him, it might be safe to assume that FFNY had been eliminated, and that Howison had either been working alone, or his fellow operatives were on lockdown.

He kept digging around for a few more minutes, then

moved on to another pile. He remained in search mode for another half an hour, now in constant contact with J.T. and Catherine. They had new suspects to add to the list—Heidi Schwann and David Mazursky, Ph.D., Sara's new boyfriend. Vincent couldn't help a grunt as he parsed that Dr. Tenure was probably a bad guy.

He compared his vial to the image Catherine sent him. His appeared to be significantly smaller than the container she had just retrieved. So they weren't uniform. They might not even contain the same substance.

She called him as he left the warehouse. "Listen," she said, "what if each of the victims has one ingredient of the serum? Let's say they were in on it together but they didn't trust each other. Six victims, six parts of the formula? Seven if you count Indira Patel, but I don't think she was a party to this."

"Six vials," Vincent mused. "Or a couple of vials, maybe a jump drive with the formula, other things they needed. It makes sense."

"J.T.'s got a lunch date with Heidi Schwann. He's going to wear a wire and I'm going to follow him."

"I'll come too."

She started to say something—maybe suggest that he continue searching for more vials at the five other crime scenes they were suspicious of—but after last night, there was no way Vincent was going to stay back while J.T. met up with a suspect. Maybe Cat knew that. Whatever the case, she said, "I'm going to J.T.'s place now."

"Meet you there."

He put the phone back in his pocket, blurred to conduct a few more passes of the grounds, and decided not to bother covering over his footprints. He had to get to J.T.'s.

He had a feeling things were going to go sideways very soon.

\* \* \*

By the time Vincent arrived at the gentlemen's club, Cat had just finished wiring J.T. Then Tess checked in. She sounded slammed. The press was really beating her up.

J.T. had just completed a hack into the bank's protected archival system, and the good news was that Sky hadn't received the footage he had requested. J.T.'s program would divert any email from the bank's address to his desktop computer and blind-copy Tess so that she would know it had been done. However, as a safety measure, she wouldn't receive the footage herself—there would be too many risks that someone else might see it. Then he could examine it for beast images, doctor it if need be, and send it on to Sky. The Malibu cop would be none the wiser.

Checking in with Cat, Sky told her that while he was waiting for the footage, he had moved on to deepening their dossier on Indira Patel. He had come up with some troubling information: Aliyah Patel had been admitted to the emergency rooms of at least two hospitals and three urgent care facilities. Some New York City medical facilities had joined a pilot program to share information about individual cases, and there'd been reports of two broken bones and numerous contusions.

The picture was very grim, but in Tess and Cat's line of work, not unique. They dealt with the dark side of human nature. Still, after seeing the excited little girl in the photo with Mr. Riley, clutching her gift certificate for an ice cream cone a week for a year, Cat's objectivity went out the window. Sensing her distress, Vincent put his arms around her and held her. She breathed in the essence of him and allowed his warmth into her sad heart. It was so very hard to live the life of a protector, because you had to face, to *know*, what you were protecting people from. To fight injustice, you had to call it by name.

Most days, she could steel herself against softer, more

nurturing emotions if they got in the way of her purpose. But just as her humanity had served as a beacon for Vincent as he subdued his beast side, he had lowered her defenses with his love. Before Vincent, Cat's life had been black and white, and guys had disappointed her because she'd picked disappointing guys. After some trying times between them—horrible times, really—she and Vincent had found their way back to each other. Fear, jealousy, and mistrust had served as a crucible for the oneness they now shared. Cat knew with every bone in her body that Vincent was the great love of her life. Her only love. Her one true love.

"I love you too," he murmured against her hair, even though she hadn't spoken a single word of her thoughts aloud. That was how it was with them. Their connection gave life a whole new meaning. She wasn't just a cop, a friend, a sister, and a daughter. She was Vincent's, and he was hers. And if anything ever happened to him...

*I want all of this to stop*, she thought in a rush, but that wasn't true. She wanted to stop all the threats to Vincent's life, to their privacy and safety, because of what had been done to him. But she didn't want to stop helping others. Vincent's lifeblood lay in serving and protecting, the same as hers. If they didn't dare all, be willing to give all, they wouldn't be living their true lives, be their true selves. She understood that, but it was so difficult to let him walk into danger, and in a way, to walk into danger herself, because she knew it would crush him if she died. And if *he* died—that wasn't a thought she could even contemplate. And so the only way they could survive was to walk into danger *together*.

"Let's go," J.T. said as he put on his Summers coat. "I'm not getting any younger. Or less terrified."

* * *

Heidi Schwann had chosen to meet J.T. in the Founders Room, a clubby old ivy-covered dining hall that had once been reserved for male professors only, then professors only, and now for professors and graduate students only. J.T. assumed she had asked to meet there because she wanted to emphasize that she moved in academic circles—and the fact that she cared what he thought gave him hope that she truly wanted to impress him and not run him over with a car.

With Vincent on the job, he'd argued with Cat that there was no reason for him to wear a wire. Vincent would be able to tell if Heidi was lying. But Cat said they might as well go ahead and record the meeting because if Heidi said something incriminating or useful, they would be able to hand it over to the DA. J.T. was still unimpressed. Being involved in criminal cases didn't usually help with your tenure application.

Heidi was seated at a table in an alcove and when she saw him, she half-rose. He hoped the deference wasn't an act because it was kind of nice, and he could easily see himself accepting her as a TA if only to get some of that respect. Face it, his self-esteem needed a recharge.

"I'm so glad you're all right," she cried.

"That I'm… all right," he said slowly, mostly to buy time. It was not at all what he had expected to hear her say.

"I had my glasses off," she said, "so I didn't see the accident happen. That's why Dr. Mazursky told me not to bother talking to the campus police." Her cheeks went pink. Something in that statement was untrue. He wanted Vincent to have a good, clear shot at narrowing it down so he said, "Dr. Mazursky. So he was there at my… accident? I thought he and Sara had left."

"He was walking Dr. Holland to her car. He heard the collision and came running back. But by the time we caught up with you, you were gone and that friend of yours was driving your car out of the way so it wouldn't block traffic."

"My friend."

"Yes. He said he'd get you checked out and you went into his car."

J.T. worked overtime to remain casual. "Oh. So that was all you saw?"

"I was freaking out! But Dav—Dr. Mazursky—went over and talked to the witness and he said you were okay."

*Vincent, J.T. to Vincent, J.T.* thought. *You reading this?* He couldn't wait to find out if Heidi was lying. Because if she wasn't, then maybe David Mazursky was. And Sara *hated* lying. J.T. was the walking wounded proof of that. There were three possibilities for Mazursky's version of what had happened: one, that he *had* been told by someone that he, J.T., was okay; two, that he had lied to Heidi because he figured J.T. was okay or else he didn't really care, and he was trying to keep out of it; and three—the big kahuna—that Dr. David Lying Mazursky was in on it. If only he could let Sara know...

*Hey, whoa, who cares?* he asked himself.

"Do you remember who he talked to?" J.T. asked her. *That should be "whom."*

"No. It happened so fast."

In that case, moving on to Polygraph Exhibit B.

"So you want to be my TA. What are your areas of interest?"

A waiter came and took their order: a burger for J.T. Boom, simple. Heidi had a thousand questions about how each dish was prepared and if it contained a huge list of things she was allergic to, from peanuts to shellfish to strawberries.

"Sorry," she murmured, playing awkwardly with her silverware. "I'm allergic to air, it seems." She tried to smile. Despite all the cloak and dagger stuff, he was touched. It had to be difficult going through life like that.

If it was true.

"Is it genetic?"

She shrugged. "My great-aunt's the healthiest woman I know. She lives here, you know. In the city."

Mrs. Steinway. He had that name wrong. Steinway was a piano. It didn't matter. Cat knew her great-aunt's name.

"Do you see her often?"

It was a clunky question and a more suspicious person might wonder why he asked, but Heidi simply nodded. "Yes. I go there a lot. We—we have tea and cookies, and we talk…" Her voice grew faint. She was editing out the fact that David Mazursky usually went with her. J.T. wasn't sure how to proceed.

"That must be nice for *both* of you." He took a sip of water to collect his thoughts.

"Um, yes." She touched her silverware nervously. "We're close." Then she looked up at him with those gigantic glasses and behind them, her piercing brown eyes. She was very pretty. "One of her tenants was murdered. You know those awful attacks that have been happening? He was one of them."

"Really?" He kept his eyes wide, his tone shocked. "She owns the building it happened in?"

She nodded. "It's where she lives, too. A few of the other tenants have moved out. She's getting worried about paying the bills."

"That's tough. You must be worried about her, too."

She sipped her water. Her hand was shaking. "She was out of town the night it happened. Visiting my other great-aunt. Aunt Alice is in assisted living in Rochester. Aunt Lydia pays for most of it. Her financial situation is already tough. That building is so old and there are always repairs to be made. I've been hoping to make things easier for her."

She took a breath, and J.T. knew she was going to make her pitch. "If I could make a name for myself in biotech, write my own ticket…" She kept her gaze glued to her water glass. "It's a competitive field and everyone is looking for profitable products…"

He was pretty sure he was hearing David Mazursky's words coming out of her mouth. He knew he shouldn't scare her off so he bit his tongue in order to keep himself from asking her straight out what was really going on.

"Why come to me, then?" he said. "I'm not working on anything that's going to set the world on fire." He couldn't resist adding, "Are you?"

"Well, I was thinking about something," she began. "I'm sure you've read about the new nail polish that responds to the presence of Rohypnol. The date rape drug." He nodded. "I have so many allergies, and I've always been careful, but just recently a little boy died at summer camp because he didn't realize there were peanuts in a cookie a friend gave him. So I was thinking, what if we could assign markers to common ingredients people are allergic to? Maybe like a specific smell?"

"This is research adjacent to *pheromones*," he said for emphasis.

"Exactly. And David… Dr. Mazursky," she amended hastily, "tried to help me but he's bioluminescence. Then he told me that Aunt Lydia's tenant, Dr. Tiptree, had published a paper on pheromones a long time ago and we—we talked to him about it at Aunt Lydia's." Splotches of purple crawled up her neck and over her face. "He was very excited about my ideas. He even said that once I got my Ph.D. there might be a job waiting for me."

"Well, that would be great," he said. "A job with what company?"

She sighed. "I think it was some kind of government contract. He didn't say. And now, well, there won't be a job."

"Maybe not that particular job, but biotech is a growing field. And you probably know that allergens are a real problem. And there's amazing research being done on immune deficiencies."

Their food came. Heidi inspected hers very carefully before taking a bite. J.T. picked up the ketchup bottle and gave it a few shakes, but nothing came out. He said, "I hope you don't think this is rude," and inserted his silverware knife into the neck of the bottle. Just as victory was about to be his, he dropped the knife on the floor.

"Oh, darn it," he said, and began to look around for their waiter.

"Here, use mine." She picked up her knife and held it out to him.

"Thanks." He got the ketchup flowing and set her knife down beside his plate. "Well, Dr. Mazursky might still have something to contribute. What if you could use some kind of bioluminescence that makes the allergens glow? And the detector could be a device or maybe even some kind of phone app? It would be the same situation as labeling on packages, only updated, and with tech."

"I thought of that." Her eyes shone. Her glasses *were* very thick. It struck J.T. that if her glasses had been off when his car had been hit, she actually could have missed the whole thing. "But he thinks—and I agree with him—that glowing food in any case would weird people out."

"And peanuts already have a smell," he countered. "If you could simply boost it, or trigger a hormonal response of dislike…"—leaning over his food, he smiled at her to take the sting out of the word "dislike"—"…which could be done." His mind began churning the possibilities. It was a bit of a *Brave New World* scenario, but of course he would never actually participate in it…

"Like an additive that triggers the survival mode at the most atavistic level," she ventured. "Think what that would mean for parents of toddlers, or whose kids are at summer camp."

This was cool. A nifty problem to solve. A pretty woman who wanted him to help her solve it. For a little while he could dream the dream...

And then he thought of Tess. And all the murders. And their suspicions. And the fact that it was possible that Heidi was seeing her thesis advisor's boyfriend behind her back. For all he knew she was some new kind of beast that Vincent couldn't detect.

But mostly he thought of Tess.

His smile fell and he pulled back. Heidi didn't seem to notice as she took a tentative taste of her very plain salad and gluten-and-dairy-free pizza. "Maybe we could work on this even if I wasn't your T.A."

Despite everything, when she smiled at him hopefully he started melting again. Just a little, and he began to wonder if *she* was exuding some kind of pheromone.

"I'll take it under advisement," he said. "I'm also waiting for my budget for next semester."

"Oh, I know Sara will make sure there's money in the budget," she blurted, and then she flushed again. "I don't mean to imply that Dr. Holland would pressure you."

*Right, even though she's the assistant chair of my department and on the tenure committee,* he thought archly.

After they parted, he met Catherine and Vincent at the appointed spot—well out of visual range of the dining room and anyone who might have followed Heidi there. From the somber looks of Cat and Vincent, he knew something was up, and he bid a wistful farewell to the half-formed daydreams lunch with Heidi had conjured in his head. No groundbreaking pheromone research. No cute TA.

"Fill me in," J.T. said.

"She was nervous and sweating from the time she sat down until when you two left. And her heart was going a mile a *second*," Vincent told him.

"Could you tell which parts were lies and which parts were the truth?" J.T. asked.

"You know it's easier for me when people answer yes or no questions. Which I know you couldn't have done," Vincent hastened to assure him. "Catherine verified as many facts as she could on her phone. Heidi *is* related to Lydia Steinmetz and she *is* a grad student here."

"I'm waiting on a warrant to go deeper," Cat said.

J.T. nodded at her, then looked at Vincent. "All that pheromone stuff?"

Vincent shrugged. "I'm going on my intuition here. I think Mazursky put her up to it. Maybe he's feeding her a bunch of lines but I think she knows it's window dressing for something else. But she's going with it to please him."

"So Mazursky's the one we want?" he asked hopefully. He didn't want Heidi to be a bad guy.

"Not sure yet. Let's go check your office. Let me see if I can figure out who broke in," Vincent said.

"Here's the knife." Wrapped in his napkin, J.T. handed Cat the knife Heidi had picked up when he had "accidentally" dropped his on the floor. He had scooted it into his lap when Heidi wasn't looking. "And I've got a little bit of pizza crust."

"Thanks. I'll dust the knife for prints and we can get her DNA off the crust."

J.T. tiredly rubbed his face with both hands and dropped them to his sides. "We're going to find out she's the beast. Or that she's had plastic surgery or she's a clone or something."

"Or maybe she's just a young, ambitious grad student," Vincent said. The three looked at each other for a moment, as if such a thing would be stranger than any of the other possibilities. J.T. could tell that each of them was mentally gearing up for another installment of Adventures on Steroids. Or, as he liked to call it, daily life.

Cat's phone rang. She looked at Vincent and J.T. as she

said, "Hi, Tess. Okay, thanks for the heads-up. I'm glad it worked. Yeah, J.T. just had lunch with Heidi. Inconclusive results, but we know that something's off." She nodded. "Okay, I'll tell Vincent and J.T."

She ended the call. "Tess says she just got the blind copy from the bank's email. That means the footage is in your inbox. We need to view it and either forward it to Sky as is or alter it."

"Okay. I need to be at my command central to see the footage. I'll take you guys to my office so Vincent can do his tracking thing while I go home. We still don't know who broke into my office."

They reached the door, which only appeared to be locked. J.T. showed them the doorstop he'd crammed under the jamb to keep it shut until he could install a locking mechanism. Like many of the professors, he had an agreement that the cleaning staff wouldn't come in his office.

"If I report the break-in, university security will inventory all my information and IT will examine my computer. It's much easier for us if I just take care of it myself and tell them later that I broke it."

"Smart," Cat said, as she went in first. She didn't have her gun out but J.T. knew she kept it within grabbing-and-shooting distance.

"I haven't touched anything," he said, and along with Vincent and Cat, he took in the magnitude of the mess. "I don't know what they were looking for."

"Howison wanted to know if I'd been changed," Vincent said. "Maybe he or his operatives were looking for evidence that I was a Muirfield experiment."

"We can go on the assumption that they didn't find what they were looking for. If they had, they wouldn't have abducted you to ask you about Vincent," Cat added.

"In that case, I'm going to make up a whole slew of

fake files. All kinds of misinformation. How about you're a Martian, Vincent? Do you want to be in the NSA, Cat? Then when people break into my office they'll be satisfied and *not try to kill me for information*." He bent to pick up half a dozen file folders that had been fanned out like playing cards on a casino table.

"Don't," Vincent ordered but the word came out more as a growl. His eyes were glowing, his face altering. He was beasting out so he could do his tracking thing.

J.T. held out his hands to show Vincent he was still leaving everything as is. "Or how about I say in your file that you're in the CIA?" he asked Cat.

Cat turned to shut the door while J.T. kept his eye on Vincent. Yep, fingernails extending.

"What about the FBI?" a voice said from the hallway.

## CHAPTER TWELVE

D avid Mazursky, Ph.D., briskly entered the room and closed the door. Cat whipped out her gun and took a bead on him while Vincent's growl deepened.

"Easy, big fella," J.T. said to Vincent. "That head cold's really kicking your butt."

"You're FBI?" Cat asked Mazursky.

"I am. So put the gun down, Detective," Mazursky said calmly. "I pose no threat to you."

"Two things," Cat said. Her heart was thundering. If Mazursky was FBI, she didn't dare take her eyes off him for a second, or he would disarm her. But it took every ounce of self-discipline she possessed not to check on Vincent. If he beasted out in front of this guy—

"Yes?" he asked, waiting.

"The FBI has posed many threats to me. And if you were really FBI, you'd know that."

"Fair enough," he said. "Of course I know about your father, Special Agent Reynolds. What's the second thing?"

"I'm NYPD, and we don't take orders from the feds. We are your equals in every way," she said. "So I will keep this gun up."

He smiled. "Everything I've heard about you is true."

She tensed and made sure her finger was on the trigger. If he made one wrong move, she would take him down. "And what have you heard?"

"That we're lucky to have you on our side."

"I think you guys should take this out into the hall," J.T. said in his singsong *I am warning you that Vincent is transforming* voice.

"It's all right. I know about Dr. Keller," Mazursky said.

Shocked silence met his declaration. Cat remained locked and loaded, although her arm muscles were beginning to tire.

Then Vincent growled more menacingly than before. Cat said, "It's okay, Vincent. Please stay calm." To Mazursky, "We're going into the hall."

Mazursky cocked his head. "You're going to hold a gun on me in the hall?"

"Turn around, put your hands on the wall, and spread your legs," Cat ordered him. He paused and she pointed her gun at his face. "If you know anything about me, you know that I'll use this if I have to."

He complied, putting himself in the deliberately awkward pose. Cat searched him and took his weapon, a Glock 27. She kept patting him down and found his cell phone, keys, and a second gun—a Sig Sauer 9mm. While he was vulnerable, Catherine took off her muffler and draped it over her own weapon, effectively concealing it.

"Okay, let's go," she ordered Mazursky.

As they left the room, Vincent growled again. He was being protective, worrying about her, but he had to be quiet or the other people in the building would think there was a wild animal on campus and call security. She wondered if J.T. had the tranq gun in his office.

She strode forward and Mazursky preceded her, his hands half-up. Raised too high, and it would be suspicious to onlookers. But too low, and he could grab something to hit her with and deck her in seconds.

She shut the door behind herself and tried to kick the doorstop into place with her heel. "Talk," she said.

"I need to speak to Dr. Keller," he said.

"He'll hear you just fine."

He arched a brow, impressed. "All right, simply put: We've been on parallel tracks with you three. We believe the first six murders were committed because the victims were working for an outside organization that has successfully created... something new. That this new thing emits a pheromone that elicits a chemical response in its victims, incapacitating them with fear."

Cat maintained a poker face. "You can say you're FBI, but truthfully? I have no idea who you are."

"I can show you my badge." When she looked at him blankly, he smiled wryly. "Which I could have bought off the rack at FAO Schwarz." That was the world-famous toy store on Fifth Avenue in midtown Manhattan.

"The Bureau and I have a complicated history," Cat said. "FBI badges do nothing to reassure me. You mentioned six murders. What about Indira Patel?"

He grimaced. "We think Patel is the first time this new weapon has been deployed. The first six... we have no indicators that any sort of cross-species activity was present."

That jibed with their own findings. But that still was no reason to trust him. "So did you take out the first six?"

"Why would we do that?" he replied. "We wanted them alive so we could learn about this new... development."

New beast. Monster. Weapon.

"If you'll recall, your father went to extraordinary efforts to shut down the prototype project. We're committed to continuing his work."

"His work included murdering innocent people."

He clenched his jaw as red crept across his cheeks. The mention of her father's heinous acts clearly angered him. Maybe he was one of the good guys after all.

Still, she did not lower her gun.

"As we both know, innocent people are being experimented on while we're standing here," he said. "And not by the Bureau."

"The soldiers of Delta Company were innocent people," Cat shot back.

"They volunteered for the experiment. They had already sworn to give their lives in service to their country."

"Some gave all," Cat said harshly, thinking of Mr. Riley and the portrait of Lafferty that hung above his mantel.

"*You've* sworn to protect and serve," he said. "Does your oath come with strings attached?"

"Unknowingly becoming a weaponized beast is not a string, it's a lie," she said. "Orchestrating the deaths of some people so that others may live is wrong."

"There's collateral damage in any war," he observed.

"I'm a police officer, not a soldier."

"The only difference I see is semantics. You *are* a soldier. A warrior. What our world has become… we can't afford these fine divisions anymore. People like us—committed and honorable—we must take on this greater evil. Everywhere these people go, everyone they touch—they're our jurisdiction, our business."

She opened her mouth to argue, but he went on. "You've worked outside the law for three years, Detective Chandler. You've used your badge and your gun contrary to the rules and regulations you swore to uphold."

"I don't have to explain myself to you. And I won't."

"So what then? Are you going to kill me?" He raised his chin, betraying his wariness. Then he said, "I'm willing to die, for the same reason that Major Howison gave his life to save

Dr. Forbes: to find and stop the people who made this beast, and to destroy that beast."

She still didn't give ground. Years—a lifetime—of betrayal had solidified her resolve. "Are you talking about FFNY?"

"The people we're targeting created FFNY as a cover for their operations. The FFNY's mission was to locate and capture the beast and to find the serum that enabled it to secrete a complicated set of pheromones that evokes a fear response in anyone within a fifty feet radius.

"The organization in control of FFNY is called the Thornton Foundation. They've been attempting to extend the field of influence. For obvious reasons, of course. Let one of these things loose on a field of engagement and you can not only force your enemy to retreat, but to also keep a healthy distance from you in the first place. Like a force field."

"Why kidnap Dr. Forbes?"

"You mean, do they know that he's shielding Dr. Keller?" He lowered his voice. "We think they suspect, but we don't think they know. Dr. Forbes was mentioned prominently in some correspondence that remained intact when Muirfield was destroyed. I believe he was pretending to cooperate with your former medical examiner, Evan Marks. Who *did* give his life in service of the greater good."

"What kind of correspondence?" she asked sharply. "And why do you know about it?"

"Emailed discussions of their research, a set of notes about Dr. Marks's findings and Dr. Forbes's opinions, and about Dr. Marks's plans to present his findings at a symposium. And his secret deal to ally himself with Muirfield, which, as you know, he recanted."

Though she retained her stone face, she took a moment to grieve Evan's death. Flirtatious and brilliant, he had been a bright spot in some dark days. Until he had decided to destroy Vincent to "protect" her. More than one man had gone down that route... and died because of it.

"And of course, it's no secret that Dr. Keller was in Delta Company and served in Afghanistan during the time period that Muirfield was engaging in testing. That he disappeared for a decade, and only recently resurfaced. Excellent grounds for conjecture that Dr. Forbes is... privy to the inner workings of a clandestine project no longer acknowledged by anyone who participated in it." He smiled as if to indicate that she knew exactly what he was getting at.

"To sum it up, Dr. Forbes is on the front lines, Detective. And so are you. And so is Dr. Keller."

She was aware that he hadn't mentioned Tess. That was good.

The door opened and Vincent appeared on the threshold, utterly human, his dark eyes boring into the FBI agent's face. His broad shoulders were squared and he stood poised as if to strike. Beast and man, Vincent was a protector first and foremost. J.T. appeared behind him, clearly not loving the situation.

"J.T.'s office wasn't ransacked by anyone we're acquainted with," Vincent announced. Cat translated: not Heidi Schwann, Howison, or... this guy.

"How did you ever get a cover as a Ph.D. at a university?" Cat asked Mazursky.

"With tenure?" J.T. added.

Mazursky smiled. "In my case, it was the opposite way around. I was recruited after I got my Ph.D." He smiled at J.T. "But before tenure. By the way? Sara misses you. I think if you tried, you could win her back."

J.T. blinked. "*I* don't think you and I should talk about Sara." He hesitated. "Unless she *knows*."

"About all this?" He gestured with his still-raised arms at the four of them, himself included. "She doesn't. And honestly? The situation has escalated to the point where I'm going to have to make some changes in my cover. Such as leaving the university."

"Escalated," Vincent said.

Mazursky looked at the three of them. "I've been compromised. Before he was killed, Major Howison got word to me that someone in the Thornton Foundation suspected I was undercover, too. He didn't know if they had proof, but my handler wants me to get out of here."

"Gee, that's too bad," J.T. muttered. "What about your career?"

"J.T., are you kidding? He's in the FBI now. He'll have lots of opportunities for research in biotech," Cat said harshly.

"Your tax dollars at work," Mazursky replied.

Cat's phone buzzed. She said to Mazursky, "You can put your hands down." He did, and she checked her phone. It was Tess. *OMG. HURRY! WORK ON FOOTAGE. SKY'S ABOUT TO CALL THE BANK.* She held up the phone so that Vincent and J.T. could see the message... but Mazursky couldn't.

"I have to get home," J.T. said.

"I'll make sure you get there," Vincent said, but Cat could hear his hesitation. There was a lot to discuss with Agent Mazursky.

"Houston, we have an elephant in the room," J.T. said.

"The problem is," Mazursky ventured, "we don't have a lot of time to get to know each other. To figure out if we can trust each other. That thing is out there somewhere. Killing people. Even if you decide I'm a bad guy, I'm one hundred percent human. Easily contained. That thing? Not so much."

"He's right, Catherine," Vincent said.

Cat said, "Agreed. But we move slowly. You give us cause to regret trusting you... and I won't consider you an innocent anymore."

"And neither will I," Vincent said.

Fear flared in the man's eyes. Then he nodded. "Both of us have some puzzle pieces but so far, I don't think either side knows what the picture on the box is supposed to look like."

Cat tried to imagine what this new beast could look like. Aliyah Patel had seen it. It was time to make that visit to the little girl a priority.

"Okay, question," she said. "Is Sky Wilson one of your operatives?"

"Who's she?" he asked, and Vincent grunted appreciatively.

*Just because he acts ignorant doesn't mean he is,* Cat reminded herself.

"Okay, so get off my case. Literally," Tess said into the phone, just as Sky leaned his head in the door and gave the jamb a jaunty rap. She hung the phone up. "Yeah?"

"It may be true that all things come to he who waits," he began, "but I've been waiting a long time for that ATM footage."

*Not by New York standards,* she thought. But she couldn't risk having him call the bank to complain. "I'll call the bank myself." She picked up the handset. "How's the forensic accounting coming?"

"Well, I told you about the abuse issues with Aliyah Patel," he said. "I thought maybe her social worker had been bribed by her aunt to leave it alone, but I don't see any unusual deposits in her checking or savings."

"I doubt she was even paying attention," Tess said sourly. "Or maybe Indira promised to do better and Hogan let that suffice."

He frowned. "I know social workers are overworked and their caseloads are unreasonable, but how do you ignore a stack of evidence like that?"

She pursed her lips. "I guess that's what the public's saying about the one-twenty-fifth. Seven murder victims, and we're guessing you've found an eighth. What do you think, some crazy gangbangers on PCP?"

"Aliyah Patel could tell you about that," he ventured.

"I called the hospital. She's still catatonic. They won't clear us to talk to her right now. Not even if we bring crayons or hand puppets," she muttered. She was lying. She didn't want Sky Wilson anywhere near a witness to a beast attack.

"Please don't judge me too harshly," he said pleasantly, "but what about bringing in a shaman? I know a couple."

"Don't even." Tess glared at him. "That's all I need. The clear sign that Captain Vargas is unfit for command." She held up a hand. "I'm not fishing for reassurance. Just, let's leave the woo-woo stuff for Malibu, all right?"

He smiled and bowed his head. "Yes, ma'am. About the first six vics. I assume this citywide homicide task force has filed detailed reports?"

"Yes." But not in the context of beast-makers and beasts. Of course she couldn't tell him that.

"Do you mind if I read them over? I'd have a fresh perspective. Detective Chandler's taking personal time so I'm without my Yoda." He smiled at her again, this time as if she really should smile back. She didn't. "Or... I did notice a large stack of files on her desk, speaking of an overwhelming caseload..."

"I'll leave it up to you," she said. "Either way, you're earning your paycheck."

"Okay." He turned to go, then turned back. "I know it would be inappropriate for me to give you a neck massage—"

"Goodbye," Tess snapped.

He shut the door and she sighed and picked up her phone to make yet another call. Because life, you know? Just never complicated enough.

\* \* \*

Vincent and J.T. returned to the gentlemen's club while Cat and Agent Mazursky decided to pay a visit to a very frightened witness—Aliyah Patel. Cat was glad. It was past time. Plus she wanted Mazursky to see first hand the toll this was taking on innocent people. It was all well and good to frame the situation in terms of the rich and powerful versus cops, soldiers, and government agents. But as with the first wave of Muirfield experiments—poor orphaned children whom no one would miss—Aliyah Patel was being given a raw deal. Maybe Mazursky and the Bureau were all about finding the serum and investigating the monster, but her priority was protecting the citizens of New York. The rest of the world, yes, if possible. But New York was her home, and these were her neighbors.

The sky was low and gloomy gray; pine trees dipped in a bitter wind that stung Cat's cheeks and nose with frozen needles. She rubbed her gloved hands together, reminding herself to be grateful even for this hard, brittle day: For so many, there were no more days at all.

A dozen emails and text messages came in and she prioritized them, smiling at an e-card Heather had sent her: On the screen was a diva in a black-and-silver evening gown smoking a cigarette in a long, black lacquer holder and arching one penciled-on brow at the viewer. The text read *I'm not apologizing, dahling. Well, not exactly.* Chandler women were stubborn and proud. She still couldn't believe Heather had mixed it up like that. She wanted to be proud of her but the only thing she felt when she replayed last night in her mind was pure, unadulterated fear. Heather could not be part of this bleak, dangerous world. Heather was the porch light, the sunflowers in the garden.

Mazursky scrolled through his own smartphone missives— Cat imagined that many of the questions she and he had about the other would be answered if they simply swapped phones for thirty seconds—and then he put it in his pocket.

Mistrust sleeted against Catherine's heart and then they reached their first stop: a low concrete building at Vanek Memorial State Mental Health Facility. One window was lit and a security guard stood behind a sheet of bullet-proof glass, waiting for them to step right up. They had to present their credentials and relinquish their weapons in a metal tray at the bottom of the window. The man examined their pieces of identification carefully, then made a call. Mazursky stamped his feet for warmth and flashed Cat a little smile.

"How suspicious of me were you? I mean, before I identified myself as an agent?" he asked her.

"I'm still suspicious of you."

The guard sent back their IDs with two visitor badges and told them sternly to wear them at all times.

"And don't lose them, or you might wind up in here," he finished. Maybe it was meant to be a joke, but Cat didn't laugh and neither did her companion.

They were about to enter the mental health holding facility where Aliyah had been admitted. A clutch of narrow grimy windows, all of them covered with wrought iron bars, alleviated the grim face of the building. A trio of smoking chimneys coughed into the air, coating the scene with a Victorian, sepia look. A hundred years ago, this place would have been called an insane asylum.

After the intake guard stowed their guns, a buzzer sounded and the main gate opened. It was metal and it creaked and squealed on rusted hinges. A guard in a gatehouse asked them to wait until an escort arrived—a heavy-set matron named Lena Mueller with short gray hair and matching eyebrows, who didn't smile or say hello as she shepherded them into the main building.

The interior was more depressing than the exterior. Few lights were on; the white paint on the walls was peeling. A bulletin board contained out-of-date safety flyers and a faded map of the facility with fire escape routes marked by red arrows. There were innumerable doors with buzzers, and guards, and orderlies, and finally they were walking down a gloomy corridor signposted PEDIATRIC CARE UNIT. Cat was appalled at the idea that Aliyah, who had already suffered so much, was incarcerated here. There was no better word for it.

Finally they came to a door with a tiny square of glass in the center. Chicken wire veined the window, obscuring their view. Beside the door was a file in a holder. *Patel, Aliyah.* The silent, cranky Ms. Mueller pressed a buzzer, which was answered. Then she used a swipe key as well as a metal key and the door swung open like the beckoning fingers of a witch with an oven and an appetite.

In profile, Aliyah was sitting in a medical gown on a cot with her back against a brick wall. She was staring down at her hands, and her hair hung in front of her face, effectively shielding her from view. She was so small that her feet didn't reach the edge of the narrow bed. Her shoulders were slumped and she made no effort to acknowledge Cat and Mazursky's entrance into the room.

Just as she did not acknowledge the man seated on an orange plastic chair facing her:

Sky Wilson.

"What the heck?" Cat demanded, as Sky smiled calmly and got to his feet.

She had the presence of mind to glance over at Mazursky, to see if he recognized Sky. If he did, he kept a very good poker face.

"Detective Chandler," Wilson said. "I thought you were taking time off or I would have let you know that I was coming here." Was that a veiled dig that she hadn't informed him of the same thing? "I think I'm making progress with my friend Aliyah here. I've been working on her throat chakra, the seat of communication. I can feel her increase in connection." He smiled at Agent Mazursky. "Are you one of her doctors?"

Cat gave Agent Mazursky a long, hard look. If he said the wrong thing—*anything*—in front of Wilson, they were going to have a big problem. Mazursky seemed to get it; he inclined his head and said, "I'm David Mazursky. I've been brought in as a consultant on this case."

Cat turned to the matron and pointedly thanked her. The woman told Cat that she'd be outside the door. She showed her where the panic button was—big and red and up too high for Aliyah to reach.

"I'm sure we won't need it," Wilson said to the woman's stiff, retreating back, then looked up at Cat. "Well, it's catatonia. That much is evident."

He rose from his chair and indicated that she should take it. There were no other chairs in the room. When she remained standing, he sat on the cot beside Aliyah instead. Aliyah didn't move a muscle.

"I did my time in violent crimes," Wilson said. "This is trauma, pure and simple. But Aliyah wants to talk to us. She's melting the wall between us with her laser-beam eyes. It's her superpower." He smiled at the little girl, who didn't smile back.

"I thought we were going to leave the interviewing to Mrs. Kuhl," Cat said. She took the chair so that three adults weren't hovering over the little girl.

"You don't perform delicate surgery with a table saw," Wilson replied. "Mrs. Kuhl simply doesn't have the proper tools." He waved a hand in front of Aliyah's wall of hair. "I can feel the heat of your laser eyes melting the wall, Aliyah. Your words are floating in the bubbles, just like we talked about. Once the wall has melted away, the bubbles will pop, and your words will be freed."

He turned to Cat and Mazursky. "Hold out your hands.

You can feel the heat from the wall as it melts away."

Catherine wanted to brain him. But there was no way she was going to argue with him in front of Aliyah or Mazursky, so she held out her hands.

She *did* feel heat. A warm strip of air between Aliyah and her. Mazursky didn't seem to feel anything, or if he did, he gave no indication. His face was a combination of annoyance and curiosity.

Cat glanced upward to see a vent in the wall. She heard a puffy little blowing noise. The source of the heat, then, and no New Age woo-woo.

"Okay, Detective Wilson," she said firmly. "It's time to—"

"Mmmm," Aliyah mumbled to the floor.

Cat was galvanized. She glanced toward Wilson, who was beaming at the little girl.

"Pop," he whispered. "There goes a bubble. And out comes a word."

"Mmmm." Her thin fingers flexed. "Mmmon…"

*Monster.* That was what she was going to say. Cat caught herself sitting on the edge of her chair in anticipation. She held her breath.

"Mmmo." Her legs twitched.

"Pop, goes another bubble," Wilson chirped. He clapped his hands. "Way to—"

Aliyah flung herself at him and raked his face with her fingernails. Fissures of blood sprang open as he fell backward and she landed on his chest, clawing at him. She was kicking and shrieking, and screaming one word, over and over again. Not monster, no:

"*Mommy! Mommy! Mommy!*"

# CHAPTER THIRTEEN

As Aliyah attacked Sky Wilson, Mazursky pressed the panic button and a siren like a ship's klaxon whooped. The door was open in two seconds and the matron rushed in with two attendants in white uniforms. They dive-bombed at Aliyah and hoisted her off Wilson. She kicked and screamed as the three adults tried to contain her. Her eyes were wild. Spittle flew from her mouth.

Wilson grabbed at his face and said, "It's all right, Aliyah. You're safe."

They were pressing her against the bed, holding her down. A flash of movement and then she went limp. The matron wheeled around with a syringe in her hand.

The older of the two attendants knelt beside Wilson and barked at the other one to get gauze and antiseptic. But Wilson pushed himself to his feet and, covering his face, edged past the man and sank down beside the cot. He put his hand on the crown of Aliyah's head.

"It's all right. You're safe. You are divinely protected. No one can harm you. Don't be afraid. Nothing can hurt you here."

Aliyah whimpered.

"Wilson, you need to be looked at. That's an order," Cat said.

"Jonas, take him to the nurses station," Ms. Mueller told the man who had already been attempting to help him. "Dr. Lewis should be there. She can take a look."

"We'll go with him," Cat said.

Each attendant slid an arm under Wilson's shoulders, as if he were an injured football player being helped off the field. Cat held open the door while Jonas spoke into a radiophone. By the time they got to the nurses station, a doctor in a white coat was waiting for them.

"Wow, I would never have expected this from Aliyah," the doctor said. "She hasn't moved a muscle since she was brought in." She applied a square of gauze to the bloody tracks, tossing it into a bin marked BIOHAZARD. Cat sidled over and plucked it out. Mazursky quietly picked up a paper drinking cup and Cat dropped the gauze into it. Then he slipped the cup into his coat.

"That was before the bubble machine was plugged in," Mazursky said dryly. Cat couldn't help her quick grin.

"I got through to her." Wilson puffed out his chest. "Someone finally broke down the barrier."

"Better you than me. You may have scars." The doctor appraised his wounds. "I'm thinking a few sutures."

"Once you're fixed up, you should take the rest of the day off," Cat said.

"I'm fine," Wilson insisted, but he looked ashen. "The plumber is coming today. A white sage smudge…"

"I can drive you home," Cat said. "Dr. Mazursky can drive my car to the precinct and wait for me there." She just hoped she hadn't left anything incriminating in the vehicle.

"To the precinct." Wilson tilted his head. "I assumed that you worked here, Dr. Mazursky."

"No, I'm a consultant," was all Mazursky said, and Cat

didn't elaborate either. It was clear from Wilson's bunched shoulders that he knew he was being kept out of the loop.

As the doctor numbed and stitched up Wilson's face, Cat glanced at her phone to see a text from J.T.: *FOOTAGE DANGEROUS*. She was dying to know exactly what that meant, but J.T. had prudently not attached it. She replied to say she'd come right over after dropping off Wilson.

The gray-haired matron appeared and informed the doctor that Aliyah was sleeping now. They had administered a powerful sedative.

"What did you say to her?" the matron asked Wilson.

"I provided a safe place for her to re-experience her trauma, in hopes of exorcising it." He frowned as the doctor tied off one of the sutures. "She said 'Mommy.' Right, Detective Chandler?"

As was usually the case with beast-related situations, Catherine chose to be very selective about her reply. "I think that's right," she hedged.

"It was definitely what she said."

"Her mother's been dead for most of her life," Cat said. *Or has she?* Could it be that Lucky Number Seven, the first murder to feature the new beast DNA, had nothing to do with serums or government scientists and everything to do with revenge for Aliyah's abuse at the hands of her aunt?

The three fell silent. The doctor applied bandages to the stitched areas, then handed Wilson two small white pills and a paper cup filled with water.

"Painkillers," she said. "Take them."

"So if the mother is dead," Wilson murmured as he took the medication and chased it with his water, "maybe this triggered a memory of her mother. How did her mother die?"

"That's an excellent question," Cat said, easing up on him a little. "One I think is worth finding out. For all we know, Indira Patel's death is related." She glanced at Mazursky, who was chewing the inside of his cheek. He looked as uneasy as she felt.

"But you can find it out tomorrow," she added. "I want you to go home."

"Meanwhile, Aliyah is in here, suffering," Wilson said.

"She's unconscious," the matron said flatly.

"The spirit still suffers," he replied. "It still suffers."

After Dr. Lewis wrote Wilson a prescription for antibiotics, Mazursky, Cat and Wilson walked back through the labyrinth of buzzing doors and gates. At the guard gate they returned their badges; then they got back their guns and walked to the parking lot. Wilson pulled out his phone.

"Hi, Mom. Listen, I accidentally cut myself. Do you have aloe vera growing in the apartment? That's great." He was pressing his fingertips on his bandages and wincing. Cat felt truly bad for him. He had succeeded in getting through to Aliyah when no one else had been able to. She wanted to chastise him for doing it without her but she could also understand, and countenance it. They were in the middle of a crime wave, and he had been relegated to financial forensics and waiting for ATM footage. It showed initiative that he had gone to visit Aliyah. Truly, he should have checked in with her and Tess, too, but both of them had been too busy to pay much attention to him.

Mazursky said, "Do you have any evidence bags on you? I'll take the gauze square into our lab."

"You're going to be at my precinct," she began as she handed him a bag, but he shook his head.

"I know you managed to process samples at your lab but we have a lab that's fully protected. I'll retain possession." He put the square in the bag and sealed it shut.

"Dr. Forbes can examine it."

"Not at the university," he countered. "That's equally risky." He looked at her. "Short of pulling a gun on me, there's no way you're going to take this from me. A modicum of trust, remember?"

Her temper flared but she kept her cool. After all, she had the victim with his clawed face. And she could always go back to the facility. As long as Aliyah was a patient there, she would have access to her DNA.

"Trust goes both ways," she said. "We pool information."

"Yes. We do."

Then Mazursky parted ways with them and Wilson gave Cat verbal directions to his apartment. The snow was falling sideways now, obscuring visibility. Cat watched the bars on her phone decrease one by one.

She didn't know what she had expected, but Wilson lived in a charming old brownstone with a bay window. The house was filled with plants and stained glass. A large statue of the Virgin Mary stood in an alcove that had been painted sky blue. That surprised her; she'd thought he and his mother were into Buddhism.

Cat helped him to a gray velvet Victorian settee. On a curved wooden coffee table there was a handwritten note paper-clipped with a plumber's business card. He picked it up and nodded to himself. With his cheeks bandaged and his back rounded, elbows resting on his knees, he looked less like a smug California kale-juicer with a fake tan and more like a stunned person in pain who was still trying to understand what had happened to him. In other words, traumatized.

"Can I get you something?" Cat asked, removing her coat and hat. "You wanted some aloe vera?"

He smiled, the cocky Californian returned. "I think I'll start with aloe vera. I have some other herbal remedies but I think I'll wait until you leave to break them out. You already think I'm a crackpot."

"No," she began, then laughed and shrugged as he rose from the couch. He was unsteady. The painkillers, she guessed.

His gait was measured as he led the way into the kitchen, which was a jungle of potted herbs crowded into another bay window and hanging in clusters from the kitchen ceiling the way some people hung pots and pans. He seemed to regain some of his bravado as he picked up a large ceramic pot of aloe vera—she recognized it—and showed it to her.

"This is the universal healer," he said. "It helps with sunburns, cuts, scars…"

The blood drained from his face. He looked absolutely white. His eyes widened to the size of dinner plates and he half-fell, half-leaned against the kitchen counter.

"What is it?" she asked him. He was looking past her; she drew her gun and whirled around—

—as the ceramic pot came crashing down on her head. Stunned, it took her an extra half-second to regain her footing and launch a back kick, and by then he had smashed the pot into the back of her head a second time. She went sprawling on the ground, her gun skittering away. As she tried to scramble toward it, his shoe came down hard on her wrist and she cried out.

He said nothing as he grabbed handfuls of her hair and dragged her to a small wooden door. He threw it open; muzzily, she expected a broom closet. But it was a flight of stairs to his basement.

"Get away from me, stay away!" he cried. And then he flung her headfirst down the stairs. She went airborne into the darkness for a second that lasted a lifetime; then her chin impacted with wood and she was bumping down a staircase into pitch-black nothingness. She flailed for a railing; finding none, she tried to tuck in her chin and cover her head, but only succeeded in slamming her forehead into something hard. The searing, slicing sensation was only one pain among many. She thought she heard the door crash shut but in the cacophony she couldn't be sure.

She kept sliding down the stairs and landed hard at the bottom onto bare concrete. Every part of her body crunched and crumpled, and then she was out.

"This is bad," Tess said as J.T. replayed the grainy, black-and-white ATM footage for her. J.T. had summoned her to preside over the doctoring of the film so they could put it in Wilson's email inbox without his ever seeing what they were seeing:

Julia Hogan, in a padded winter coat, boots, and a Cossack hat, was standing at the ATM machine. She looked left, right, then over her shoulder like a good New Yorker before she put in her card.

Her only mistake was in not looking up.

From above, a huge shadow fell over her. *Then* she looked up, screamed... and the blackness completely engulfed her. As it yanked her backwards out of frame, a shimmer of sparkles played over it.

"Rewind," Tess said. She caught her lower lip between her teeth and jerked her forefinger at the screen. "What the hell? What is that?"

"I know, right?" Vincent said. "This is weird even for beast weird."

J.T. opened his arms in a "ta-da" pose. "That, my friends, appears to be bioluminescence. Glowing organic material. The specialty of our friendly tenured FBI agent, David Mazursky."

"So that's a beast?" Tess said. She leaned forward and squinted at the screen. "It doesn't look bestial, at least like we're used to."

"Not human," Vincent said quietly. He went cold. He had always wondered if the people behind Muirfield had pushed the envelope past human-beast hybrids to manufacture creatures so foreign and terrifying that they could be said to be alien. The beast skeleton that was hidden in a large wooden chest in the gentlemen's club was thousands of years old, and resembled nothing on this earth. That creature's DNA had been injected into Vincent. What if the shadow organization had found other, even more violent or bizarre creatures and created hybrids from them?

"Hmm." J.T. tapped the screen. "This is why. Whatever that matter is, it's affecting the recorder and distorting the image. It could easily be human-shaped. We just can't tell."

"How do they do that?" Tess muttered. "I guess it's like when they beam up on *Star Trek*."

J.T.'s smile was so loving that it was a shame Tess couldn't see it from her vantage point. It was obvious to Vincent that she was trying so hard to see life from J.T.'s perspective. Surely they must know that the love they shared transcended knowledge of TV shows. He and Cat had accepted their differences—and there was no one on the planet more different that Catherine Chandler and Vincent Keller.

J.T. reached up and took Tess's hand. She leaned over him and kissed the top of his head.

Vincent wanted Cat here.

"So what you're saying is that this creature contains bioluminescent cells that affect attempts to take pictures of it. Cell phones too?" Vincent asked.

"One would theorize yes, but of course, we can simply ask the lying bastard who's been sent to keep tabs on it."

"I agree. Mazursky's got to be in on it." Vincent continued to focus his predator senses on the recording. The hair stood on the back of his neck and his heartbeat picked up. "My fear response is kicking in."

"From just *looking* at it?" J.T. swiveled around in his chair. "You okay, big guy?"

Abashed, Vincent took a couple of steps away from the monitor. "Not so much, J.T." He ran a hand through his hair.

"I'm moving into fight or flight."

J.T. looked at Tess. "What about you?"

She shook her head. "I guess we aren't affected because we're not predisposed. But if all it takes is just *looking* at it… they could flash pictures on TV, or on smartphones…"

"Maybe they already are. What if they're sending this beast to take out specific targets? Triggering it to kill would be like changing a channel on the remote."

"It would be really good if Cat showed up." J.T. eyed Vincent warily. "I thought she was just going to drop off Sky Wilson and then come over."

"You mean, it would be good if she were here so she could calm me down," Vincent said.

"In a word, yes." J.T. pushed back from the desk and walked to the bar. He bent down and murmured, "Oh, right. Heather has it."

Vincent frowned. "The tranq gun?"

"We should stock up. It's not just you and me anymore. Everyone should have an equal opportunity to knock you out if you go beast."

At the computer, Tess had put on a pair of sunglasses and was staring at the monitor, leaning forward, moving her head in a circle. She took them off and then clicked a picture of the screen with her smartphone.

"So look at this," Tess said, walking up to Vincent with the smartphone in her hand. He did. Fear rattled through him like a cold wind. With a low growl, he looked away. Then she dialed a number and put the phone to her ear. "Yeah, hi, Cat, listen," she began, then mouthed "voicemail" to the guys, "call me ASAP. I need to talk to you. A lot."

Where was Catherine? Something was wrong. Vincent just knew it. His anxiety levels rose higher. He remembered the top-secret website of Major Howison's that they had inadvertently opened. Mazursky had already told them that he had been working with Howison, but Vincent had gotten such an honorable vibe off him. The unending battle for the control of beasts and beast technology was like a series of Chinese puzzle boxes.

Back to looking at Howison's home page. Had seeing it poisoned him somehow, programmed him? Could he trust himself to remain in control?

Tess dialed another number. "Wilson," she explained, and waited. Vincent could hear the unanswered ringing, and then Wilson's smooth-jazz invitation to leave a message.

"Call me immediately," Tess barked. "And tell Detective Chandler to call me too. Also immediately." She put her phone in her pocket.

"What's Sky Wilson's address?" Vincent asked. His tone sounded gravelly and inhuman, at least to his super-sensitive ears.

J.T. did some typing. He'd hacked into the NYPD databases and was pulling up Sky Wilson's files. Tess took a nervous step toward him, as if she was afraid that there was classified data in the file that she didn't want J.T. and Vincent to see. Vincent went on alert, but J.T. was unaware.

"Malibu, California," J.T. read off. "His new address hasn't been inputted yet."

"Someone will pay for that," Tess muttered. She gave Vincent a look. "But I will be the one who collects the payment, got it?"

"Yeah." He put on his jacket and hat, and fished his gloves out of his pocket. "I'm going to look for her. Do you have *any* idea what part of town he lives in?"

"His mom does," Tess declared. "She's still at the Malibu address."

J.T. pulled up the phone number for the Wilsons' address in California, and Tess punched in the 310 area code. She shifted her weight on her hip and rolled her eyes. "*Why* do people have phones if they don't use them? Yes, hello, Ms. Wilson," she said in a polite tone of voice. "I'm Captain Vargas, Sky's new chief. Sky was mildly injured on the job today and I want to send a uniform over to your place in the city to check on him. Unfortunately, your Malibu address is on his paperwork. Would you please call me back and give me the New York address?"

She hung up. "No one in law enforcement can know this is happening. I'll be booted for sure."

Vincent walked out the front door.

Blurring and then blurring again; raising his chin to sift through the layers of odors that were New York City— sewage, roasting chestnuts, expensive perfumes and car exhaust; tuning his hearing to ignore the *clacka-clacka* of the subway trains, the incessant honking of horns and the squeal of air brakes. The bustle and yelling; the sizzle of sausages and mini-explosions of popcorn emanating from food carts. Through it all, Vincent's predatory beast-mind assembled Catherine's scent. In one of the largest cities in the world, only one living creature carried that unique signature.

And he would find her.

## CHAPTER FOURTEEN

It was freezing in the brownstone basement.

And pitch dark.

Cat smelled blood and all at once, terror crawled up her body like hungry, desperate rats. Digging in claws, ripping at her—

She shrieked, windmilled her arms, and kicked as hard as she could. A shape was looming over her, staring at her only inches away from her face, its mouth stretched into a maniacal grin bristling with pointed, blood-stained teeth. Pincers snapped together; she could hear them.

"Get away from me!" she screamed.

Only... she didn't scream. Her throat was closed and sandpapery syllables roughened her lips. Her teeth ached. Her head rang. Her breath stuttered out of her chest in weak gasps. The fright mask was there. The monster was there. It was going to kill her.

She flopped onto her stomach and put every ounce of strength she had into crawling. It was coming after her, grabbing her ankles. Its knifepoint pincers were gouging the backs of her hands.

She scrabbled fast, gaining ground—and saw stars as her

head collided with something hard. Wall.

She went down again, surrounded in her mind by monsters and demons and beasts. Hundreds of them. Pinpoints of light danced behind Cat's eyelids and then something advanced slowly, stealthily. It was coming for her. It was going to tear her apart and eat her.

*The beast. Oh, God, it's here!*

*Gun.* She reached for her holster. Empty. Fighting down wave after wave of fear, she tried to replay the attack in the kitchen to account for her gun. When he'd knocked her with the pot, had her gun dislodged? Was it down here in the icy dark? Upstairs in the kitchen? She would have to search for it.

While the beast was searching for her.

The idea paralyzed her. She told herself not to be afraid, but it was no good. Her teeth chattered with fear and cold; she pressed her hands against her chest in a vain attempt to slow her heartbeat. If she couldn't get her autonomous nervous system under control, she was going to die of fright. Meantime, she had to look for her gun. If she could even distract the monster, startle it long enough to escape...

*Stairs!* she recalled. A way out.

And at the top, a door, and a madman. But if she had her gun, she could kill him.

In the ice-cold blackness, she made a vow: *I will kill anything in my way.* Then the fear overtook her and she fell to her knees, panting.

Vincent was circling the city. Closing in, but not fast enough. In his desperation, he allowed more of the beast out, and then more. He kept his gloved hands in his pockets and his ball cap down low, and all the feelings of anxiety and caution sleeted over him with the downpour. Walking these streets, these mean streets filled with people who would kill him if they knew what he was. Who were the beasts then? Who was inhuman? Anger surged through him.

*And one of them has my mate...*

No. Catherine was a person. And he was a person. Stress was doing this to him. And this awful new experiment... that shape... bioluminescence... would they never *stop*?

"Hey, man, you okay?" asked a guy seated against a wall. He was wearing a worn army jacket, jeans, and half-gloves that revealed blue fingers. He had a sign indicating that he was a homeless veteran and a golden retriever was sitting next to him. It cocked its head at Vincent and let out a low growl. Big dogs did not like him. "Buddy?" the guy persisted.

"They did this to you," Vincent rasped.

"Who?" the man asked. "Oh, you mean the army?" Ruefully, he shook his head. Then with great effort, he got to his feet. The dog whined and the man reached down a hand to scratch it behind the ears. "No one did this to me except me, man. Got out, had a few rough patches, started with the drugs. But no one put them in my mouth." He narrowed his eyes. "But I'm doing okay. I'm getting it back together. What about you?"

Vincent regarded the man, shivering on his pencil-thin legs, comforting his companion. He said, "It's cold out here. You should be at a shelter."

"They won't let me bring Dudley. He don't go, I don't go." The dog wagged its—his—tail. Vincent repressed his impulse to give the dog a friendly pat. Instead, he took off his jacket and draped it around the man's thin, trembling shoulders. On him, the jacket was enormous, more like a cape. The man caught his breath and looked down at himself as though he had been magically transformed into a king.

"Oh, hey, no." He shrugged and grabbed the sleeve in an effort to pull the jacket off. "No, man. You got places to go."

"So do you," Vincent said. "You and Dudley. You need to get him off the streets."

The dog studied Vincent and lifted a paw, then set it down on top of the old man's instep, just not quite able to connect with the scary stranger.

"It's okay." The man's red, rheumy eyes welled. "It's what it is, you know?"

"But you're getting it together. For Dudley. So he can have a yard. And a doghouse."

The man's lips parted. He needed dental work. And better nutrition. In other words, he needed help.

"Is this your corner?" Vincent asked. "Your territory?"

The man nodded. Dudley chuffed.

"Okay, then I'm going to come back and see you," Vincent informed him. "I'm going to make sure you don't sell that coat."

"You should take it back *now*," the man said anxiously. "Just in case."

"I'm going to come back and visit you. But I have to go now."

"You have places to go." He pressed his back against the wall and tried to slide down to the sidewalk, but his legs quivered. Vincent wrapped his hands around the man's forearms and gently eased him to a sitting position. Then he pulled the jacket around the man. Dudley sat down too and put his head on the man's knee. Without missing a beat, he gave his dog another loving scratch behind the ears.

"Yes. I have to leave," Vincent said. He tipped his ball cap to the man and brought it down low again. Then he melted into the crowd, his anger quelled, his fear tamped down. Helping the man had brought him out of himself. He couldn't afford to lose himself in beast-intense drives. And of the hundreds of people around, they did not fear *him*. They feared monsters and things that could hurt them. That was as it should be.

The snow came down harder and he was about to blur when his phone buzzed. It was Tess.

"Wilson's mom called," she said. "I have an address for you." She gave it to him.

"Send a squad car?" he said.

"I was thinking along those lines. But if something *else* is happening…" She trailed off, and he knew she meant beast activity. "Get there as fast as you can and call me back."

It was a compromise, one he wasn't very happy about, but he said, "Got it," and hung up. Then he blurred into the snow, around the crowds. He didn't need a map; now that he had a general direction to go in, he flew. The snow fell harder, as if trying to match his pace. Traffic bunched up and pedestrians hurried toward the subways.

He was many blocks away when he caught her scent. Sky Wilson's, too. Putting on a burst of speed, he reached a two-story brownstone. Catherine's car was parked in front. The smell of fresh blood was overpowering. The front door was locked; he forced it open and ran inside. In the kitchen there was a broken pot on the floor and Catherine's blood. No sign of Sky Wilson. And a door…

…behind the door… *Catherine*…

He jerked and stumbled away from it, suddenly terrified. He rotated in a slow circle, *feeling* the fear seeping into him. And then he remembered the ATM and the bioluminescence, and he talked himself back out of it. It wasn't real; it didn't matter. And Catherine was in there.

"Catherine!" he called, and turned the knob. Locked; he kicked it open. It took less than a second to process that in the deep black void there were stairs… and that Catherine was lying halfway up them.

He raced down and found her. Blood and bruises mottled her face, and she was barely conscious. A doctor, he feared moving her because of possible spinal injuries. And then he felt her trembling, and heard her heartbeat. She was rocketing past fear into possible catatonia.

Holding his breath and praying that he was doing the right thing, he picked her up in his arms, carried her through the kitchen and into the living room. He laid her on a Victorian settee and chafed her hands. She opened her eyes and half-sat up.

"There's something in the basement," she said, and then she stopped. "Wait. I don't think there is."

He smoothed her hair from her forehead and checked her pupils. Then he felt under her jaw and took her pulse again. It was slowing down.

"How's your back?"

She twisted left and right, and gave him a nod. "I'm good." Using his shoulder as support, she got to her feet. He caught her hand.

"Easy, Catherine."

"We have to find Sky. He's completely out of control." She touched her holster. "I think my gun is in the kitchen."

Vincent helped Catherine up and through to the kitchen. She stood at the open back door, gulping in the snowy air. Vincent picked up her gun and she holstered it.

"Are you okay?"

"I'm not going to be running any marathons. *Ow*."

He was examining the cut caused by the pot. It wasn't too bad, as cop injuries went. Catherine hated to be coddled. There was a reason she was a police detective, and it wasn't to avoid getting hurt on the job.

"It's bloody," he said.

She reached over to a paper towel dispenser, grabbed a paper towel, turned on the faucet, and dampened it. She blotted the back of her head.

"Okay. Let's go," she told him.

He went back into the living room to retrieve her coat and hat, and shoved the front door deadbolt into place, securing it. He helped Catherine on with her coat, but she was doing pretty well under her own steam. Still, as they clambered down the kitchen steps, he could tell she was holding back a little.

The snow was a few degrees away from turning into a storm and the wind was fierce. He was without a jacket… but glad that he had given it to the old man. He should have looked for one of Sky's.

"I have his scent," Vincent half-yelled to be heard. "He hasn't gotten very far."

"Then he's probably not the beast," she yelled back.

"Doesn't seem so."

The snow was thick and wet. They took each other's hands as they lifted their legs up out of the drifts.

"Where's your jacket? You must be freezing," she said.

He was. Beast he may be, but he had to get out of this weather. The faster they found Sky Wilson, the quicker that would happen. He closed his eyes and concentrated. Then, as he opened his eyes, he saw a thermal flare behind a row of trashcans, and heard a thundering heartbeat.

Two quick taps on Catherine's shoulder and a gesture in that direction, and they cautiously approached. She said into his ear, "He's probably armed. I didn't see him take off his holster when we entered his house." As she spoke, she drew her gun.

By unspoken mutual consent, they each took an end of the line of trashcans. Vincent circled right and Catherine took the left. A galloping pulse increased in volume as Vincent approached. He gestured to Catherine, but he was certain she couldn't see him through the heavy curtains of snow.

Tuning out the rush of the wind and traffic, Vincent heard Sky muttering over and over:

"Just stop. Just stop it. Don't come near me."

It was almost a chant. Then the telltale *snick* of metal warned Vincent that Wilson was about to open fire. He leaped over the nearest trashcan on a trajectory with the distraught man and the two skidded backwards. The can tipped over and trash cascaded over Vincent's shoes and the backs of his legs.

In an instant he had Wilson's gun, which he handed to Catherine as she approached. Through the near-blinding snow, she kept her weapon trained on Sky as the man fought against Vincent and, defeated, curled into a fetal position, whimpering.

"We think something's been manufactured," Vincent told her. He was trying to be discreet, even though he doubted Wilson was listening to him. "To induce fear. J.T. is on it." He looked at her. "And we're assuming that our new friend is, too."

Catherine gazed down at Wilson. "I doubt a hospital could help him. The place where Aliyah's being kept sure isn't helping her."

"Then we take him to J.T.," Vincent said. "We could meet him at his lab at Northam."

"Too unprotected and too far away."

"Agreed."

Vincent stood and hoisted Wilson to his feet. He said to Catherine, "You drove here, right? It'll be slow going but we've got to get him contained."

They began to walk back toward the brownstone. The whimpering subsided and Wilson obediently trudged between the two of them. Vincent sat with him in the back of the car as Catherine drove. New Yorkers were struggling on the roads and sidewalks.

"At least this bad weather will cut down on the protests over the homicides," Catherine observed. "Give Tess some breathing room."

They arrived at J.T.'s. When they walked in with Wilson, J.T. took an anxious glance at his bank of computer screens and got to his feet. Tess moved protectively in front of the screens. Vincent steered Wilson to the couch and Wilson buried his face in his hands as he sat.

"What the hell?" Wilson muttered.

"What's going on?" Tess asked.

"I attacked Detective Chandler."

"*What?*" Tess cried.

"And tried to shoot her boyfriend," he added.

"Well, we've all been there," J.T. said.

Wilson held out his hands. "I'm ready to submit to arrest."

"Not so fast," J.T. said. "First I want some blood."

"We think you've been subjected to some kind of hallucinatory drug," Vincent said, choosing his words carefully. "I'm not sure how you ingested it, but J.T. would like to test for its presence." That was basically accurate.

"J.T.?" Wilson said, gazing at J.T., who was putting on some gloves. "I'm sorry, but who are you? Why don't we go to a hospital?"

"Okay, here's the deal." Tess sat down on the arm of the sofa. "We think this drug is behind this rash of ultra-violent homicides. And we also think that someone in the precinct may be involved. We're not sure who so we're keeping our investigation on the down low. Dr. Forbes is a biochemist who's consulting with us."

Wilson wearily leaned his head back on the sofa. "And I've been in the way. *This* is why you've been acting so resentful towards me," he said, turning to look at Catherine.

"Yeah," she replied, startled. "Caught me." She flashed him a weak smile.

"Have to say, you were a suspect when you showed up early," Tess told him.

"See, I didn't," Wilson replied. "Captain McAllister said you needed me as soon as possible." A shadow crossed his face. "You know, I try to be positive about people, give them the benefit of the doubt. But if you know something about why this job offer came my way, I wish you would tell me."

Tess cleared her throat. "That's official business between you and the department, and best discussed privately. In my office."

"Okay, I'm going to take your blood now," J.T. announced. "Can you roll up your sleeve?"

Wilson complied, unbuttoning his shirt cuff. "She said it was just a drink."

Catherine and Tess traded looks, and Vincent raised a brow. J.T. wrapped a blue tourniquet around Wilson's bicep and began to tap for a good vein. Wilson made a fist.

"But after that, I started getting crap assignments. It's obvious to me that she's punishing me…"

"Detective Wilson," Tess cut in. Her heart rate was picking up. Vincent was sure she was hiding something. Covering up for *Wilson*?

"…for turning her down," Wilson finished. "Ouch," he said to J.T.

"Sorry. You'd think I'd be super-good at this. I do it so often," J.T. mumbled.

Catherine and Tess looked at each other again, then at Wilson. Tess frowned.

"Captain McAllister. She… approached you?" Tess said carefully.

"Hey, no." Wilson grimaced. "Please forget I said that. I shouldn't have said anything. I'm not myself. I'm NYPD now and I wish her all the best."

"But she did approach you," Catherine repeated. She looked at Vincent and he knew that she wanted him to listen to Wilson's heartbeat and tell her if he was lying.

A vial filled with his blood. J.T. stoppered it and set it in a tray on the floor.

"Yeah." Wilson sighed. "She started coming to work all dressed up, taking lots of calls with the door shut, and her lunch hours got really long. I figured she had a new boyfriend.

A few weeks went by and she asked me to come into her office to discuss a case. She pulled out a bottle of scotch and a couple of glasses. I mean, we all drink with the boss now and then, yes?"

Both Catherine and Tess nodded. Vincent listened intently. The man was nervous and upset, but so far he was telling the truth.

"Her dress was low-cut, inappropriate for the office, I thought, but again, I'm about positive energy. But her *aura* was a swirling mass of lust combined with duplicity. She put her hand on my knee and really started coming on to me. But I could see in her aura that while she *was* attracted to me"— he couldn't help an egotistical little grin—"she was trying to manipulate me. Get me to make a pass."

"Why?" J.T. asked.

"So she could accuse you of sexual harassment," Tess said slowly, "and move you out of the department." She looked a little green around the gills. Vincent was bewildered, but he dutifully kept listening to Wilson's built-in lie detector.

"Yes, I think so." Wilson looked grateful to Tess for giving voice to the words that he didn't want to utter. The things he was saying were damning; he was speaking to his new superior, and if they got back to his old captain, she might consider suing him for slander. At the very least, she could mess him up if he needed future references.

"Do you know why?" Catherine asked.

"I got to thinking about the phone calls and the long lunches. And I figured that the new man in her life was jealous of me. He wanted her to get rid of me."

A sour, bitter grin flashed across Tess's face. Sotto voce, she said, "Or she wanted to give her new man a job."

Catherine looked grim. Vincent still wasn't following and he had the feeling he might never know what was going on. It wasn't necessarily his business unless it had something to do with the beast situation, and he didn't think it did.

"All done," J.T. announced, slapping a bandage over the puncture area. He looked at Vincent as if to say, *Now what?*

Right. What were they going to do with Wilson?

Tess said, "I don't think you should go back to your place tonight, Wilson. I can authorize a hotel or take you to a safe house. Either way, you're not going to be alone tonight. I'll stay with you, keep watch." Her gaze remained steadfastly averted from J.T.'s line of sight. Something was way up. Something personal. But of the four of them, it made the most sense for Tess to guard him. J.T. had serious work to do on all the leads they had gathered, including the two vials Vincent and Catherine had brought him. Vincent himself could be put to far better use investigating the brownstone and the crime scenes of the other murder victims.

Catherine's phone rang. "Chandler," she said as she put it to her ear. Vincent could hear the conversation on the other end:

"This is Dr. Lewis from Vanek Memorial. I met you earlier today when I attended Detective Wilson."

"Yes." Catherine squared her shoulders, listening hard, in full detective mode. Vincent could practically see her shifting her weight onto the balls of her feet, ready to spring into action.

"Aliyah Patel is missing. The orderlies did bed checks forty-five minutes ago and we've been looking for her ever since."

"Have you caught anything on your surveillance cameras?" she asked.

Vincent grabbed up Cat's coat, hat and gloves and laid them on the coffee table beside her, then went into J.T.'s bedroom and plucked J.T.'s heaviest coat off the rack. He was putting on his gloves when Catherine met him at the door, ready to go.

"Aliyah's been taken," Cat said to the group. "They don't know who did it."

"How?" Wilson blurted. He began to rise. "They have six layers of security. Who signed her out?"

"We're going over there now," Cat said. To Tess, she added, "I'll call in, keep you informed. We'll probably have to use landlines until the storm clears."

"But it's snowing like crazy. You can't go out in that," Wilson said, and the New Yorkers all smiled patronizingly at him.

"I checked and there's no Snow Emergency Declaration," Cat said. "Public transportation's still running and we can get there by subway."

Wilson was agog. Tess said to him, "*We're* going out in that. To the nearest hotel."

"Yes, ma'am." He started to get up, then caught his breath and sat back down.

Tess said, "Dr. Forbes, do you have any juice? Maybe some crackers? My officer needs to get a little something in his stomach."

"Sure, Captain Vargas. I'm sure we can find something in my kitchen. If you'll follow me?" The two moved quickly across the room.

"We'll stay in contact," Cat promised. Then Vincent opened the door into the blizzard. A little girl wouldn't last in this. If Aliyah had snuck out on her own, she was probably already dead.

# CHAPTER FIFTEEN

Considering what she'd already been through, the few steps from the subway to Vanek Memorial would have taken a debilitating physical toll on Catherine if Vincent hadn't been there to carry her and blur. No one was around and the snowfall would surely cloak them from any video cameras.

They were expected and their entry was expedited, which in one way was ironic, since a gap in their security had resulted in the loss of one of their patients. It would have been useful for Cat to take notes on their procedures when they were being demonstrated at their best. All that was moot, however, because Cat had brought the world's best tracker with her. And while she discussed the situation with James Farris, head of security, and they laid out a strategy, Vincent walked the oppressive corridors of the facility alone. She could barely contain her impatience; she wanted him to text her his findings as soon as he had the answer, but their cell phones weren't working.

So she went through the motions of lining up interviews with the staff and requesting footage—she wondered if there would be a sparkling monster on it—reminding herself that it was possible that Vincent would return to her empty-handed.

She was sitting in the otherwise deserted cafeteria with a cup of tea and a candy bar, across from the night orderly who had done Aliyah's bed check and discovered her missing— her second interview in the cavernous, dimly lit space—when Vincent poked in his head. She could tell by his expression that he knew what had happened.

"Excuse me one moment," she told the man. It took her an extra beat to push back her chair and walk over to Vincent because her injuries were beginning to make her stiffen up.

Vincent shepherded her over to the double doors that swung out from the industrial kitchen. He kept his voice low.

"It was an inside job," he said. "Lena Mueller used a coded passkey that hadn't been assigned to anyone to get into Aliyah's room. She knew exactly where to move to avoid being caught on camera. Her timing was perfect. She'd been planning this.

"She walked Aliyah out the back entrance into her car. I haven't quite figured out where the parking garage guard was. He wasn't in on it. I asked him straight out if he was and he was telling me the truth when he said no."

Cat took everything in. She said, "That's it, then. Do you know the motive? And where she took her?"

"Not yet. But it makes more sense for me to start looking by myself."

"Agreed. I'll steer everything toward that scenario without revealing that we know. If you find anything call the chief of security's landline or J.T.'s, and I'll do the same."

He pushed open the double doors and eased her into the darkened kitchen. He held her very gently but she could feel the passion in his taut muscles, the way his breath caught. He studied her face with the intensity of a man who was leaving on a long journey, and never wanted to forget what his beloved looked like.

He kissed her, softly at first and then with more urgency. He ended the kiss with a sigh against her hair.

"I don't want anything to happen to you," he murmured. "*Ever.*"

"I feel the same. But these are the cards we were dealt, Vincent, and we both have to play them."

"Then I'm doubling down because the joker is *wild*."

"Every time we turn around, the stakes are raised," she agreed. She kissed him twice more, and then the real world rushed back in and they were two protectors on a mission once again.

They returned to the cafeteria and Vincent left. Cat sat down at the table where the orderly waited. He was playing with a ring of keys.

"So how well do you know Lena Mueller?" Cat asked him.

Blasé, he leaned back in his chair. He looked tired, maybe even bored. It was unimportant to him that a pediatric inmate was missing.

"Man, she's like a prison warden or something. Rules, rules, rules. By the book. I don't even think she has a heart."

That didn't sound like someone who might bust Aliyah out of there for altruistic reasons. Signs pointed to abduction, possibly by the beast-maker. Maybe he—or she, or they—didn't want any witnesses. No one who could explain what the newly evolved beast looked like... or could do.

"I heard Mueller was in the army, you know? Man, she should have stayed there."

Cat's face tingled. "The army."

"Yeah. The battleaxe." He smirked. "She looks like a guy, you know? Like a sergeant."

That was ten kinds of sexist, but Cat didn't have time to worry about setting this guy straight. She stayed neutral, but her brain was already trying to connect Lena Mueller's army career with the beast activity.

The man went on, "She has way too many friends coming and going here, like this was party central, and I'm pretty sure a lot of them were into some seriously bad stuff."

*Pay dirt.* Cat remained neutral. "Like what?"

"I think some of them were mercs." He waggled his brows, very excited.

"Mercenaries?" she elaborated, and he nodded. *Members of FFNY?*

"They were hard asses, you know? They had these crazy magazines with tricked-out soldiers on the covers. *Camo and Ammo*," that's what I called them. He grinned faintly at his own cleverness.

"Do you happen to have any copies?" She kept her voice steady and cop-like but she knew, she could feel, that she was onto something.

"Yeah, actually, I saved them." He pushed back his chair. "I'll go get them."

He left and returned with a large stack of magazines with covers featuring a desert landscape and a tank, men in camouflage holding enormous assault rifles, and even a close-up of a grenade, lovingly photographed as if it were a Fabergé egg.

Cat reached in her pocket and slipped on a pair of gloves. She picked up the first issue and flipped the pages. It was chock-full of ads for assault weapons and body armor, and the articles were on subjects such as training non-English-speaking troops and building a homemade drone detector. There were also columns of personal ads in minuscule type advertising mail-order brides from Russia, Thailand, and Cambodia, and "Merc Sought" classifieds consisting entirely of strings of numbers.

"I don't know what those are," he said. "It's been driving me crazy."

"Usually, it's a check-in service. You call a number and

then input the string of numbers. That takes you into the system. My guess would be that there are a bunch more hoops after that," she added, in case he might be feeling particularly adventurous and decided to call in.

"May I take these?" she asked. "I'll bring them back." That might be soon, or maybe in ten years, if the People of the State of New York developed a strong case against Lena Mueller for kidnapping.

"Yeah," he said grandly. "Sure."

She thanked him, pulled out her business card, asked him to call her if he could think of anything that might help her investigation, and left the room.

She went to James Farris's office and asked to use his desktop computer. He logged her in and left the room to give her privacy. He had aged five years in the last thirty minutes, and Cat sympathized. If he kept his job after this, it would be a miracle.

Cat knew her way around databases—New York City detectives took lots of seminars and classes, and she had spent hours watching J.T. hack into system after system—and in short order she had pulled up Lena Mueller's personnel file and clicked it open. Lena Mueller had made it to captain in the army, and had not re-enlisted. She had attended graduate school to become a psychiatric social worker. This was her third placement.

*Another social worker*, she thought, typing furiously, scrolling, and clicking, seeking a connection, a clue, anything that would move her case forward. They were so frequently more than cases: Aliyah was a terrified little girl.

One ear out for a call from Vincent, she drilled down through Nurse Mueller's addresses and other jobs. She typed multiple searches into Referendia. And then she found a promising court case that Mueller had been involved in. The family of a little boy had sued a private clinic called

Grace Hill because their son had died during a round of electroconvulsive therapy—a procedure they had not given consent to. He had been sedated, and then electrodes had been applied to his temples and a current sent through his body. During the procedure, the little boy's heart had gone into defib and could not be stabilized. The defense argued that the ECT had nothing to do with his heart attack.

Lena had testified on the behalf of the family… and against her employer. A transcript of her testimony also revealed that she had observed "experimental procedures of a classified nature" of which she did not approve while she'd been in the army. But she hadn't spoken up. This time, she had, and had lost her job over it.

Lena Mueller had left the army well before Vincent had joined up. Had Nurse Mueller observed earlier Muirfield experiments? Or those of some other program?

Cat added these new pieces to her puzzle. Maybe Aliyah had been scheduled for electro-shock therapy or something similar and Lena had kidnapped her to prevent it. The former army nurse would see that as a rescue, not a crime. Could she do it alone or would she need confederates?

A few more keystrokes and Cat had confirmed that Vanek Memorial did administer electro-shock therapy, and that Aliyah had been put forward as a candidate. Her case was under review, but Dr. Lewis herself had recommended that they move forward.

The picture became clearer. It could be that this abduction wasn't beast-related, even though Aliyah had seen the beast and Lena Mueller had served in the army.

She put in a call to J.T. and told him what she had found. She also asked him if he'd heard from Vincent. He hadn't. Tess had transported Wilson to a hotel and J.T. had taken advantage of the time alone to examine Wilson's blood as well as the two vials Cat and Vincent had given him.

"And I think I've found something pretty amazing," he concluded. He paused dramatically. Cat wanted to humor him and beg him to reveal his discovery, but she was tired, cold, sore, and worried. So when she didn't play along, he said in a slightly hurt voice, "The vials are part of a very complicated formula. If we consider multiple alleles at a diploid locus—"

"J.T., *please*."

"Okay, all right, jeez. You remember how Mazursky hinted that the first six murders might have occurred while some faction was trying to find the individual ingredients to create the new beast-making serum? The fear-factor special?"

"The Thornton Foundation. Yes." She waited for him to confirm Mazursky's suspicion.

"Well, that's wrong."

"*Wrong?*"

"Yes. And I think Mazursky knows it."

He had her full attention now. "Wrong how?"

"After examining Wilson's blood and the two vials, I think what we have is two parts of an antidote. Cat, I think those people died *protecting* that antidote."

"Why? What's in the vials? What's in Wilson's blood?"

"In the vials, there are two of the chemicals that were present in the serum your mother used on Lafferty and we used on Vincent when he started to have his violent blackouts. In the blood, there are antibodies that look similar to the ones that presented in Vincent's bloodstream when he was almost cured."

Cat blinked in surprise but forced herself to remain silent.

"Here's what I think happened," J.T. said. "The beast's blood got into Aliyah Patel's bloodstream during the attack on her aunt. When she went crazy at the facility, she scratched Wilson, which made him go all fugue and attack you, and then his blood got into the wound on your head when he clocked you in his kitchen. Then you went psycho in the basement. You were all responding to the beast's biological makeup. In my sample of Wilson's blood, antibodies began to react against the contamination. His body was attempting a cure. I'll bet I'd find the same thing in your and Aliyah's blood, although you're pretty far down in the contamination sequence."

"A cure?" She had barely heard anything J.T. had said after that.

"Don't jump to conclusions," he warned. "This is the cure for the fear-factor."

"The fear-factor, or the fear-factor beast?" she pressed. "If this antidote were given to the person who was experimented on to become the fear beast, would they lose their beast side?"

"I knew you'd go there. If I had the entire antidote, which I don't, and Vincent took it before another encounter with the beast, would he succumb to the fear pheromones? I don't think so. And then he could kill it."

"But you don't think the antidote would…" She licked her lips, too hopeful to finish her sentence. Because yes, she *was* jumping to conclusions. How could she not?

"Would the serum de-beast him forever? I don't know. Maybe yes." His voice dropped as he moved into thoughtful scientist mode. "Maybe the triggers that induce the change could be deactivated. Vincent reacts to stress and threats by beasting out. If, when he began to feel stressed, he had something in his body that shut down response to some of the physiology…"

Cat winced. "Are you talking about some kind of tranquilizer, or a chemical that makes him less… him?"

"A cure would make him less… him." He cleared his throat. "I do know what you're asking," he said more kindly. "But right now, we need to find all the pieces of the antidote before anyone else does. I think the six people on the list each had something, and I think you and Vincent need to find out what the other five had, and collect the items if you can."

"But first we find Aliyah."

"Any leads?" J.T. asked.

"They were going to shock her brain, J.T. Because she saw a beast. Because it emitted pheromones that scared the wits out of her, literally. And I know how she felt, because I felt it too. I think I didn't succumb because I was able to think logically about what was happening, and as you say, I wasn't contaminated by beast blood, like she was. But she's just eight years old. She's probably still trying to figure out if monsters are real. And Santa Claus."

"What, *what* about Santa Claus?" he cut in, and Cat took a second to smile.

"What I'm saying is, she didn't have any defenses to put up. I did. I think that's why I could fight the fear away."

"Then what about Sky Wilson? He *is* more impressionable. Look at all the woo-woo stuff he's into. And by the way, *what* was going on between you and Tess while he was telling us about his boss from hell?"

Cat knew he'd ask, and she'd already known that she would guard Tess's privacy. She and Vincent had made a promise not to keep secrets from each other, but she did believe in the concept of the kind lie and the harm you could cause in the name of full disclosure.

"You know how it is, J.T. It's really infuriating when you're a woman in a traditionally male-dominated field and you're dedicated to playing fair, but then you see another woman doing all the stereotypical 'femme-fatale' maneuvers to get her way." That much was true. It was just that there was more. "And we knew her at the academy and we were very supportive of her, so it really pissed us off to hear about her behaving that way."

"Got it," he said and to her relief, he sounded as if he had bought her explanation and would let the matter rest. "You know, I thought Sky was some kind of a plant. He's so over-the-top I figured it had to be an act."

"What I've learned is that it's the nice, normal, friendly ones you have to look out for. People you wouldn't look twice at. You bump into them at parties or while you're ordering a coffee." People like her biological father.

"Hey, I have a call on the other line," J.T. announced. "Hold on."

*Let it be Vincent.*

J.T. came back on the line. When he didn't speak right away, she pushed back from the desk and got to her feet, as if bracing herself for the very worst news she could hear.

"That was Vincent. Lena Mueller's dead. Shot at point-blank range. By Mazursky."

"*Mazursky?*" Her blood ran cold. So not the news she had been hoping for. "And Aliyah?"

"He took her. Vincent said he's trying to track them and he's not staying in one location long enough for you to rendezvous. He did ask me to call Mr. Riley, which I did, but he isn't answering his phone. It could easily be out of service because of the storm."

"Or he could be in trouble." She typed in his address and got directions and subway schedules. "I'm going there now."

"The mayor just announced that the city might issue a Snow Emergency Declaration. If that happens, all public transportation will stop. You might wind up stuck someplace. Vincent said you were hurt pretty badly at the brownstone. Are you sure you're up for this?"

She was touched. Of the quartet, she and J.T. had perhaps the most prickly relationship, a holdover from when he saw her as nothing but a threat to Vincent's safety. It meant something to her when he dropped the sarcasm and showed real concern for her.

"I'm fine." She had to be. That was the way she did her job... and ran her life.

After she hung up, she found Farris and told him that she had a lead and she'd share it as soon as she could.

His expression darkened. "I would never have hired Lena Mueller in the first place. In fact, I tried to get her transferred to another facility, and that was only because I knew I could never get her fired. Her union is too strong."

"Why didn't you like her?" She heard herself using the past tense. "Don't like her?" she amended. Mueller's body had not yet been discovered by anyone except Vincent. As far as this man knew, she was alive.

"There's just something about her, I could never trust her."

"Your instincts about her were right," she said. "You're good at what you do."

"Yeah, that'll look great on my application for food stamps."

*There are a lot of steps between there and here*, she wanted to tell him. Maybe he'd be able to keep this job... or get another in another state. If they were right, that's what Joe Bishop had done.

He gestured to the magazines. "What are those?"

She filled him in, and together they paged through one. He was quiet, intense, angry. "Those men who came around. I figured them for old army buddies."

"They could have been."

"Let me put those in a bag for you," he said. "Hold on."

She didn't want to cool her heels any longer than was necessary. But she couldn't exactly hand-carry half a dozen slick magazines under her arm in a storm, so she waited while he left his office, then returned a few minutes later with a nicely plasticized, reinforced shopping bag from an organic grocery store chain. He held it open while she slipped the magazines in. Then he added his card. She had already given him one of hers.

"I'd appreciate any information you can share," he said.

"I only saw that little girl a couple of times, but when these poor folks are here, they're mine, you know?"

"I get that. We are doing everything in our power to find her."

"And *I* get *that*."

## CHAPTER SIXTEEN

S ince Lena Mueller had left the facility via the back way, Cat did too. The guard gave her a wave as if he knew her. He didn't ask her for any identification, nor to sign out in his register. Lax. Did Farris know that one of his weak links was sitting right here?

The back way was a parking garage. That meant security footage with license plate numbers—Christmas, to a cop. She made a mental note and added it to the list of items she would request if and when she found it necessary to give Vanek Memorial another look.

She went through a door into what was becoming a full-fledged blizzard. Her battered bones ached with the cold and she half-walked, half-hobbled to the subway entrance with her fingers crossed. The heat and a squeal of brakes told her that the trains were still running. So far, so good.

Had Mazursky shot Lena to get Aliyah away from her? If his intentions in doing so were good, why hadn't he informed Cat of what he'd done? Why didn't he call her now? There was always a chance that his and Aliyah's safety would be compromised if he checked in. She had to table that for now.

She got on the next train and headed for Mr. Riley's.

Although she was underground, she whipped out her phone and checked it. No bars. Then she awkwardly dropped it in the shopping bag, and decided to leave it there. It was actually easier to get to.

The car was nearly empty. A scrawny kid cocooned in a selection of hoodies scrutinized her, then looked away. A man wearing a thick overcoat was determinedly reading a newspaper. The rhythm of the car lulled her; she was exhausted and sore. It was tempting to transfer to the B train for Bleecker Street, which would take her mere feet from her building.

Determined, she made the necessary transfers to Mr. Riley's house, oriented herself, then climbed to street level, grimacing when she entered an Arctic blast. She was the equivalent of six city blocks from Mr. Riley's front porch and now, with all her heart, she wished she'd dared to drive so she wouldn't have to do this. Supremely glad that she told J.T. she was going to Mr. Riley's, she imagined herself lying half-frozen in a snow bank, and Vincent discovering her and digging her out. Everyone had limits, and maybe she should have been more honest about what hers were.

Except… Mr. Riley might be in trouble. And maybe she could have asked Tess to send a squad car, but what if the beast sent out its pheromones on unsuspecting unis?

She slipped the grocery bag over her shoulder as she sank up to her thighs in the snow, which was still falling. Glowing squares bobbed like balloons—windows. She pictured the houses on either side of Mr. Riley's home—the one that would be closer to her sat approximately fifty yards away. Next came the tree swing and then the path to the porch. Almost there, then.

Shivering, she quickened her pace as best she could, but felt as though she was staggering along at a snail's pace. She kept her hand extended to feel for landmarks and as her gloved hand made contact with fence posts, her numb fingertips burned.

She had to stop twice to catch her breath, and then she groped her way onto the porch. This time, her boot went through the porch. She grabbed onto a wooden post and slowed her descent just enough to save her ankle from twisting. Then she fell forward against the door, the noise serving as her knock.

"Mr. Riley!" she shouted, but the wind swallowed up her words. She knocked with a double fist and then grasped the doorknob to extricate herself from the hole in the porch.

The knob turned; the door swung open, then canted sideways as it ripped away from the topmost hinge. The room inside was dark and as icy as a tomb.

Cat reached behind herself and closed the door as much as she could, which wasn't much. She pulled her gun and with her free hand, searched the magazine bag for her phone, intending to use it as a flashlight. Her fingers closed around what felt like a fuse. She set it on the floor, then pulled out her phone and shone the light on the object.

It was a transmitter.

Catherine repeatedly smashed her heel against it. Rapidly she searched the house, clearing each room as she went. And then, in the back bedroom, there was a shape on the floor. Mr. Riley.

She cleared the room, holstered her gun and crouched beside him. She laid two fingers against his neck. He had a pulse.

"Mr. Riley, it's Detective Chandler," she said clearly. "Are you hurt?"

"Men," he rasped. "The flag."

She panned her phone across his face. There were bruises on his forehead and cheeks. A cut on his cheek.

"Where is the nearest phone?" she asked.

"Nightstand."

She rose, grabbed the handset, and called 911. She identified herself, described Mr. Riley's condition as best she could, gave his address, and added that a home invasion had been committed. The dispatcher promised police and rescue units but cautioned Cat that they would be delayed because of the storm.

After she hung up, she returned to Mr. Riley's side. He rose to a sitting position, rubbing his head.

"Are they still in the house?" she murmured.

"I don't know. I guess I fainted. They wanted Roxie's flag. I told them I never got it." He made two fists and pressed them against his forehead. "Then these *other* men came."

Her detective's mind ran possible scenarios: *The Rileys never received the flag that had draped Lafferty's casket at her military funeral. Someone intercepted it. Sounds like two different groups came after it tonight.*

She grabbed the blanket off the bed, wrapped him in it, and murmured in his ear, "Stay down."

"There's a flashlight in the nightstand drawer," he whispered.

She found it but didn't turn it on. Despite the darkness and the wailing of the snowstorm, she moved silently into the hall. She didn't know if the power was out because of the storm or because Mr. Riley's attackers had cut it.

Methodically she cleared the rest of the house as best she could, on high alert as she assessed her situation. All her subway transfers had been below-ground. The snow had been falling relentlessly while she'd walked to the house, and she'd destroyed the bug soon after. But given the level of technology their adversaries were capable of, Cat had to assume that they knew exactly where she was.

Farris had to have put it in the bag. *He's involved in this. Whose side? How many sides are there?*

She had to get Mr. Riley out, but first priority, of course, was his immediate safety. Mr. Riley had prudently put on his storm windows—she hoped he'd had help—and they served as barricades, but the broken front door was an invitation to danger. She ran into the kitchen on the balls of her feet with her hand over the flashlight to subdue the beam, and rummaged around for a screwdriver to work on the hinges. She then grabbed a wooden broom from his pantry and laid it between two chairs, threw her weight on it and broke it into two jagged pieces. She hurt all over.

She took both pieces and wedged them under the door to keep it in place, then attempted to fix the upper hinge. No luck. Her hands were shaking, she was too injured and the hinge was ruined. The best she could do was push furniture up against it. She went back into the kitchen and put a chair underneath the knob of the kitchen door. There was another phone attached to the kitchen wall; she grabbed it and called J.T. She quickly filled him in.

Then she said, "Has the Snow Emergency Declaration been announced?"

"No. And I haven't heard from Vincent."

"Okay. Mr. Riley has a car. I'm going to check it out. I'll keep the line open but I'm setting the phone down."

"You have a gun, right?"

"J.T., I'm a cop. I always have a gun."

"I have such mixed feelings about hearing that. But right now… don't you think you should just wait for help?"

"J.T., *I'm a cop*. I *am* the help."

"Right."

"I'm putting the phone down. Keep the line open." Then she pulled out her gun and waited. If someone was listening in, she didn't want them gathering around Mr. Riley's garage for a welcome party. Instead she went back to the bedroom to check on Mr. Riley.

He was unconscious, but he had a pulse and he was breathing. Cat sucked in her breath and gently shook his shoulders.

"Mr. Riley? This is Detective Chandler. Can you hear me?"

No response.

She made sure his air passage was clear. Then, instead of disturbing the barricaded front and back doors, she snuck back into the bathroom, put her gun away, and opened the window beside the sink. There was no storm window, so that was a blessing.

A gale of snow raged in at her, pushing her backwards. She planted her feet and forced her way through. At least her landing was soft. She couldn't even see the garage, which meant she couldn't see anyone coming after her. She didn't have a built-in thermal imaging system like Vincent.

As she had anticipated, the garage window was still unsecured. She scrambled into the garage and got into the car, jammed the key in the ignition... and nothing. Not too surprising, so she methodically ran through all the protocols for starting a car in winter in New York before she sat back in the seat for just an instant and took stock.

Back in the house, she bent over Mr. Riley and passed her flashlight over his face. His skin looked gray, but his eyelids flickered, and then he opened his eyes.

"I think I'm okay now," he said, "except that I'm very cold."

"Did your power go out because of the storm?"

"I don't know." His voice shook.

And then she heard a noise from inside the closet. *I cleared that*, she thought. Doors that opened outward, which meant an intruder would have the advantage if she attempted to open it.

She said calmly, "Mr. Riley, do you have any pets?"

"Not anymore."

As she moved in front of him, she set her flashlight on the

floor in front of herself. It would illuminate her target and make it more difficult to see her. Then she stood in a good, wide stance and held her gun straight out. It was ready to go.

The door burst open and she pulled the trigger. A black shape flung itself at her and she raised her knee and shot again, aware that Mr. Riley lay directly behind her.

"*Move!*" she bellowed at him.

When she fell, she smacked against his shoulder but that was all. As the weight of the attacker toppled onto her, she rolled sideways, hitting him—it was a man—as hard as she could on his temples with her gun. She kept hitting him and then she shot him again. Suddenly the flashlight was on him—Mr. Riley was holding it. She patted the perp down for weapons and found nothing but a .45 on the floor, already sopping wet with blood. She'd shot him in the chest and he was bleeding profusely.

His eyes were lifeless and she tore off the balaclava. The dark brown face was mottled from the pummeling she'd given it, but it was not one she recognized.

There was a noise on the roof. Both of them started. Then to her amazement, Mr. Riley put the flashlight on his bed, leaned over, and picked up the bloody .45. He had to use both hands to lift it but he had hold of it.

"Are there any other exits?" she asked him as she arranged the blanket over his shoulders.

"It's an old house," he said, as if that were an answer. She took it as a "no" and realized that the only exit that made sense for them was the kitchen door. It would be too difficult to get him out the bathroom window and she had barricaded the front door.

"Let's go." She kept the flashlight aimed toward the floor, counting on the ambient light to keep him closely behind her. She couldn't afford to check on him; this was the best way to save his life.

There was loud pounding on the roof. She kept her cool and tried to count footfalls. Maybe one target, maybe two.

They got to the kitchen door. The phone handset was still lying on the counter. She picked it up and said, "J.T. One dead. Holing up here until help arrives."

"*One*... right. Got it," he said tersely.

Then Cat replaced the handset on the counter, put her finger to her lips, and saw that Mr. Riley had lost his blanket. No time to do a thing about that now; she pulled the chair away from the doorknob. When she opened the door, she caught it so that it wouldn't slam against the house. The wind was still blowing, but not as hard.

They got outside and the first thing she processed was that it was no longer snowing, but visibility was bad. She moved right, her intention to skirt around the front of the house. It was dark and frigid and she had no idea if the old man was behind her. She got to the path with the barren bushes and he bumped into her. Good.

She grabbed his hand—it was as spindly as a branch—and half-led, half-dragged him along the path. The tree with its swing was ahead but she wasn't sure where. She needed both hands free to feel her way, and if he was going to keep hold of his slippery, heavy .45, Mr. Riley did too. A tiny part of her brain nagged that he might trip and accidentally shoot her with it, but again, all that mattered was the next step forward into the snow. And the next and then next.

She had no idea if the people on her roof were still up there, or if they had figured out she and Mr. Riley were attempting an escape. If the man she had killed was important to them, or just a foot soldier. No time for that now. Thinking would just get in her way. She had to strategize.

Her knees knocked into the swing. She knew where she was now. Mindful of the .45, she grabbed Mr. Riley's shoulder and pulled him around the tree. The .45 slipped from his hands and thudded half an inch from her toes. She held onto him and felt him swaying.

"I'm okay," he whispered.

She squatted down and retrieved the gun. They staggered toward the street. She was pretty sure she'd reached it when her feet didn't sink down as far. She turned left and quickened their pace. If the subway was still operating, the station's bright lights would give them away. But if it wasn't still running, they would be sitting ducks.

Blue-white underground illumination gave her some hope. Steamy heat gave her more. She flashed her badge at the station agent, who helped her guide the sick, shivering man through the turnstile. He was having trouble moving. As best she could, as quickly as she could, Cat helped him descend the stairs.

One man stood on the platform, gazing at them with interest. Catherine kept her arm holding the .45 down at her side.

"No trains have come in the last fifteen minutes," he said. He was bundled up against the cold and wore a hunter's cap with earflaps. "But it's warmer down here than it is up there."

"That's for sure," she replied. She covertly slid the .45 into her coat pocket, took the coat, and laid it over Mr. Riley's shoulders. She chafed his hands, alert for hostile movements on the part of their platform mate. "It's a bad storm."

"Hey, is your dad okay?" he said.

Before Cat could reply, shadows of figures blossomed on the tile wall. Too many people were clattering into the station. Cat guided Mr. Riley to a pillar. He was so bedraggled that he obediently staggered over and leaned against it, nearly collapsing. The memory of intense, debilitating fear seized her and she shook it off, hard. That was not happening, not now.

"Oh, my God!" the man in the hat yelled.

The shadows became armed soldiers in ski masks. One group raced in, followed by another. Two factions. Submachine guns were raised; pistols aimed.

Cat shouted to the man, "Get down *now*, sir! Get down, get down! *Fall down!*"

The adversaries opened fire on each other, and someone was aiming at *her*. She returned fire at the first target she made. She might have clipped his shoulder; she didn't know, so she kept firing at him; and more figures swarmed, guns exploding like cannons as sound and cartridges ricocheted wildly. Then fear did spark up her spine, but it was that special kind of fear that cops felt: *Protect the civilians, assess the odds, the odds are terrible, improve them.*

Improve them by taking out more bad guys or evacuating the civilians or acquiring more weapons. She could only shoot one gun at a time and the other one was with Mr. Riley. One cop, thirty soldiers...

She'd been shot before, and she'd lived.

Her mind filled with an image of Vincent. She forced it away and concentrated on surviving. Bullets zinged around her, pitting the tile, the metal, the concrete. They sent showers of sparks up from the third rail.

One of the assailants crumpled. But only one. An incoming bullet struck Cat's gun and tore it out of her grasp, nearly breaking her fingers. She pushed herself backward toward the pillar, to find Mr. Riley lying on the ground.

*No no no no no*

She stuck her hand in her coat pocket and was just about to withdraw the .45 when the pillar exploded. She covered Mr. Riley with her body.

Footfalls and gunfire and a fusillade of bullets; if she stayed like this she'd take a dozen bullets to the brain. If she didn't, Mr. Riley might. She extended her gun and squeezed off rounds.

And then through the chaos she heard the most wonderful sound in the world: Vincent's bestial roar. It echoed through the tunnel; then he was rocketing into the station from below the platform, rushing up behind her like an avenging angel. She only heard him; she dared not raise her head. She heard more bullets and shouts and shrieking. The echo of falling bodies. She smelled blood.

"Catherine."

He was around her, holding her, easing her up off Mr. Riley. She immediately got to her feet to check on Hunter's Cap; he had passed out but appeared otherwise unhurt.

As she lifted her head to look back at Vincent and Mr. Riley, movement among the bodies caught her eye. She raised her gun, and found herself locking gazes with a man with a bloody face.

"Don't shoot," he said. "Please."

She kept him firmly in her sights. "Take out your weapons and hold them over your head." She didn't want him to throw them to someone who was playing possum—pretending to be dead. He did as she asked.

"Now walk very slowly toward me. Why were you after us?"

His steps took him past fallen comrades but he didn't look down at them. He knew that one false move would lead to his own death.

"Orders," he replied stiffly.

"More," Cat warned him, raising her gun an inch to make her point.

"The flag at the Riley house. There was something in the case. We were told to get it by any means necessary. My superior sent a squad, figured it would be easy, but there was already a group from…" He trailed off.

"From?" she urged.

"Thornton. Freedom Foundation."

"And you are?"

He lifted his chin. "I've been ordered to die rather than reveal that information."

"I have no problem with that," Vincent said.

The man paled. "Delgado Industries."

*So two groups want the antidote in addition to the FBI. And us.*

"What did the flag case contain?" she asked.

"I don't know, ma'am. I'm just a merc."

*As I suspected*, she thought. "The case you were sent to retrieve was never delivered to Mr. Riley's home."

If he was shocked, she couldn't tell because of all the blood on his face. But he went silent and she could see the wheels turning. Those wheels could be fatal.

To him.

By then he was out of range of the bodies on the floor, so she said, "Put your weapon down and kick it toward me."

Instead, he aimed straight at her. He was dead before he had time to pull the trigger.

Vincent saw to that.

Vincent quickly checked the vitals of the man in the hunting cap. "He just fainted," he told Cat. "We'll take him in for medical care. Which is exactly what we're going to do for Mr. Riley."

# CHAPTER SEVENTEEN

There never was an Emergency Snow Declaration, so Heather celebrated by ordering a pizza. She doubled the order when Cat called on their ancient landline and told her that she and Vincent were on their way. Vincent had been tracking a kidnap victim but he'd lost the trail in the storm, and once J.T. told him that Cat was in trouble, he'd gone in search of her instead. Good thing, too, because there had been *another* massive firefight and Vincent had saved her.

Vincent and Cat tumbled into the apartment and they looked terrible. With barely two words to Heather, which, okay, she *did* understand because they were exhausted, they went off to take a shower together. They were discussing the beast case, and Heather got the distinct impression that things had gone off the rails again tonight. This time, frankly, she was glad they'd left her out of it.

They were still in the shower when the pizza guy came.

"I don't have enough money," Heather yelled through the bathroom door. "And my credit card is... tired."

"Use the emergency stash," Cat said. "In my top dresser drawer. Five twenties in Dad's cheesy money clip."

"Got it," Heather said, as she sailed into Cat's bedroom and pulled the drawer open. She looked in and didn't see it. Rooting around, she grinned when she found a photo booth filmstrip of Cat and Tess as well as a gift certificate for a facial she'd given Cat last Christmas and she *still* hadn't used—but no money clip.

"Huh," she said, stumped.

And then she remembered the night when Walker had come over. After she had awakened alone, she had noticed not only that one of her garments was ripped but that this drawer was open.

*He stole from us.*

Her heart thudding, she shut the drawer and leaned against the dresser. *He stole Cat's money, and our dad's money clip. And then he left Silverado.*

She couldn't tell Cat. It was too awful and humiliating. Cat would never take her seriously if she told her about this. She thought about how judgmental she herself had been back when she thought Cat was dating a semi-fictional guy named Vincent Zelansky (semi-fictional because he was actually Vincent, only with fake details about his life). *So* sure Cat was making a mistake that she had talked Tess into helping her stage an intervention at the precinct. So what happens? Vincent is a hero and Walker is a thief.

*I can just replace the five twenties*, she thought. But she couldn't do anything about the money clip. Her father had won it in a golf tournament and her mom had had it engraved with the date and the words *Pro Husband*. It was one of her and Cat's most treasured mementoes.

"Heath?" Cat called. "Did you find it?"

Heather saw Vincent's pants draped over a chair. She shut her eyes tightly, dove her hand into his pocket, and found his wallet. Feeling sick, she grabbed forty bucks and put the wallet back.

She paid for the pizza and set it on the table, by then Cat and Vincent were out of the shower. As she sat down to eat Cat looked to be in a lot of pain and Vincent was hovering, very concerned.

"I'm okay. Sort of," Cat said. Then she held out a hand to Heather. "Heather, I'm sorry I came down so hard on you for getting involved. You saved Vincent and Tess. And all I did was yell at you."

"Oh, no big," Heather murmured. About to lose it over the money she had stolen, she went in the kitchen and opened a bottle of Cab. One of the perks about her job as an event planner was lots of free samples of food and drink. She could afford to have a nice brimming glass of wine in the kitchen without letting it breathe. So she chugged it down and then she poured glasses for Catherine and Vincent and another for herself.

"So, Mazursky," Cat said to Vincent. "I wonder what his agenda is."

"As soon as I've had some rest, I'm going after him," Vincent declared. "I'm going to get Aliyah back—" he looked at Cat "—*we* are."

"But rest first," Cat insisted, and he nodded and sat with her. Heather could see that he was about to fall over from tiredness. "Who do you think intercepted the original flag? Because if whatever was in the case was a component in the cure, it's going to be the most difficult part of the antidote to find, obviously." She scowled. "Now we know why the Rileys never received the flag."

"It was sent through the regular mail?" Heather topped off her glass. She poured some more for Cat and Vincent too.

"Yes. And Lafferty died over a decade ago," Vincent said, sipping. "It'll be impossible to trace."

"Only difficult, not impossible," Cat retorted, and she smiled a little. Vincent smiled faintly back.

"Now that's the wine talking," Heather said.

A little later, *her* wine was talking: She clutched a full glass in one hand and Walker's business card—her only reminder of their last night together—in the other as she worked up the nerve to call him. She dialed his number, leaving a very slurred, pissed-off message. She also called the number written on the back—whoever "L" was—for good measure and got no answer. There wasn't even a way to leave a voicemail message.

So she hung up the phone and burst into tears. She was drunk and sad and she had stolen money from Vincent.

*I am getting our stuff back from Walker,* she swore. *Me. No matter what it takes.*

She cried a whole river of tears.

And then she passed out.


Like many police officers, Tess had done her share of witness protection and that usually meant sleeping on the couch of a motel room or a small safe house, in order to be close to the witness. But Sky Wilson had insisted on giving her the bed and taking… the floor. He was lying down on it with his arms down at his sides, chin raised. It was the way you slept when you wanted to give your chakras room to breathe. She couldn't help a grin.

Meanwhile, she had discovered some amazing things while staying alert and awake, using the laptop she had borrowed from J.T.'s place. He had so many of them that he passed the extras out like some people give away subway cards.

She left the room, went into the bathroom, and dialed Cat. She didn't look at the clock but she knew it was sometime during the middle of the night. It didn't really matter. They were cops on a case. You did what you had to do and that meant calling when you had something to share with your partner.

*I miss being your partner so much,* she thought, as the phone rang.

"Yes, Tess," Cat said, muffling a yawn.

"Aliyah's mom Gheeta was murdered by Aliyah's dad. She was home at the time and may have seen or heard it. His name is Shyam Badal. He's doing twenty to life so I decided to see how he's doing and guess what. His prison file is sealed." She waited a couple of seconds for Cat to process that. After all, it was late at night and that was weird information.

"Sealed," Cat repeated, and Tess chuckled. Dangling interesting leads in front of a detective was like pointing one of those little French pigs at truffles. "But he's serving his sentence *now*," Cat mused. "How can it be sealed? *Oh.* Perhaps with a little help from some friends?"

"Yes. My first guess? The FBI."

Cat drew a breath. "Vincent, wake up," she said. There was muffled noise in the background. In the phone, she asked, "What prison is Badal in?"

"Our favorite. Rikers."

"Tess… what if…"

"With you," Tess assured her. "Homicide number seven: Indira Patel was abusing Badal's daughter. Number eight: Julia Hogan did nothing about it. Two deaths. And the family was close to Lafferty, who gets a beast makeover."

"Right. We were thinking Lafferty could be our beast, but it could be Shyam Badal. Remember how I told you that Aliyah started screaming 'Mommy' when Wilson was trying to communicate with her? Maybe she has trauma from that as well, Tess. And *that* was what he reached, not beast memories."

"That poor kid," Tess muttered, blowing air out of her cheeks and shaking her head. "She's what, eight years old? If the universe was fair she'd win the lottery every single week for a year. The heck with ice cream cones."

"Let's get J.T. on the sealed file," Cat suggested. "That's a higher priority than tracing Lafferty's missing flag. I think. I wish we could clone J.T."

Tess grinned wolfishly even though Cat couldn't see her. Double J.T. meant double so many great things. "I'm thinking the flag wound up in the hands of Muirfield, or maybe the scientists who have been protecting the antidote. And? Just because there were six homicides doesn't mean there were only six ingredients."

"We need J.T.," Cat said.

"We need J.T.," Tess replied. Then she thought in a rush, *I need J.T.*, and suddenly she missed him so much she could barely stand it. Accompanying her heightened emotion was a huge sense of relief. She'd thought she'd lost her special bond with him, and that their relationship was waning. But he had become part of her world, and she couldn't imagine that world without him in it.

"I'm going to leave Sky here and go to J.T.'s," Tess said. "Thank God it's stopped snowing. Or maybe it's just the calm before the storm."

In the morning, Heather was grateful beyond belief that although New York was clogged with snow, the plows had cleared the roads for driving and the subways were running. It took a lot to mess up New Yorkers' lives.

More than one thieving charmer could dish out.

Wearing green again, she swept through the front doors of the academy. There was Elaine, being all receptionista in a really badly designed outfit. Worse than yesterday. It was so bad that Heather actually stopped walking and stared in amazement.

"Is something wrong?" Elaine asked.

"Yes. Yes, there is," Heather blurted, feeling a little guilty because she'd been thinking so harshly of Elaine's outfit. But judging was part of the fashion biz. "I have to get in touch with Walker. It is very, very serious business."

Elaine's perfectly arched brows lifted a thirty-second of an inch, as if she couldn't quite be bothered to look surprised. She leaned back slightly in her desk chair.

"Maybe if you tell me why I should violate school policy and get myself fired by handing out his personal information…" She trailed off and smiled at Heather.

"It *is* personal."

"Sorry." Elaine shrugged and picked up her cell phone. Heather narrowed her eyes.

"He stole something from me and I want it back."

Elaine's eyes grew huge. "*What?*"

"Uh-huh, yeah," Heather snapped. "Something irreplaceable. My parents are both dead and he stole something that was my dad's."

"Are you sure? I mean, could it have been someone else?" She touched her shiny nail to her shiny lips. She seemed like an entirely different person. One who actually cared about what Heather had just told her. "An accusation like that…" She leaned forward. "It could harm the school's reputation, know what I mean? Has anyone else been in your apartment who could have stolen it? Your super? A repair person?"

Heather thought back. The super *had* come up because she and Cat had complained that the heater wasn't working. They hadn't been home, and of course he had a key.

*The drawer was open the night J.T. was kidnapped*, she reminded herself. *The last night we slept together.* That didn't mean that *Walker* had opened it. Cat could have easily left it open, or even the super or one of his assistants after they worked on the heater. But what about her garment?

"No," Heather insisted. "It was him. *He stole from me.* My sister is a cop—"

"I didn't know that," Elaine said, swallowing hard. "Huh."

"A *detective*," Heather added for emphasis. "And she'll find him and she'll bust his ass."

*All I have to do is tell her about this.*

She knew that she should. The trail was hot right now. But it would grow cold fast. He might move out of his place; he might leave New York—but he was getting somewhere, right? Making a name for himself? So why leave?

Her brain was a boiling cauldron of indecision as she went to Silks and Rudi reminded them all that they had one week left before the New Looks competition was closed.

"And I'm getting some early entries, and let me say that they are ama-zing," he cooed. "You are my most talented class ever."

Winning the competition took on new importance because she felt like such a loser. She called Walker and L a dozen times. Nothing. She thought about asking J.T. to track down the number, but what should she say if he asked her why?

The truth. She should come clean so they could bust this guy and get back their stolen possessions. She should tell Cat.

"Yes," she said aloud, and a weight lifted. Given how upset she was, just that little kick of euphoria was enough to carry her through the day. Her last class finished, she was about to leave when Mr. Summers himself came out of his office and raised a hand in greeting.

"Heather in green," he said. "Elaine asked to go home early and I'm expecting a few end-of-day calls. Would you possibly mind playing receptionist for a few minutes? The system is a little complicated, but all you would need to do is wait for some calls. You can let the rest go to voicemail. I'll show you how."

Her mouth dropped open. Her face prickled. Was this really happening?

"No problem." She smiled at him and forced herself not to make a mad dash for the glass desk. She scooted around behind it and picked up the headset. "I know how to use this. I'm good to go."

"Wonderful. *Merci*. I'll email you a short list of calls to let through. The email address is 'receptionist at Silverado dot com'. The password is 'silverado' backwards."

"Got it."

She sat down and got situated. Mr. Summers went back in his office. She made sure the email was open on the screen and checked the buttons on the phone. Then, just as she was about to bask in her good fortune, she noticed a stack of pretty business cards embossed with a big L on the right side of the keyboard. No, it wasn't L. It was *eLaine Tugong, Designer*. And the phone number looked very familiar. Heather pulled out her cell and checked her recent calls. She'd called that number at least a dozen times.

It was L's phone number.

Elaine was L.

Heather wanted to throw up. She sat for a few seconds in complete stupefaction, and then on a hunch she started scrolling through the receptionist email account. At all her jobs, she had occasionally forgotten to open up her personal email account and used her work account to send and receive messages. She had to assume Elaine had done the same.

There. And there. And there. Messages to and from Walker. With no guilt whatsoever, she opened all of them.

*Hi, babe, you were right. It's a winner! Thank you.*

There was an attachment of a photo of her corset. Heather checked the time the email was sent: Walker had taken a picture of it and sent it the night he had slept over.

A winner...

She gasped. Elaine had to be referring to the New Looks competition. Were they trying to steal her design?

She began to scroll through Elaine's emails to Walker. There was another attachment of her muslin pattern for the corset. Her throat tightened as it became abundantly clear that Walker had feigned interest in her to gain access to her costume submission—for Elaine.

"At least she steals from the best," Heather murmured. Her heart was shattering, but rage was rushing in to fill the cracks. The freaking *nerve*. All she had to do was copy these emails and show them to Mr. Summers and—

There was one from *Couture Bleu* magazine:

*Dear Ms. Tugong,*

*Thank you for forwarding your designs to us. They were fresh and original—exactly the caliber of work Mr. Summers described when recommending you to us for our spring internship program. We are happy to tell you that we have accepted you into our program, which will begin on April 10th. We appreciate your efforts to scout for other promising students at Silverado. Some of them show real promise and we'll be contacting them as other opportunities open up.*

Heather caught her lower lip between her teeth. So was Elaine claiming credit for other people's designs—hers, for one?—or was she secretly trying to help them? And what did Mr. Summers have to do with it?

This was all seriously messed up.

An email dinged and she jerked, startled. It was Mr. Summers' list of approved callers. Just as Heather skimmed it, a call came through from an allowed name and Heather transferred it.

Another call followed, then another, and she was about to forward some of the emails to herself and take pictures of the screen with her smartphone when Mr. Summers approached and said, "Okay, that's it. Thank you, Heather."

Her hands hovered over the keyboard but he was just

standing there; surely he would see what she was doing. Should she tell him?

"Mr. Summers…"

His cell phone rang. He put it to his ear and said, "You can go. I'll log out."

"But…"

He raised an imperious brow, clearly displeased that she wasn't leaving.

*I know the password,* she reminded herself. *I'll try to find out what's going on tomorrow.*

"Thanks. It was fun to route the one call." She smiled at him as if everything was fine with her. But inside, she was a boiling cauldron of freakout. Whatever Elaine's ultimate goal, Walker had totally used her. She'd had such a crush— still did—and he was after her design… for Elaine. She had to get real; it wasn't to help her, Heather, in any way.

*I will not cry.*

"So good night, Heather," Mr. Summers said, impatience bleeding through.

She got her purse and rose. Coat, hat, gloves, right. If her boots touched the floor, she didn't feel it. The world was orbiting around her and it took every ounce of willpower to push the front door open. The tears were threatening; it was sleeting and miserable and she was crushed and humiliated.

She was about to jaywalk to get to the subway station when a black low-rider slipped up to the curb and a window rolled down. She was about to walk past it when a familiar voice said, "Hey, baby, wanna buy a gun?"

Heather actually smiled. "No way," she said. And then she wiped her eyes of the tears that had won the battle for her face.

J-Bag's smile fell. "Heather? What's wrong?"

He sounded like a different person, like just a guy, not some banger, and she pressed her lips together. She just stood there like an idiot.

Leaning across the seats, he opened the door. "Get in," he told her.

"Why? So we can go murder someone?" she said, agonized. Men were awful; they were thieves and felons.

"Shit, girl, get in." He held out a hand.

And Heather took it. She got in and he zipped away from the curb into the icy downpour and the gray, fierce traffic. He glanced over at her and she pressed her fingertips to her forehead, lips quivering.

"Hey, so, what's going on?" he asked.

"First-world problems."

He snorted. "Man problems. No woman cries like that because her tiara delivery is late."

"Wrong." She was done in. She needed a good sob session. Instead, she found herself telling him the entire horrible story.

"Did you snag one of eLaine's business cards?" he asked when she was finished.

"Damn it. No. I got flustered."

"Well, get one tomorrow and we'll figure out where she lives. And then I'll pop her for you." When she stared at him, he grinned impishly. "I wouldn't do that. But he did steal your shit. My guess is it's still at her place, including that cheating dirtbag. We can start with the money clip and see what's shaking with your corset once I tie them up and threaten to blow their heads off."

"J-Bag," she began and he waved her off. "Seriously. No violence. And, um, why are you doing this?"

"Seriously? I like you," he replied, and when she blanched, he added, "Not in that way. This is a friend helping out a friend, if you want it like that."

*My life is so odd*, she thought. She inclined her head a smidgen and murmured, "But no beating them up or vandalizing their homes."

"We'll get back your hundred bucks, too," he said. "And?

I'll only take twenty percent off the top."

That made her smile. "Deal," she said.

Yes, her life was odd, but that was just another word for "interesting."

Right?

## CHAPTER EIGHTEEN

"Shyam Badal is listed in the Riker's internal records as dead," J.T. said as he looked up from his computer screen.

"Beast," Cat and Tess said at the same time.

"Seems most likely," J.T. agreed.

"If it's him, maybe he's taken Aliyah himself. Or has a confederate who rescued her from Lena Mueller," Tess suggested, sounding hopeful.

"Or maybe someone is trying to use her as a bargaining chip. Get Badal to come in," Cat said.

"Mazursky," all three said at once.

"I hate that guy," J.T. muttered.


Meanwhile, across town...

"Going somewhere?" Vincent asked James Farris as the man sat in his Audi and uselessly cranked the ignition. They were in the garage where Farris stored his car, which many New Yorkers did. Cars were a pain to drive and park on the crowded island of Manhattan. Public transportation made more sense. However, if you were trying to flee the fury of a beast whose lover had been put in danger, it made sense to grab your own set of wheels.

Just as it made sense to disable that Audi by pulling out the distributor cap, if you *didn't* want it to go anywhere.

With the abatement of the storm, it had been easier for Vincent to track Farris to this garage. He was hopeful that he would soon pick up the scent of Aliyah Patel.

"Who—what?" Farris said, but his look of abject horror betrayed him; if he didn't *know* who Vincent was, then he had a pretty good idea.

Vincent reached in and pulled him out, then placed him on his feet against the side of the car. The man was shaking. Vincent could hear his pounding heartbeat and made some mental calibrations. If this guy lied to him he might give himself an aneurysm.

"Who are you working for?" Vincent asked him. "And don't lie. I will know."

"Lena took her on her own. We hadn't received orders to do anything but keep her under observation. I don't have the first idea where she took her."

He was telling the truth. "Who," Vincent said impatiently, "do you work for?"

"I'm new at this. Lena brought me in a couple of months ago. She got herself transferred to New York because they'd found out about the antidote. They knew the FBI was looking for it, too." As Vincent opened his mouth, he said, "I don't know who they are. But they're rich." His breath stutter-stopped. "I was going to be set for life."

"For doing what?"

He looked down, then away. Vincent smelled fear on him, that and something else. Maybe it was shame.

"People at Vanek are forgotten," he said in a voice that would have been barely audible to anyone but Vincent. "And we have access to equipment, drugs…"

Vincent was disgusted down to the depths of his soul. "You were going to provide test subjects for the fear project?"

Farris nodded. "I swear to you, I was told it was for an anti-anxiety medication and the FDA was dragging its heels about approving human trials. Until Aliyah Patel was brought in, and Lena told me she was suffering from the effects of the experiment. And I wanted out. I was on the verge of telling you and Detective Chandler all about it. But they threatened my life."

*He doesn't know about me,* Vincent realized. "What exactly did Lena tell you?"

"That the murders in town were being committed by a test subject. Someone who had been driven insane by the experiments he had undergone."

*He.* "Did they specifically say 'he'?"

"No," he said wretchedly. "It was all this weird legalese. 'The subject' this and 'the subject' that. Never identified. I thought it might be Aliyah when they first brought her in. When she attacked that police officer, I was sure of it."

Vincent was stunned. Why had that not occurred to any of them? He had smelled the beast scent for the first time in this entire case when he had gone to her in the interview room. What if instead of the scent being an artifact of the crime scene, it was a biological part of her?

"I'm telling you, Lena took Aliyah on her own," he said. "Honest. We weren't given the order. She was trying to save the poor kid…" He exhaled, and it was as if all the oxygen in his body simply left. "I told her not to do it. I said she'd pay."

"She has," Vincent said. "She's dead."

"Oh, God." The man's legs gave way, and Vincent allowed him to sink to the floor of the garage. He buried his face in his hands and let out a wracked sob. Vincent felt absolutely no pity for him. A less evolved beast would have torn him limb from limb right there and then.

"Did they tell you to put a trace on Detective Chandler?" he asked.

Farris nodded. "I got a call while she was in my office."

At this, Vincent had to turn away. Sheer rage threatened to call out his beast side, and he couldn't afford the luxury of a loss of self-control. Once he was fully human again, he turned and loomed over the distraught man.

"You didn't ask why?"

"No," he whispered. "Don't you get it? These are not people you ask questions. You just do what they say." He swallowed hard. "Lena's dead, oh, God. But what about Aliyah? Is she dead, too?"

"She's been taken."

He covered his mouth with his hand. Then he said, "Let me help you find her. Please. Let me do something."

"You've done enough," Vincent retorted coldly. The man's face crumpled, but still pity did not come. "Do you know who Agent Mazursky is?"

The man's heartbeat told Vincent that he did. "We're supposed to call a number and report in if we hear anything, especially about him. They're after him. He has something they want. But I don't know what it is," he added anxiously.

He was telling the truth about being ignorant. Vincent said, "Give me the number. If there's a code word or something you have to do to prove who you are, tell me what it is. *Now*."

Farris cringed. "They'll kill me."

"We'll protect you," Vincent said. He wasn't sure what they would do with him afterwards, but that wasn't his immediate concern. "You said you wanted to help."

"Of course."

"All right, we're going to call them," Vincent said. "I'm going to write down exactly what you should say."

Farris dialed in and inputted the code.

"What have you got?" said an electronically disguised

voice on the other end of the line.

"Mazursky found a vial on Howison's body," Farris said, reading from Vincent's script. Vincent had him lie to shake things up. Delivering misinformation was a time-honored war tactic.

"How do you know this?" the voice demanded.

"Lena Mueller told me." May as well make it something they couldn't verify.

"How would she know?"

Farris looked at Vincent, who pantomimed shrugging in ignorance. "I don't know. She mentioned it tonight." Then he said on his own, "Is Aliyah Patel all right?"

"What do you mean?" the voice snapped.

Vincent's stomach dropped to the floor. *They don't have her. They didn't take her.*

"Hello?" said the voice. "Answer the question."

Vincent mouthed *Lena.*

"I thought you knew," Farris said. "Lena Mueller took her out of here earlier tonight."

"*What?* How would we know that?"

"The other operative in the facility," he replied, and Vincent frowned at him in surprise. This was news. But Farris gave his head a shake.

"We don't *have* another operative in the building." Vincent was surprised the voice would be so forthcoming. "So you're saying Aliyah Patel has been abducted?"

"Or rescued." At a sign from Vincent, Farris hung up.

"That was almost fun," he said.

*I will not kill him,* Vincent thought. *At least, not now.*

Vincent returned to J.T.'s with Farris in tow and told Cat, Tess, and J.T. everything that had happened. Cat and Tess traded somber looks. Their best theory continued to be that

Mazursky had abducted Aliyah and murdered Lena Mueller, but for what specific purpose, they didn't know. Leaving Farris in J.T.'s custody, they divided up and began the search of the five crime scenes they had not already examined for components of the antidote. Cat and Tess took the two near each other in Greenwich Village: one on Houston Street, and one near the Mulberry Street branch of the New York Public Library.

To their dismay, they discovered hiding places at each domicile, one in the wall and one in the floor. And no vials, jump drives or other items that could have been used in the formulation of an antidote.

"Someone's beat us to it," Cat said into the phone to Vincent.

"I was luckier in crime scene number four," Vincent announced. "That's Attenborough on the list. I'll send you a—"

And then he was cut off.

"Vincent?" Cat half-shouted into the phone. "Are you there?" But she was speaking to dead air.

"Not good," Tess said. "Keep trying, and let's go to the scene."

The squad car's lights and sirens fully engaged, Tess wove through traffic while Cat hit redial a dozen times, two dozen. Her stomach was clenched in knots. She had a terrible feeling that Vincent was in real trouble and she couldn't shake it no matter how hard Tess tried to talk her out of it. Tess ran down possible scenarios: Cell phones in New York were notorious for dropped signals. Someone may have arrived on scene and Vincent cut the call so as to remain concealed. All those things had happened to them on cases. There was no reason to expect the worst.

"I can't shake it," Cat said, and they looked at each other with sudden realization.

"Fear pheromone flashback," Tess suggested, and Cat nodded.

"I guess I need that antidote too," she replied.

"Number four" was where a man named Nils Attenborough had been found shredded to pieces. It had not been his home, only where his homicide had occurred. They drove through the city into blocks of abandoned, burned-out buildings mixed with occupied structures. The ones that were being used were in no better condition than the ones that weren't. Brick and sooty snow, trash, rust and neglect greeted them at every turn. Deeper they went, past chain-link fences guarding empty lots and a huge, snowy pit that might have been the start of a massive construction project, long abandoned. There the traffic thinned and Tess took off the lights and siren, opting for the element of surprise in case they needed some kind of advantage. They didn't know. Vincent hadn't returned any of Cat's calls.

Cat verified the address as they pulled off the street and trundled into a grid of disintegrating factories and storage facilities. As she opened her door, it began to snow. She looked up at the angry gray sky and crossed her fingers for a quick, light snowfall. She and Tess drew their weapons and kept to the shadows as they approached the front door of their destination. The body had been discovered on the ground floor about thirty feet to the east of the foyer.

They went inside with flashlights on. The floor had once been covered with small, white octagonal tiles. Hundreds of them had come loose and the wind must have bunched them into ominous little piles like arcane hex signs. Their feet crunched over broken glass. The walls were weeping with decay and mold.

They moved past a stairway toward the crime scene. Then in the darkness, Cat heard a sound that thrilled her heart then froze her blood: the fierce roar of a beast.

A beast who was not Vincent.

Answered by a gunshot.

Followed by a howl of agony.

\* \* \*

Gasping, the monster lay in a pool of blood, and Aliyah shrieked and clung to the man in the coat, the one who had taken her from Nurse Mueller. The monster had handed the man a little metal bottle and then it had tried to attack him.

Now it was changing. Now it was becoming the man Aunt Indira had taken her to see in the jail.

Her daddy.

She screamed and shrank back against the man in the coat. Then her daddy looked up at her and tried to stretch out his hand.

"Ali, I didn't kill your mama," he groaned. "They made it look like I did it. But I didn't. I loved her. And I love you."

"Daddy?" she whimpered. Now she tried to push against the man in the coat but he held her fast.

"Stay here. He'll kill you," the man whispered.

"Let her go to him," another man said as he stepped from the shadows. Aliyah recognized him. He had come to see her in the hospital.

The man in the coat let go of Aliyah. She stood uncertainly, staring down at all the blood and the man who had been a monster, who had killed Aunt Indira. She knew that in her heart. And yet, somehow, she also knew that he had done it for her.

The nice man stepped forward and took the gun away from the man in the coat. He had shot her daddy with that gun.

Aliyah was bewildered, and she began to cry.

And then the nice lady from the hospital ran into the room with another lady, whose skin was close to the color of Aliyah's. And their arms were around her and the nice man was kneeling on the floor beside her daddy, trying to help him, and the man in the coat was on the floor, too, and they were tying him up, or something.

Her daddy said to the nice man, "You don't know what's

coming. You don't know." The nice man looked very unhappy and the darker-skinned lady walked Aliyah out of the room. Then the nice man came out and the other lady walked with the man in the coat.

And her daddy never did come out of that building again.

As Catherine kept her gun pointed squarely at Agent Mazursky's back, Vincent examined the two vials they had just taken from him: he'd beaten Cat and Tess to two of them, but Vincent had gotten to Attenborough's first. That made four they had retrieved from the first six homicide victims, plus Howison's. Two were still missing, as was whatever had been concealed in the case with Lafferty's flag.

As they walked out of the building, Tess, who was carrying a weeping Aliyah, said, "Where to now?"

"My brownstone?" Sky Wilson said from across the walkway.

"What the hell?" Catherine blurted.

He was straddling a motorcycle parked beside Tess and Catherine's squad car. He shook his head at their looks of surprise and said, "You *do* remember that I'm a police detective, right? And that I know how to follow a trail of clues?"

Vincent's default wariness kicked in, but Wilson raised a hand and said, "I haven't figured out all of it but I know you're more than my Yoda-partner's boyfriend in every sense of the word *more* and it's cool. Your secret is safe with me. Whatever it is, exactly."

Not at all convinced of that, Vincent knew they didn't have time to argue the finer points of secret-keeping, and J.T.'s was out of the question while Farris was held there.

"We should take Wilson up on his offer. J.T. has company and we need to figure out what's going on asap."

Catherine and Tess concurred. With Aliyah in Tess's arms, they drove Mazursky to the brownstone in their squad car. Wilson rode his motorcycle and Vincent took Mazursky's vehicle, a white panel van. The inside was tricked out with beast-strength restraints, a cattle prod, and a tranq gun. Shyam Badal's mobile prison. He remembered how unhinged he had become when the fear beast—Badal—had lurked nearby. Badal must have somehow repressed the release of the pheromone just now because Aliyah had been there. Nor had it triggered as he lay dying.

They alerted J.T. that more pieces of the antidote had been found, then convened at the brownstone for a debriefing before Tess took the vials to J.T. It was still snowing, flakes heavy and gray, and Vincent's sense of urgency kicked in. Tess would have to leave soon.

"So Badal was the fear beast," Vincent said to Mazursky as the group placed their prisoner in a chair and Catherine kept a weapon trained on him. "And he killed Indira Patel and Julia Hogan in revenge?"

"He was only supposed to look for the antidote. He promised to do so if I let him loose. But he went after them immediately."

"Aliyah was your leverage. You got him to resume looking by bringing her to him."

"Yes."

Wilson had taken Aliyah to a bedroom and was offering her snacks from the stash of organic vegan offerings in his fridge. She had apologized a dozen times for raking his face.

Mazursky blew air out of his cheeks. "You have no idea what's going on. There's another world out there, one that blows past your notions of beasts. What we're dealing with has gone way, way beyond the scope of your understanding."

"Then make us understand," Cat said coldly.

"We've been working day and night to get fully informed,

but we know we don't have all of it. Badal was in jail for murder and we used that leverage to get his consent for experimentation. We attempted to duplicate what we knew of this new beast's genetic makeup using Badal. We had some success, as you have all experienced. But it is *nothing* compared to what's out there. Trust me when I tell you that." He looked straight at Vincent. "It will make Afghanistan look like a picnic."

"Which is why you murdered people to collect all the pieces of the antidote," Tess said.

"Same old FBI," Catherine drawled, and Mazursky shrugged, unapologetic.

"As I said before, extraordinary times require extraordinary measures. This thing was imprisoned here in New York City by its makers, but it escaped. We had three operatives on the inside but they never got close enough to actually observe it. And they died when it broke out. We don't know where it is, but we do know we have to get rid of it."

"Why should we believe you?" Catherine asked.

He pulled out his smartphone. "Here. This is why you should believe me."

The screen revealed a close-up of a soldier's face. Vincent had seen fear before, but nothing like this. The man's face was distorted, jaw distended, eyes about to pop from their sockets. Fear was turning this human being into another entity, something never human again. Agonizing to see, unbearable to imagine. Sweat poured down the man's face, and then blood, as a shimmering arm stretched forward and with talons instead of fingers, gouged into his forehead and pulled his face down like a sheet of wrapping paper. What was beneath...

The person holding the camera was crying. Then there was shrieking as the camera pointed to a ceiling, whirled, revealing a room of immobilized soldiers dropping one by one into gouting pools of their own blood and organs.

"This is the escape. I have more footage."

Vincent nodded. "We should watch it all."

"Agreed," Catherine said thickly, and he loved her for her courage and her commitment to what clearly was their mission. It was coming time for Team Beast to step up.

"We need to destroy this thing," Mazursky said.

"How can you, even if J.T. can recreate the antidote?" Tess cut in. "If no one can get near it to inject the serum…"

"Pheromones," Mazursky said. "Once the antidote is created, we'll release it in its air space."

"But you just said that you don't know where it is," Tess argued, and then Vincent saw the light dawn on her face. "Vincent…"

"Can track it," Mazursky finished.

*And will,* Vincent thought. He saw the tension in Catherine's face and heard her accelerating heartbeat; he knew how afraid she was for him… for them… and he also knew that she would never ask him not to do it. It was what they were, who they were, and it was what they did. Catherine would throw her lot in with him, do everything she could to back him up and keep him safe, his partner in every sense of the word.

"We'll back you up," Tess said, and his heart was warmed.

"And me too, of course," Mazursky added.

It was settled then, and all parties in the room took a moment to process the nature of the threshold they were about to step across. It was one they might not come back across. But it meant the world to Vincent that they would do it together. For so many years, he had been utterly cut off from the world, and everything that he had been had been put in stasis: a man who cared, who wanted to make a difference, to find meaning in service to others. Like his brothers, who had died saving lives.

Vincent gazed at Catherine, and she raised her chin slightly and nodded at him. It was the most intimate gesture they had ever shared.

*She is the best of me.* Something moved inside him and he thought, *Whatever happens next, it was worth it. Even if I die.*

The moment passed, their pact sealed. It was time to get down to business.

"How many parts of the antidote have you collected?" Mazursky asked them.

Catherine told him that they had two, Howison's and Tiptree's. He looked mildly disappointed. "I had Badal seek out the vials that you now have in your possession." He turned to Vincent. "His drug protocol enhanced his sense of smell to a degree possessed not even by you. He literally sniffed them out like a bloodhound.

"The flag has been a problem for us. We suspect Muirfield got wind of an attempt to smuggle out evidence of the beast experiments in Afghanistan and intercepted it en route to the Riley home. From what we have gleaned, it's a catalyst that sets the transformative process in motion, common to many of the formulae used on the subjects. We think it's needed to trigger the antidote. That without it, the serum won't work. And we need it. Desperately."

"Which I suppose should explain the attack in the subway," Catherine drawled. "But how did you *dream* you would get Vincent's cooperation if you killed me?"

He stared at her. "What are you talking about?"

She told him about the attack on Mr. Riley's house, and the firefight in the subway, and he gaped at her in astonishment.

"They said *I* sent them? No."

"Then it was the group Lena Mueller and James Farris were working for," Catherine said, sharing a grim look with Vincent.

"The Freedom Fighters of New York," Mazursky filled in. "Howison was undercover with them. You know this, right?"

"They implicated you."

He shook his head. "Misdirection. Trying to confuse and distract us. The *real* threat that stalks this city is out there and no one has control of it."

*When will you stop?* Vincent thought. *When will you human monsters stop twisting innocent people into beasts and putting the world at risk?*

# CHAPTER NINETEEN

J.T. was relieved to see everyone arrive at his house in one piece. The snow was like a beast itself, crazy and raging, and the mayor's office was telling people to get off the streets; last night had only been a dress rehearsal.

Wilson had stayed home to watch over Aliyah, and she would not leave his side. Which was great, because no one particularly wanted him around. Team Beast was used to working under the radar by themselves, especially in a crisis. Wilson had yet to see Vincent beast out; he didn't really know what he had gotten into. Now that he had Aliyah to tend to, maybe he would be benched permanently.

With the others keeping an eye on James Farris, J.T. got to work on the antidote. He kept the news streaming on his desktop in the background and, given the violence of the storm, was sure that this time an Emergency Snow Declaration would be called. There had been some backlash that the mayor hadn't done it last night. Naysayers said it was more evidence that the city wasn't looking out for the safety of its citizens.

"An ESD would be the best thing," Vincent observed. "It would keep more people off the streets."

"Yeah, it's not like we're going to be taking the subway,"

Tess said. J.T. raised his head and looked at her. Really looked, at his brave, fierce woman.

*I will do whatever it takes to make it right between us, if you will do whatever it takes to come back to me from this,* he thought. His throat tightened. His hands trembled on his keyboard.

Then he looked back down at the monitor. It was his silent act of courage, and as he felt eyes on him, he realized that Vincent had seen it. His oldest, best friend dipped his head and J.T. shrugged with mock resignation: *What are ya gonna do?*

Time to get to work.

He was aware that he was missing two key ingredients, and that he was trying to figure out what they were without access to the sophisticated equipment at his university lab. As a trained biochemist, he had developed his own set of beast protocols over the years, and he got out his voluminous notes about Vincent's physiology as he attacked the problem. Taking a sample of Catherine's blood as well, he began to categorize the chemical reactions that had occurred in their bloodstreams in order to deduce the likely solution that had catalyzed the event.

It was guesswork, but scientifically based. He was as careful as he could be, running computer simulations rather than risking the precious droplets of chemicals in the vials. *I wish I had help,* he thought. He thought of Heidi Schwann, which made him think of Sara.

And his heart led him back to Tess.

As he worked, the weather report took a back seat to calls coming in on Mazursky's phone. Fast, furious. The agent had a body to cover up and a beast to track down. J.T. strained to listen in but Mazursky kept pacing the hall and murmuring.

Vincent walked over to J.T. and said, "They've spotted it. The good news is that it's left the city. The bad is that it's in the forest."

J.T. understood immediately what Vincent was implying. "It's hard to use pheromones as a delivery system in the great outdoors."

Coming from behind Vincent, Catherine said, "We need to find a cave."

"Yes," Vincent agreed.

"Wait, *what*?" J.T. cried. "You can't do that. You can't go *inside* a cave with that thing!"

"Let's see," Tess said from the sofa with a laptop on her knees. "Caves. Are there any abandoned structures out there?"

J.T. let out a slow exhale and propped his forehead on his hand. Then he felt pressure on the back of his head as Tess kissed him gently and laced her fingers through his.

"J.T., you know how cops are. We gotta pump it before we go in sometimes, get primed. But Cat and I are *smart*. We're great cops." She brushed a curly strand of hair away from his temple. "And we've both got a lot to live for."

He caught her hand. His chest hurt. He said, "Yeah, we do."

She favored him with one of her quirky grins. "Glad that's settled."

And it was.

It really was.

As they stood before the open door of Walker's empty apartment—*not* a cold-water walkup, just a normal, basic apartment—Heather stared at J-Bag in utter frustration. "How can they have *left*? They did all this so they'd get big magazine jobs!"

Her words echoed in the barren space. J-Bag snickered. "Girl, you mentioned your sister was a cop, right? Figure they got all freaked out and bailed. Or for all you know, they've traded up to some fine place because they already have those magazine jobs in the hole."

"Great," she said.

He crooked a finger. "Come with me."

"Why? So we can knock over a liquor store together?" she asked.

She followed him out of the building and back into his car. He smiled and moved into the traffic. It took her about five minutes to realize that he was driving her to the offices of *Couture Bleu* magazine. He gave his keys to a valet who pointedly looked him up and down—J-Bag had on a black hoodie with a red fist on it, a pair of baggy black jeans, high tops, and large leather wristbands on each wrist. J-Bag turned to Heather and said, "You're good for the valet parking, right?"

As she sputtered in protest, he took her hand—*they were holding hands*—and walked through the revolving door head up, shoulders back, as if he owned the place. The receptionist looked startled.

"Yo, this designer is from Silverado and her Nude Look design was stolen from her by another—"

"*New* Look," Heather corrected, smiling. "Really. It's okay."

J-Bag looked at her in horror. "*Okay?* My kitten woman is no wimp." He turned back to the receptionist. "This is Heather Chandler, you know, and—"

"Oh. Right." The receptionist smiled. "We received your submission. And the note from someone named Walker that there'd been a mixup when it was sent in. The wrong name was on it. Yes? Elaine something?"

Heather gaped at her. "Um, yes," she said slowly.

"Oh. My. God," said a voice. "*Look* at those cheekbones. Did the agency send you over, you luscious thing?"

Heather and J-Bag both turned. A man with a camera around his neck was slinking toward them. He held his hand out to J-Bag and said, "This time they got it *right*."

J-Bag blinked, and then he grinned at Heather. He said, "So maybe a happy ending, eh, baby?"

Then the photographer said, "The mayor just called the Snow Emergency Declaration. We're all going to be stuck in here together for a long time. Why don't we get started? I love what you're wearing. What's your name?"

"J-Bag."

"Let's just start with working poses." He looked over. "Janine," he called. "Look at this hunk. I'm thinking cover?"

And Janine Deveraux, the editor-in-chief of *Couture Bleu*, glided over on her skinny high heels and her perfectly cut little black dress and beamed at J-Bag. "Move over Tyson Beckford," she drawled. She grinned at J-Bag. "*Love* the look. We'll have to build a wardrobe. Tux?"

"Tux," the photographer agreed.

And Heather just started laughing as hard as she could.

"I have it," J.T. announced, holding up the vial. It was clear, and somehow Vincent imagined it would be the color of blood. So much blood had been spilled to obtain it. "I don't know if it's going to work, though."

"I don't know if this is, either," Vincent said, holding up his fighter pilot's helmet.

Each of them was holding a helmet. The antidote would be mixed with oxygen and circulated through their systems. This had been the last thing that Major Howison had been trying to tell him: "Bone do" had been his attempt to say "bone dome," the military term for helmets. "Oxygen" signaled that it was a fighter pilot helmet.

Ever since Howison had died in his arms, Vincent had wondered how Major Howison had withstood being in Shyam Badal's proximity when the fear pheromones had been released. The clearest answer was that he had to have been given some version of the antidote. Mazursky claimed ignorance and of course he was believed. Why would he have ordered so many murders to get the vials if he already had the formula?

But mulling his words coupled with remembering the smell of the warehouse—like the flight deck of an aircraft carrier, or flight helmets that had been burned in the fire—had yielded this answer. He hoped it was the right one.

"We'll be back soon," Tess said, wrapping her arms around J.T. "You know we will, right?"

He swallowed hard. Vincent watched him struggle to remain upbeat. He knew it was bothering him that he was "babysitting." But surely he had to comprehend that his creation of the antidote was nothing short of miraculous. There had been no way to test it. Like so much else, they would have to chance it in the field—daring to give all if it didn't.

"Be careful," J.T. ground out, and he walked through to the door.

The snow cascaded like supernaturally thick rain. New York was under siege, and there was no one on the streets. Mazursky had ordered Humvees, and as Catherine, Vincent, and Tess joined him inside the lead vehicle, Vincent sensed deep, palpable fear tugging at every nerve ending in his body. They all put on their masks. They had on body armor and heavy boots. They buckled in and trundled off in a world of pure white. Vincent and Catherine held hands and took deep breaths of the mixture.

Mazursky said through his microphone, "The Bureau won't forget this."

And Catherine retorted, "It escapes me why we should care."

They drove, Vincent eavesdropping on every call Mazursky sent or received on his radiophone.

Before he regained his composure, Vincent suffered a

moment of panic. *They're coming for me. To take me from Catherine.*

*No. That's over.*

They went on a winding road that Vincent had never been on before, despite innumerable trips to these woods. He and his brothers had cross-country skied here. He had brought Catherine here for picnics in the spring.

Suddenly, birds billowed into the air and scores of wild animals darted in front of the Humvee. The driver slammed on his brakes, slowing, swerving, as the terrified animals panicked and fled. Deer, raccoons, possums, wild turkeys shot across the road.

The fear spread more deeply into his bones. Catherine held his hand tightly and took heavy, rattling breaths. He tapped her forearm, asking after her status.

"I'm losing it," she said.

"It's not real," he replied. "Catherine, you know it's just chemical. It's not real."

But it was real. It was monstrous; they came across the eviscerated carcass of a deer, and then of a man, and then of another man... and then of twenty men, one of Mazursky's scouting parties. Their deaths were so recent that blood steamed from the snow. Thick and richly red, there was so much of it, so much.

More dead.

The Humvee driver started screaming. Catherine sagged, and Tess and Mazursky were gripping each other by the shoulders as the miasma of horror invaded them.

Vincent said, "Stop the vehicle. Here."

Doubled over, Catherine said, "No, Vincent. It will kill you. I will die if it kills you. I won't be able to live."

"You're okay," he insisted. "It's just the pheromones."

But inside he was agreeing with every word she uttered.

It would kill him.

The plan had been for them to get as close to the fear beast as they could, and then Vincent would get out of the Humvee and lope through the snow, inviting it to track him. Over his shoulder, he had slung a rocket launcher, and in the payload, there was a hollowed-out projectile filled with the antidote in gaseous form. When the rocket was aimed at the fear beast and launched, it would burst open and deliver the pheromone ammunition. Or so it was hoped. Mazursky had supervised the engineering of the device, as, he conceded, the United States military had used similar devices against other enemies.

There were more rocket launchers in the Humvees, but all of the vehicles had stopped in their tracks, their occupants too terrified to proceed. Their weapons, therefore, were useless.

Soon the snow was blinding, and Vincent directed his circulatory system to feed his thermal imaging capabilities. Trees glowed orange; more animals bounded out of the forest, some colliding with him. He stayed on target, focused, one leg following the other through the blizzard.

One leg…

One…

*Afghanistan. Guns shooting. Men shooting. Beasts perishing. Death, death. Destroy. Retaliate. Fight back. Rend. Dismember.*

He had to find the cave. Get to the cave. Draw the fear beast inside. If only it would come.

*It can't come after me. It will kill me.*

Vincent shook as his jaw clacked against the bottom of the helmet. Rage coursed through him. Rage was better than fear. Let others fear him. Let them quail and quake. He would tear them apart with his teeth. He would…

*Muirfield. Hunting him down. Years. Years waking up in the dead of night in a cold sweat: Is it them? Are they here? Do I hear soldiers? Choppers?*

He was tiring. The snow blocked him. Ice was freezing the

blood inside his veins. In the oxygen hose, he tasted something metallic and wondered if the antidote was changing because of the cold. If it would stop working. If he would get inside the cave and launch the payload and nothing would happen and he would die in agony. He would be ripped—

His beast side threw back its head and roared.

And it was answered.

"I can't stand it. We have to retreat," said the Humvee driver. Cat was seated by the passenger door, half-turned toward him. "Where's my gun? Defend!" He whipped out his weapon and pointed it at Cat. "Enemy!" he screamed.

"No!" she cried. She lifted her own weapon. The driver was sweating. He began to laugh and cry. His hand wobbled but Cat could see that he was preparing to pull the trigger. Her world telescoped to his fingers on the metal.

She was about to open fire when her door burst open and someone dragged her bodily from the vehicle. She fell into the snow just as the driver opened fire—and Mazursky went down, bleeding from a dozen wounds. Blood spurted onto the snow.

The driver kept firing. Cat flipped herself over on hands and knees and crawled toward the side of the Humvee just as Tess leaped out. She reached down and took Cat's wrist; without a beat she began to drag her as she moved on instinct, fight or flight. They both had on their helmets; Cat forgot her words, her thoughts. She scrabbled in the snow to keep up as they madly charged into the black woods, the dense branches, the icy pond with a thick crust…

…and the liquid, unfrozen water beneath.

They crashed in.

And they went down.

* * *

Bullets and bombs. Guns pointed at him. Death. Kill first.

*Run.*

*Run.*

*Run.*

In a sheer panic. Trying to remember the mission; there was a mission; he was a man—

Beast-Vincent roared and caught the scent. Left, right, up the hill, through the copse of trees; right, right, right. Tracking his prey, running it to ground.

It roared back, more loudly, more horribly. The world became a vast star field of glowing blackness, luminescent. He kept after it, his animalistic survival instincts unable to assess the danger as he bore down on it. Huge, unknowable, revolting.

With a savage howl of frenzied triumph, Beast-Vincent threw himself at it. It fell back, then shot into the air and landed on him, and threw him fifty feet upwards; trees raced up to bombard him in the face, the neck. He cracked and broke. Then again, it grabbed him up and slammed him down with unbelievable force.

It was killing him. *Let it let it let it.*

With his helmeted head in its mouth, it began to drag him. The snow was scarlet with his blood. His arms and legs were wrenched from their sockets; his joints twisted and cracked like chestnuts in a fire.

*Let it.*

He was barely conscious. Roaring and growling and batting at it without any awareness of doing so. His mind was back on the streets when he had been the vigilante and millions of New Yorkers wanted him dead. Hunted everywhere, hated, Beast-Vincent.

And then he thought of Catherine. His half-closed eyes opened and he saw her smile. Her beautiful eyes. Heard her voice saying, "You are not a monster, Vincent. You saved my life."

Saved her life.

*Save it now.*

It was dragging him, but miraculously, he still had his rocket launcher. He clung to it with all his might as the fear beast pulled him over boulders and streams streaked with ice water. It was going somewhere; it had a destination.

He saw Catherine's face again. His beast attributes faded and he was just a man.

*With a rocket launcher.*

It took him a moment to realize that the fear beast was heading for the very cave Tess had selected for him. It raced inside. Vincent's body armor was coated with blood and mud. He held on to the launcher.

And then his helmet was yanked off, and the full force of the creature's fear pheromones assaulted him. He tried to move, to aim the launcher, but as before, he went completely limp. He crumpled to the ground and cowered on his knees, dropping the launcher to shield his face. He saw *something* coming down at him, but what it was… if it had ever been human…

He couldn't defend himself. He couldn't move even one single finger. Lift an arm.

The world fuzzed out, becoming white, becoming Catherine's beautiful face.

*If I don't do this, what happens to her?*

That was the greatest fear. The worst thing he could think of. The thing that he dreaded more than a painful death or even the end of the world: the end of Catherine Chandler, the woman he cherished, respected, loved.

For some, that fear would be their undoing. It would utterly unnerve them. Shatter them.

For Vincent, it gave him back his humanity.

And in that moment, summoning all the effort in his entire body, his spirit, even his soul, he forced himself to stand up.

He grabbed the launcher.

*Assemble, load, fire.*

He collapsed.

*We're drowning,* Tess thought. Words penetrated the sheer panic that had engulfed her. She sucked on the mask for oxygen and antidote, but it was dragging her to the bottom of the pond. In her mind's eye she saw her brothers grouped around her, yelling at her to save herself; and then she saw J.T., telling her he loved her.

There was an explosion. The water literally shook, and her eardrums pounded.

Then she was rising up through the water; someone was pulling her out. Her back arched as the faceplate was pulled up and she breathed in the heavy snowfall. Gasping in the crystalline white.

It was Mazursky, bleeding so much that she couldn't imagine how he was still alive.

"Cat?" she bellowed, coughing up water.

And Cat said, "I'm here."

When Vincent awoke, he was lying in the cave on his back, and there was a small campfire burning beside his right foot. On it was a metal coffee pot. As he sat up, he discovered a note on his chest:

*Thank you for corralling and destroying our little problem. We are in your debt. You might consider the possibility that you are fighting for the wrong side. You can't imagine the other creations we have at our disposal, or fathom what we will do next. The world is ours, and it's for our friends. And you, Dr. Keller, can be one of those.*

*We urge you to join us. If you do not, you will face horrors that will make this seem like a pleasant interlude.*

*Why did we spare you?*

*You are unaware of what you are capable. You were not engineered to stop progressing. When faced with dangers that call upon your body to evolve, you will do just that... you will become, truly, the king of beasts.*

*We look forward to observing this. And you can be sure that we will be doing so.*

*Soon.*


*With regards,*
*Howard Thornton*
*President and CEO, Thornton Industries*


Vincent crumpled the note and began to drop it into the fire when he stopped himself. Instead, he sniffed the paper and closed his eyes. Focused. Saw the soldiers hoist up the dead fear beast. Saw them carry it out.

He reached the edge of the forest just as the helicopter rose into the snowstorm and left with the corpse, dangling from a net. Even from here, he could smell that it was dead.

He stared after it a moment, savoring victory—over a monster, and over his own fears—and then he went in search of Catherine.

# CHAPTER TWENTY

## SIX MONTHS LATER

Seated at Mr. Riley's beside, Vincent leaned forward and murmured his confession into the old man's ear. Told him the story of Lafferty's request that he, Vincent, helped her escape. How he had refused, and consigned her to death.

"And I'm sorry," Vincent said. For a moment he thought Mr. Riley had fallen asleep... or worse, and he checked the old man's pulse. It was fluttering. Mr. Riley was dying.

Twin tears traced glittery tracks down the sick, careworn face, and Vincent knew he had heard it all. "I'm so sorry," he said again.

"Son, you couldn't even save yourself," Mr. Riley murmured. It was a struggle to speak. With great effort, he lifted his hand and it hovered limply in the air, as if seeking Vincent. Vincent slid his hand beneath it, and Mr. Riley grasped his fingers, his grip surprisingly firm.

"I didn't know if I should tell you the truth," Vincent said. "You believed all these years that she died a hero."

"But she did." Very slowly, Mr. Riley's eyes opened and fixed on Vincent. "She volunteered all the way. Enlisted.

Worked her ass off to get into Delta Company. I was so proud. She told me how hard it was over there. And how you kept her spirits up. Told her not to be a big baby."

Vincent remembered. His throat tightened as memories of that night on patrol flooded back, when Lafferty broke down and told him she wanted to walk into the desert and never come back. Away from the carnage and the people who hated them and the little children who begged for the scraps from their mess tent. That was before the experiments.

He wouldn't tell this old man that, ever.

But he had told Lafferty that the people there were counting on them—the freedom fighters, the civilians who needed this war to end—and the people back home, who had given this conflict their best: their young men and women. Sons, daughters, brothers, sisters.

He had told her to be brave, and to fight with valor, and he'd sworn he would survive if she would. They'd made a pact. She'd hugged him and called him her brother.

"I wish I'd never met her," Vincent said. "That she'd stayed home—"

"Hush your mouth, boy," Mr. Riley snapped. "My Roxie did die a true hero."

"For the wrong cause. They betrayed us."

"Not everyone. Some people believed they were making you safer." Like Cat's mother, Vanessa Chandler. "And Roxie stepped up. She volunteered. Who would have died in her place? Maybe an ambassador who negotiates a lasting peace in the Middle East. Or a doctor who discovers how to cure the disease that's killing me.

"She was a hero," he said again. "Like you."

He squeezed Vincent's hand again—less firmly this time—and gave him a little smile.

"You'll take care of Aliyah, you and Detective Chandler? I

left everything to her. It's not much, but it's more than she's got now."

"We'll take care of her," Vincent promised. Given all the violence and trauma in her young life, Aliyah was doing remarkably well. He and Catherine had told her the truth about beasts—that they were not magical, but a product of science, and that one day there would be no more beasts. One truth and one half-truth, then. One fond hope.

Mr. Riley gasped. "Amanda and Roxie are waving at me," he said. "I see them."

"Then go to them," Vincent said quietly. "And say hi to Lafferty for me."

"I will." The old gentleman smiled. His eyes fixed, and Vincent knew he was gone.

Outside in the hospice garden, roses bloomed.


He walked into the conference room at Thornton Industries with an easy swagger and an air of confidence. Mr. Howard Thornton, president and CEO, smiled at him and said, "Welcome aboard. I trust your journey was a pleasant one?"

"Yes, sir, but if I may make a suggestion… you need to rearrange the interior of your private jet. The feng shui is off." He adjusted the prayer beads around his wrist.

Mr. Thornton chuckled. "Californians. Now, please tell us everything you know. We're especially interested in hearing how Vincent Keller devised the plan to eliminate Experiment Z two-three-seven. Or as they so quaintly called it, 'the fear beast.'"

Sky Wilson took a seat at the beautiful conference table. "Of course, sir. I'll tell you everything I know."

Mr. Thornton beamed. "Wonderful. And in return, Mr. Wilson, I will show you… *wonders*."

\* \* \*

In Greenwich Village, in each other's arms, two lovers dreamed of rings and rainbows, and loved ones long departed; and the words of their vow sealed their soul together:

*We are better together than we are apart.*
*And we always will be.*

That vow would see them through the dark times, if more came. If the entire world came at them, as long as they stood together, they could not lose.

*We will always win. We have already won.*

Cat woke from the unimaginable joy in her heart. Propped on his elbow, hair tousled from sleep, Vincent gazed down at her, his eyes glistening with unshed tears.

*Another life that has just begun.*

"I had the most amazing dream," he told her.

And Catherine said, "Me too. I dream it every night." She reached up to hold him. "And you're always in it, Vincent."

"You *are* it, Catherine," he murmured. "You are the dream."

When the sun rose, they were still dreaming.

## ABOUT THE AUTHOR

Nancy Holder is a multiple award-winning, *New York Times* bestselling author (the Wicked Series). Her two new young adult dark fantasy series are Crusade and Wolf Springs Chronicles. She has won five Bram Stoker Awards from the Horror Writers Association, as well as a Scribe Award for Best Novel (*Saving Grace: Tough Love*.) Nancy has sold over eighty novels and one hundred short stories, many of them based on such shows as *Highlander*, *Buffy the Vampire Slayer*, *Angel*, and others. She lives in San Diego with her daughter, Belle, two corgis, and three cats.

You can visit Nancy online at www.nancyholder.com.

# BEAUTY & THE BEAST &

## VENDETTA

### By Nancy Holder

During a mysterious blackout, Angelo DeMarco, the son of New York City's most powerful family, is kidnapped. NYPD detectives Catherine Chandler and Tess Vargas are on the case when they learn of a second missing person: Cat's father has disappeared from his prison cell. Vincent is desperate to help Cat, but as tensions rise, the couple become caught in a trap where the only way out is to confront their pasts and prove their epic love.

For more fantastic fiction, author events, exclusive
excerpts, competitions, limited editions and more

VISIT OUR WEBSITE
titanbooks.com

LIKE US ON FACEBOOK
facebook.com/titanbooks

FOLLOW US ON TWITTER
@TitanBooks

EMAIL US
readerfeedback@titanemail.com